M000201830

# THE MISSING HUSBAND

NATASHA BOYDELL

BLOODHOUND
— BOOKS —

Print ISBN 978-1-913942-51-9

# PROLOGUE

There is nothing remarkable about the last time you saw your husband. It was a typical September day, a wet weekday morning just like any of the thousands that have passed before it without ceremony. You were alone in the kitchen, tidying up the aftermath of the children's breakfast when he walked in. His hair was still damp from his shower and the fresh, clean smell of toothpaste and lemon shower gel emanated from him, just as it did every morning. It was one of your favourite smells and even after all these years of marriage you still paused for a second to breathe it in.

You switched on the coffee machine, sliced some sourdough bread and put it in the toaster, while he grabbed the coffee cups and milk; years of cohabitation creating a routine so ingrained that you were hardly aware you were doing it anymore. The children had gone to school early that morning, so you had a rare, uninterrupted breakfast together, sipping your still hot coffee and talking about the mundane topics of family life. Then he wiped his mouth, stood up, kissed you and left – his mind, you imagined, already preoccupied with the tasks of the day ahead.

It has now been five months and you haven't seen him since.

You've replayed that morning over and over again in your head. You've obsessed over every single second of that day and the days leading up to it. Recently someone asked you, 'If you knew then that it would be the last time you saw him, would you have done anything differently?'

The answer is, you have no idea anymore. Because, what do you do when your husband has betrayed you? When he has turned his back on everything you built together, on your children, on your intertwined life as a family unit? When his selfishness has broken you and the life you thought was real? When every time you think you've found the answers, something happens to plant a new seed of doubt in your mind?

You carry on. You put the kettle on, you look after the kids and you get on with your life.

Because, really, what else can you do?

# 1

## KATE

K ate sat at the kitchen table and stared at her iPhone. It was a pointless exercise really. She already knew it wasn't going to provide her with any answers. She scrolled mindlessly through her Facebook, Twitter and Instagram feeds, scanning the endless conveyor belt of other people's lives without processing any of it. It was simply a habit, a distraction from real life and in particular the situation she was in. She looked at the clock on the wall and then back at her phone. She tapped her fingers on the table, her manicured nails clicking on the hardwood surface, one, two, three, one, two, three, four, five, playing scales in her subconscious – an old habit from years of piano lessons as a child.

The kettle boiled and clicked off for the third time that morning. No tea had been made yet.

The house had the stillness that comes after the whirling tornado of children – school shoes flying across the room, the frantic search for missing coats or bags, bickering over who gets the pink earmuffs – have finally departed for school and peace is temporarily restored for a few blissful hours. Normally she treasured the silence but today it was too loud and too obvious.

Something was missing and she had that horrible, sinking feeling you get in the pit of your stomach when you know that the world has fundamentally shifted but you're not sure exactly what that means yet.

Finally, she exhaled deeply, picked up the phone and called her sister Erin. As usual, it went to voicemail and this wasn't the time for pleasantries or small talk. Five words were enough, so she took a deep breath and said simply: 'I think he's left me'. There was nothing else to say and she put the phone down and stared at the clock again. It continued its steady ticking, oblivious to the chaos that was erupting around it. Time didn't stand still for anyone.

The clock was grey and elegant, an impulse purchase to fill a blank wall and the final touch to the family kitchen which had been Kate's project of passion for months. She'd finally got to buy the sunken sink, central island and huge Aga she'd always dreamed of. 'Like a modern farmhouse kitchen in the city,' her husband Pete had commented when it was finished. She'd been desperate to create a rural chic effect and the stress of the whole renovation project had nearly tipped her over the edge on several occasions, so she had been thrilled by his description.

They lived in a townhouse in Muswell Hill, north London, just a few minutes' walk from the bus stop where Pete started his journey to work each morning. He hadn't wanted to live there at first because there wasn't a Tube station nearby, but she had immediately fallen in love with the 'impressive four-bedroom house in an enviable location' pitched to them by the slick Greek-Cypriot estate agent. When they went to view it, Kate, clutching their eldest daughter Lily's hand while cradling a newborn Maggie in her baby carrier, could imagine them putting down roots here. She could already hear their children's laughter echoing around the rooms as they ran through the halls, growing up, playing with their friends and making memories. They would be so happy here, she thought.

So, just as she had always done so well in her old job in public relations, she had prepared her best pitch to Pete, painting the picture of an idyllic family life in the house, sending him links to nearby restaurants and cafés that she knew he'd like and eventually persuading him that this property was exactly what they needed. Four years on and he still moaned about the damn commute. But she knew he loved the house really and the girls, now seven and five, had got into the popular local primary school. Plus the renovation, while stressful, had given her a much-needed project to distract her from the relentless and overwhelming job of being a stay-at-home mum to young children.

Now all that was left to do was the overgrown garden and recently she had been feeling like she was almost there, that Project Family Home was nearing completion. To her that symbolised the start of a new, better life. She was slowly inching ever closer to having created the ideal home that she had dreamed of for her family, a place constantly filled with people, life and laughter for many years to come.

But this morning, as she sat in silence at their handmade pine kitchen table, listening to the monotonous sound of their beautiful clock ticking in their immaculately designed kitchen, she had never felt more alone. Her mind drifted back to the previous day and the last words she had said to her husband before he left.

The morning had started like any other. The girls had bounded into their rooms at 6.30am, snuggling under the covers for a few more blissful moments in bed before they all had to face the day. Kate had got up with them and taken them off to get dressed while Pete checked his emails. Downstairs she had made them breakfast and waited for Rachel, their nanny, to collect them and take them to school. She had asked her to come earlier than usual so that they could go to a breakfast fundraiser organised by the parents committee. Once they had left, Kate had started cleaning up the kitchen as she waited for Pete to come down, then they'd had a quick breakfast together before he left for work.

Had he acted any differently over breakfast, she wondered, casting her mind back? She didn't think so. Nothing she could put her finger on anyway. What was the last thing she had said to him as he headed towards the front door? She tried to think but she couldn't remember exactly now. It wasn't 'I love you', they'd stopped saying that to each other every day years ago. But everyone knew that was par for the course when you've been together forever and you've got children. It was a given that you loved each other.

That evening, she hadn't been surprised when he wasn't home to help put the girls to bed. He was a workaholic and in the nine years she'd been married to him she'd become accustomed to his late nights and business trips. As a director at a large media company there was always a client to schmooze or a crisis to handle. She had carried on with the usual evening routine – bath, bed and stories with the girls – before kissing them goodnight and padding wearily down the stairs, pouring a glass of red wine and collapsing on the sofa. Turning the TV on, she sent Pete a quick text to ask if he'd be home for dinner before scrolling through the channels and choosing an episode of *EastEnders*. Pete loathed soaps but she loved them, and she always indulged in her guilty pleasure whenever he wasn't around. She relished the mad, over-the-top drama of other people's fictional lives, secure in the knowledge that hers was reassuringly mundane in comparison.

At 3am she woke up on the sofa with the empty bottle of wine next to her, a horrible taste in her mouth and the immediate sensation that Pete wasn't in the house. She climbed the stairs and glanced into their empty bedroom, then pulled her phone out of her jeans pocket and called him, nearly jumping out of her skin when the sound of ringing downstairs pierced the still of the night. Pete never went anywhere without his phone. She followed the sound to the coat rack by the front door and rummaged through his jacket until she discovered his mobile nestled in a pocket, next to an envelope with her name on it. It had clearly been there all day, but she hadn't heard it go off. Looking at the screen she could see just two notifications – her own text message that she'd sent him earlier that evening, unread and unanswered – and her missed call. Putting the phone in her own pocket for now and feeling the grogginess of the red wine wearing off rapidly, she turned her attention to the letter.

She couldn't remember the last time her husband had written her an anniversary card, let alone a handwritten letter but the writing was undoubtedly his messy scrawl. Walking back into the living room and sinking down on to the sofa with a rapidly growing feeling of dread, she stared at the envelope for a second before pulling out the letter with fumbling fingers. She scanned it quickly, her heart thumping as the adrenaline kicked in. When she was finished, she went back to the beginning and re-read every line over and over again, trying to make sense of the words.

*Kate,*

*I love you, I always will, and I love our children more than life itself. I've struggled for a long time trying to make this work, to feel as happy as I should with our perfect life, our perfect house and our perfect family, but I just don't have the strength anymore. You deserve better, so do the girls.*

*I met someone else, I don't know how it happened, I wasn't looking for it but it came and I couldn't resist. I'm sorry, I know I'm weak. But I also know that I feel happier and lighter than I've felt in years. I feel free. I know you won't understand this right now but I hope that you will, in time, and that you will find the same freedom.*

*I'm going away for a while, to give us both a chance to clear our heads, for the dust to settle. I know you'll be angry with me and it's more than I deserve but please tell the girls that I'm on a business trip. I want to be a good dad to them, I need to be. But to do that we both need some time so that we can reset and start again.*

*I'll be in touch in a few weeks. I love you. I'm sorry.*

Kate stared at the letter for so long that the words started to blur and bounce around on the page in front of her. Her heart was pounding as her mind whirred through possible alternatives – this wasn't actually happening; she was dreaming; it would all be fine in the morning – before landing on the inevitable truth. This was very real and the life that she knew had changed forever. But she simply wasn't prepared.

She had been with Pete for so long that she couldn't really remember life without him. University sweethearts, she had met him in a student bar in Leeds on her first night in the city. She was high on nerves, cheap beer and the excitement of being away from home for the first time. The bar was heaving with over-eager freshers, necking lagers or alcopops as they made conversation and sized up potential new friends, future housemates and soulmates. After an exhausting day of travelling from her family home in Southampton, finding her new digs, unpacking and meeting new faces, she'd been desperate for a seat and as soon as she spotted one at the end of a table that looked free she'd launched herself at it, grinning self-consciously at the other inhabitants at the table who were all staring back at her. It was quickly established that the seat was already taken and when its tenant, Pete, returned from the bar to claim it, he suggested they solve the problem by her sitting on his lap.

It wasn't love at first sight but it wasn't far off either. He was living in the same halls of residence as her and they struck up an easy friendship, meeting in the canteen for meals and walking to campus together where they would go their separate ways for lectures – him in business management and her in communication and media. Soon they were spending several evenings a week lying on her bed together, listening to indie music (his choice), eating crisps and discussing the meaning of life. They were the very cliché of new students but she loved it. By the time she went home for Christmas, she was smitten with this new boy in her life, with his confidence, easy self-assurance and banter, and she spent the entire festive period mooning over him, listening to Mariah Carey (her choice) and using every ounce of willpower that she had not to drunk call him and declare undying love.

Meeting up with her old school friends in the local pub, she'd felt different, as though she'd somehow become a new person in those three months she'd been away, and she was aching to get back to Leeds. The holidays seemed like they would never end and as soon as term started, she was throwing her stuff into her holdall, waving at her parents and practically sprinting to the train station to make her journey back north.

To her amazement and utter joy, Pete returned in January single after breaking up with his girlfriend from back home. As soon as he heard she was back in town he was at her door with some Doritos, a four-pack of beer and a nervous grin. Within two weeks they were an official couple. By the following year their relationship was as solid, reliable and familiar to all their friends as the second-hand furniture that furnished their student digs.

The perfect couple, that's what they'd been called by the

other students during their time in Leeds. They were sociable and fun-loving, always up for a laugh and popular with everyone. They bickered of course but while other couples would have drunken, jealous spats after nights out, accusing the other of flirting with another student from their course, they seemed immune to the drama. With Pete she felt both safe and exhilarated at the same time because everything with him was more fun, more colourful, than her dull, suburban life had been before she met him.

By the time they graduated, they'd made their plan for the future and agreed that they would both apply for jobs in London and move there as soon as they were hired. Their reputation as the dream couple followed them to London where they survived the tumultuous post-university years when all the other couples around them were breaking up as their lives took them in different directions and towards new passions and desires.

They managed to navigate the tricky path to pursuing their careers and discovering new friendships while maintaining their relationship. She'd been tempted of course, enjoying the attention of work colleagues flirting with her at Christmas parties or catching the eye of an attractive man in a bar on a night out with the girls. She was sure he'd had plenty of temptations too, but she trusted him implicitly. She knew, and relished the fact, that their relationship was envied by friends and colleagues on both sides and that there were women out there determined to find a chink in their armour and claim Pete for themselves, but they had held strong for all these years, a solid couple that couldn't be broken. Until now.

Kate remained rooted to the sofa digesting, thinking, disbelieving and then believing all over again. How had this happened? What had actually happened? Why hadn't she seen it coming? What was she going to do in the morning? What should she tell the children? What should she tell their friends? She felt an overwhelming wave of humiliation. Everyone was going to be talking about this. Did people already know? Were they gossiping behind her back? Her thoughts and fears came thick and fast then, invading her mind with such force that she couldn't shake them off. She sat there, immobile and trapped in her thoughts, unable to move or to see any light at the end of the tunnel in this situation.

It was only when she heard the gentle hum of the milkman's electric van on the street outside and the clinking of two bottles being put on her front doorstep that she realised a new day had begun without her. She had to sort herself out before the kids woke up. Dashing to the bedroom she quickly showered, brushed her teeth and changed.

Lily and Maggie, ever the early risers, appeared soon after, clutching their teddies and grinding their little hands into sleepy eyes. They were so innocent and blissfully unaware of what had happened the previous day, and Kate looked at them and thought her heart was going to break. Instead, she forced herself into autopilot mode, an act that came easier than expected after years of practice, preparing their toast and peanut butter and supervising their washing and dressing, until Rachel, their lovely Australian nanny, arrived to gather them up and take them to school. Clearing up the discarded cups and plates on the table, Kate kissed them both, waved them off and waited for the front door to close with a slam. With relief, she sunk down onto a kitchen chair and considered just what the fuck to do now. Maybe she should be in tears, but she was too horrified to cry. Stuff like this didn't happen to them – only it had and now she was left to clean up the mess with very little idea of how to go about it. She bit her nails nervously and grabbed her phone.

Forty-five minutes later Kate still hadn't moved when her phone bleeped with a message:

what the actual fuck? I'm on my way.

Erin was at the house in fourteen minutes. As soon as Kate opened the door her younger sibling barged in, eyes wide, hair unkempt, and said simply, 'Start at the beginning and tell me everything.'

'He didn't come home last night,' Kate began. 'I found this note.' She passed the note to Erin who devoured it, reading each word as if searching for a clue to a cryptic puzzle. Once she had finished the letter Erin looked up at her, mouth hanging open in shock. For a split second Kate thought she saw something else pass over her face – a fleeting response so quick that she almost missed it – as though the shock hadn't quite reached her eyes. 'You don't seem that surprised? What do you know? What's happened?' she demanded.

'I don't know anything at all,' Erin protested, holding her hands up in surrender. 'I'm as shocked as you are that this has happened. He has everything he could ever need and he's thrown it all away for someone who I can only assume is a twenty-something blonde bimbo with big boobs. He's a selfish bastard.'

Kate observed her sister. Perhaps she was being paranoid. She was, after all, sleep-deprived and out of her mind with worry. And right now, she needed an ally not a row, so she decided not to push it. She sat in silence for a minute or two, staring at the note and trying to think of something to say. On the other side of the table, Erin appeared to be doing the same thing. Finally, to her relief, Erin broke the silence. 'Did he say anything to you yesterday morning? Did he seem different at all?'

'Not at all,' she replied, replaying the previous morning over again in her mind. 'That's what I can't understand. We even had breakfast together, just the two of us, and he acted like everything was normal. He had plenty of opportunities to say something to me and he didn't. He must have known the whole time what he was planning to do. I can't decide if he's a calculating bastard or just a coward.'

'Where did you find the note?'

Kate explained her middle of the night discovery to Erin, who raised her eyebrows when she heard that Pete had left his phone behind as well. 'When he says he's met someone else, do you have any idea who?'

'I can only assume it's someone from work or one of his clients,' Kate answered. 'He's never anywhere else except at the office or at home so I doubt he'd have time to find someone else. It's unlikely to be a mum at the girls' school given that he's been so busy at work he hasn't done a school run in months. I guess I know why now. Not working after all. Shagging, probably.' She started laughing slightly hysterically. Was this the first sign of madness?

'I bet it's a bloody PA,' Erin said, 'or a receptionist. This is a midlife crisis and he'll be back with his tail between his legs within weeks, I'm telling you now. But the question is, would you have him back?'

'I really don't think that is the question. I think he's gone. For good.'

'How do you feel?'

'Awful.'

The women looked at each other, so many unanswered questions between them. Kate knew that Erin was itching to probe – to ask about the state of their marriage, were they happy, how were things in the bedroom? But now was not the time and they both knew it. That would all come, in the days and weeks to follow.

'What have you told the girls?' Erin asked.

'Nothing, they didn't ask where he was: they're used to him being away sometimes in the week. I sent them off to school as usual.'

'What are you going to tell them? Are you going to say he's away on business like he asked you to?'

'I think so – not for him but for them. They'll be upset that he didn't say goodbye before he left but then they'll forget about it and it gives me some time to plan what I'm going to do next.'

'Which is?'

'I have no fucking idea.'

## 2

### PETE

Pete looked at the French countryside stretching out before him and sighed deeply. He felt at once both utter contentment and nagging guilt over what he was doing. He took a sip of his ice-cold white wine and turned to look at Claire who was lying on the wooden recliner next to him. Her dark eyes were covered by a large pair of black designer sunglasses and she had wrapped a thin blanket around her like a cocoon to keep her warm in the unseasonably cool sunshine. She had never looked more beautiful.

The B&B they were staying at in the South of France looked like something from a picture-perfect postcard. A stone-built gîte with powder-blue shutters and ivy climbing up the walls, its cobbled veranda spilled out on to the open countryside. From their vantage point they could see endless fields and beyond that, the tops of houses from a nearby village in the valley. The place was run by a friendly French couple in their fifties who had, of course, instantly assumed they were married. Monsieur and Madame Garland, they had called them when they arrived, tired and giddy, earlier that day. He knew Claire had been thrilled by this.

On the little wrought-iron side table between them lay a pile of photos of a property not too dissimilar to the one they were staying in right now. It was going to be their new home and if you looked hard enough into the distance, you might even be able to see the top of its roof peeping out from below the hills. He glanced down again at the photos, feeling both excitement and disbelief, before catching Claire's eye. She grinned at him and he grinned back, high on life. He felt like a lovestruck teenager embarking on his first trip away from home. But this was different because, if the plan came off, they wouldn't be going home again.

It was Claire who had first suggested that they move to France. Her dad had passed away a couple of years ago and had left her his house, a three-bed cottage which he had bought to enjoy his retirement in. But his plans had been cut short after he was diagnosed with pancreatic cancer and the house had been untouched since he passed away. Claire told Pete that she couldn't bring herself to return to it since the death of her beloved father. But she had spoken so fondly of holidays there while her father was still alive, describing the short walk to the bakery in the village to pick up fresh bread each morning, the summer weeks spent paddling in the nearby river, a pace of life so different to the loud, dirty, chaotic, endless relentlessness of London. If you're tired of London, you're tired of life, wasn't that the famous saying? Well, Pete was fucking knackered.

Even so, the idea had seemed ludicrous at the time. It was one thing that he was fooling around behind his wife's back with another woman but quite another to abandon his family entirely and move to another country. 'I have the girls to think of,' he had reminded Claire when she suggested it. 'I can't just up and leave like that.'

'People commute from France to London all the time,' she had assured him. 'It's so easy now. You could still see them at weekends and sometimes in the week too. And think of the amazing summer holidays they could have out here. They could come for the whole six weeks. They'd absolutely love it, you know they would.'

'What about my job?' he'd asked, still humouring her at this stage because the idea, while alluring in theory, was unrealistic and impossible.

'What, the job you've been moaning about pretty much since we met? The one you've been talking about leaving for months?'

'Yeah, fair enough, but I'd still need to work. How am I going to earn money holed away in the middle of the French countryside eating baguettes? It's a sweet idea, Claire, but come on, be realistic.'

And so of course, she had done just that. There was no denying that Claire liked to get her own way. When Kate was like this, buzzing around with a bee in her bonnet like the time she had made him buy that damn house, it annoyed him but with Claire he felt different, her gentle persuasion was somehow less offensive and more endearing. She had scoured job listings, looking for roles that could be carried out remotely with occasional travel for meetings and presented him with some frighteningly feasible options.

'It's becoming much more popular these days,' she told him. 'Lots of people work from home. You could go into London every couple of weeks for meetings and tie it in with seeing the girls. You can rent a little flat in north London and decorate one of the bedrooms for them so they can sleep over whenever you're there. And then in the holidays they'll come and stay with us in France. It would take some getting used to, I know, but we'd work it out and it could be absolutely amazing. Let's escape the rat race, Pete. Let's live the life that most people can only dream of.'

At what point did this ridiculous idea start to make sense?

When did he convince himself that he could actually do this? Was it when Claire persuaded him to apply for a couple of new roles which offered remote working and he thought there was nothing to lose? Was it when he started going for interviews, just to see what was out there, while still telling himself that it had nothing to do with going to France and more to do with furthering his career? Was it when a big tech firm offered him a role with a package far better than what he'd been expecting? Was it when Claire wrapped her long, slim legs around him, put her lips to his ear and whispered that he turned her on more than any man she'd ever known? Or was it when Kate turned her back to him in bed again and he realised he was no longer in love with his wife?

Either way, just a couple of months after that first conversation when he had all but laughed at Claire for suggesting something so stupid, he found himself accepting the new job and handing in his notice at work. As he did it, he felt like he had temporarily slipped into someone else's shoes and his life was not really his own anymore. He told his boss that it was time to move on, that he needed a new challenge and although he had worked at the company for years, she hadn't batted an eyelid. She had simply accepted his resignation, shaken his hand and wished him well. After all, people moved jobs all the time these days.

Only a couple of close friends at work knew the truth. They weren't surprised to hear about Claire because they'd known about the affair for months, but they'd still been pretty stunned when he told them the plan, over a pint in the pub near the office one evening after work. He knew he shouldn't have told them but he couldn't help himself. He was like a little child with a secret he had to share or else he would burst. His colleagues had both met Kate a few times, but their loyalty was to him and he knew they wouldn't breathe a word. Still, they had urged him to think about it very carefully.

'You can't come back from something like this,' Dan, a happily married dad of three had warned him. 'She won't forgive you. And the girls, you'll never have the same relationship with them. Just think about it really carefully. You're risking everything for Claire. Are you sure it's worth it? Is she worth it, mate?'

Even Carl, a permanently single womaniser and not usually one for morals when it came to affairs of the heart, had told him to tread carefully. 'She could turn the kids against you,' he said. 'You hear about it all the time; it happened to a friend of mine. He had to take her to court and the whole thing was a shitshow. Now he only sees them every other weekend and they act like they don't want to be there half the time anyway. He's absolutely gutted and I don't think he'll ever really get over it.'

Pete had listened to his friends' warnings, but they weren't enough to deter him. He knew what he was risking and he knew what Kate's reaction would be when she found out. Apoplectic was an understatement. But it was too late now – Claire was his drug and he was hooked, and he had already gone past the point of no return.

But the doubt still niggled at him, despite his conviction, so for a while he had been thinking about a contingency plan where he didn't give everything away at first. He would tell Kate what she needed to know, that he had met someone else, that he wasn't happy and that he was going away for a bit to sort his head out. It was all true, after all, and it gave him a way back, he reasoned, if he got to France and realised it was all a big mistake.

Obviously, Kate would be livid when he returned and he knew she might never forgive him – and even if she did it would be a long road back to reconciliation with endless bloody marriage counselling – but it didn't feel as final as telling her that he was moving country permanently to be with another woman. She'd never forgive him for that. It would be game over and he wasn't quite ready for that finality yet. Was he being a coward? Was he simply putting off the inevitable? He didn't know but right now, living in this glorious moment, he didn't care.

Once he'd hashed it out in his head, he was fairly satisfied with his plan but there was one flaw – he knew he didn't have it in him to lie to her face. They'd known each other for more than fifteen years and he'd collapse like a house of cards and give away his hand under her interrogation. So instead, he had thought of leaving a note for her which told her everything she needed to know for now, while he went to France and established if the fantasy lived up to the reality, if it was really over between him and Kate for good, and if he could live apart from the children long term. He knew these were big questions that he wouldn't be able to answer until he had tried it for real. He was protecting them, he felt, from a horrible truth that they may never even need to know about. Yes, he told himself again, it was the right course of action.

Next to him, Claire drained her wine and then leaned over and took his hand, squeezing it gently, signalling that she wanted him to refill it. He squeezed it back and reached for the bottle. It was easier for her, he thought, she had no ties at home and nothing to stop her from moving countries at the drop of a hat. She was still in her twenties and had that confidence and carefree abandon that everyone seemed to lose when they hit their thirties. All she needed was a toothbrush and passport and she was good to go. Even quitting London was straightforward because she worked as a temp and rented her flat. She never liked to stay in one place for too long, she told him, there was too much to do in the world, too much to see.

He was intoxicated by her spontaneity but also terrified,

fearing the day when she might get bored of him and move on to her next adventure. But when he confessed this to her late one night, whispering his insecurities into her ear as they lay in bed, she had showered him with kisses and assured him this was not the case – that he was the anchor she had been looking for. The problem was, she wanted to moor on the other side of the English bloody Channel. And now he had agreed to go with her.

From what she had told him about her upbringing, he knew Claire had some money which had been left to her by her fairly well-off parents – her dad had been a self-made businessman and her mum a TV actress – and that safety net allowed her to live with a kind of frivolity that many people couldn't afford. An only child, her mum had died when she was at college, leaving some money for her in a trust which had become available when she was twenty-one. Then when her dad had passed away, everything that was left had come to her, including the house in France that lay just a few miles away, waiting for someone to breathe life into it again.

They'd talked a lot about how it would work. Claire had suggested staying in the B&B while they made the house, which had been untouched and unloved for two years, liveable. They'd get wifi installed, make sure they had the home comforts they were used to and then they'd move in. He would start his new job and she would begin work on converting the outbuildings on the plot of land into holiday lets. Between them, they had worked out that they'd have enough money to get by, even with the extra cost of a London flat. He'd go back home a few weeks after he had left and arrange to meet Kate, to sit down and have it all out with her, one way or another. She would have had time to calm down a bit by then and hopefully he would have had time to work out whether he'd done the right thing.

It all seemed like a story he'd read in one of those women's magazines that Kate left lying around the house. Something that happened to other people, not him. Yet here he was, sipping wine and planning his future with the woman who had made him feel alive for the first time in years. Because that's how he felt – like she'd pulled him out of the darkness and into the light again. She had brought him back to life. And that was enough for him to risk everything to be with her.

'It's getting late,' Claire said, breaking the silence. 'Shall we go in and get changed for dinner? Maybe take a walk into the village and check out that new little restaurant we saw on the way in?'

She wriggled out of the blanket and stood up, reaching over to pull Pete out of his recliner and up towards her. The close contact immediately aroused him – she'd had that effect on him from the beginning. He kissed her, still marvelling after all these months at the joy of being able to kiss someone whenever he liked and be kissed back, such a simple gesture that married couples seem to forget how to do.

'I've got a better idea,' he said, which came out a bit more lewdly than it had sounded in his head but she simply laughed at him and nodded her agreement, turning in the direction of their room and pulling him along with her.

'There's no rush for dinner,' she said. 'There's no rush for anything, really. We've got all the time in the world, Pete.'

And in that moment, despite all of his misgivings, fears and guilt about the enormity of his betrayal, he felt in the pit of his stomach that he was exactly where he should be.

# 3

# KATE

I t was Erin's idea to search the house. Kate realised that she should have thought of it sooner but instead she'd been sitting around like a spare part, unsure of what to do with herself. What was wrong with her? She sprang to her feet, glad of something proactive to do. It might distract her from the ball of dread growing inside her.

She started in the bedroom, glancing over at their bed which hadn't been slept in the previous night, the neat silk bedspread and matching cushions lying undisturbed. She went to their fitted wardrobes first, sliding open the smooth mirrored panel on Pete's side and looking in at his messy piles of clothes, a stark contrast to her neat, orderly section at the opposite end. Rooting around in the chaos she quickly noticed a gap where Pete's brown leather holdall – an old anniversary present from her – usually lived.

Rifling through his piles of clothes she discovered that some were missing: casual T-shirts, shorts, jeans and jumpers all unaccounted for. All his work outfits seemed present and correct, she noticed, hanging undisturbed. She wasn't sure what that meant yet. She moved to their bathroom next and searched through the cabinet, looking for his travel toiletry bag. It was gone. She returned to their bedroom and went to the dresser where the family's passports were kept. Pulling the drawer open, she counted, one, two, three. His was missing. She wasn't particularly surprised that he'd taken it with him but the fresh reality of it all still hit her like a ton of bricks.

Suddenly feeling desperate to be in the company of another human being, she tore back down the stairs and into the kitchen where Erin was making tea. Instinctively she grabbed her phone from the table to check his social media accounts. He'd set up Facebook and Twitter profiles years ago when everyone had them although he hardly ever used them, save for the odd photo of a lads' night out or one of the girls' birthdays. She knew he wasn't going to post a photo of himself with his mystery woman, helpfully tagging her and their location with a brief explanation as to his state of mind. But there would at least be some comfort in seeing the familiarity of his profile. She typed his name into Facebook and waited for his profile picture, a photo from their wedding day, to appear but there was nothing. Confused, she searched her list of friends, looking for his name. It was gone.

'He's deleted his Facebook profile,' she called out to Erin who, fishing teabags out of mugs, turned to her in surprise. Opening Twitter, she searched again, but while lots of other Pete Garlands came up in the results, his profile was nowhere to be found. Finally, she went on to LinkedIn. Again, while Pete Garland the Head of HR, Pete Garland the Life Coach and Pete Garland the Senior Sales Executive all popped up in the search results, there was no Pete Garland, Associate Director at Media Corp. Her husband had digitally vanished.

'Jesus Christ, he's deleted them all,' she exclaimed. It was as if he'd never existed, his online history had been entirely erased. The thought hit her like a fresh punch in the stomach. Erin pulled out her own phone, checking the social media channels herself to make sure it wasn't a mistake. 'They're definitely gone,' she confirmed. 'Bloody hell, Kate.' Then she added: 'Have you checked your bank accounts?'

'What for?' she replied, confused for a second.

'You might be able to get some clues from his transactions.'

It was a reasonable suggestion, so Kate logged into their online banking app, searching their current account and credit card for anything unusual but there was nothing that she couldn't account for over the last few days. The bill for the supermarket delivery, the regular council tax deduction and a cash withdrawal she'd made to pay the window cleaner.

'There's nothing untoward,' she told Erin.

As an afterthought she logged into their ISAs, not expecting to see any action in their long-term investments which they had both agreed to leave untouched. It was their savings for the future, for the children's education and their retirement together. Clicking into the recent transactions, her blood ran cold as she looked at the numbers staring back at her. Surely it was a mistake? She looked again.

'He withdrew £10,000 in cash from our ISA last month,' she exclaimed, as the level of his deception became even more obvious. 'The bastard has been planning this for at least a month.' She bent forward in her chair and thought she might throw up.

'I can't believe this is happening,' Erin said, looking at her with horror. 'It doesn't make any sense. It's one thing going away for a few days to sort out your head, it's quite another to take a passport and a wad of cash and disappear off the face of the planet. Something doesn't feel right here, Kate, you need to get on to some of his mates, to people at his work, find out what they know. You need some answers.'

'But he doesn't want to be found. He's made that perfectly

clear. Maybe I should just do what he wants, give him some space?'

'And what about you?' Erin demanded. 'And the kids? What about what you want?'

What she wanted was for her damn husband to be sitting in his office in central London like he should be and for this whole thing to have been a nightmare. But that option wasn't on the table and she wasn't really sure what the next best alternative was. Certainly not this uncertainty. Anything but this. They sat in silence again, looking at each other without really knowing what to say. The ticking of the clock reminded her that she hadn't had anything to eat all morning. She was just debating whether she could stomach some toast when the sound of a key turning in the lock made her jump. For a split second she thought it was Pete and her heart leapt at the idea of him strolling into the kitchen, declaring that he'd decided to work from home and he'd pick up the kids from school later, before reality kicked in.

'Shit, it's Rachel,' she said aloud. She had completely forgotten that their nanny would be returning to the house to do some chores before school pick up. She suddenly had an unpalatable thought – what if it's her? Is she the other woman? The nanny and the husband, it would hardly be the first time, would it? But then lovely, kind Rachel entered the kitchen with a big smile and enveloped Erin in a tight hug before launching into tales of school-gate gossip from the morning's drop-off.

Kate barely listened as her mind processed the possibility of Rachel and Pete having an illicit affair behind her back, shagging in the downstairs loo while she was upstairs with the kids, before dismissing it again. It just didn't feel right, like putting together the wrong pieces of a jigsaw puzzle and finding that they won't fit no matter how much you think they should. And anyway, it would take quite some balls for Rachel to turn up at work as normal if she knew that Pete had left her.

Rachel had worked for them for five years. Kate hadn't wanted to hire a nanny at first because she wasn't working, so having extra help seemed like far too much of an indulgence. But it was Pete who had persuaded her to get help. He was doing it for her of course, he could see that she was struggling with parenthood, the anxiety and relentlessness of caring for two tiny beings who relied on her for everything. Maggie was a tiny baby and Lily was in her terrible twos, hurling herself on the floor in protest at pretty much anything and everything, wreaking havoc wherever possible.

Kate sat on the floor one evening, surrounded by a sea of toys, and dirty nappies, her nipples blistered from breastfeeding and her mind addled from sleep deprivation, and sobbed. Pete discovered her still sitting there when he got home late from work and did what he normally did in a crisis – he threw money at it.

'Just for a few months,' he had assured her. 'We can afford it, so why make life harder for yourself than it needs to be? Give yourself a break, Kate.' She had reluctantly called a few nanny agencies and a week later Rachel turned up on their doorstep for an interview, wearing an oversized yellow parka, red Doc Martens and a confident, all-knowing expression as if she'd drifted down from the sky like a modern-day Mary Poppins to save their family. Within a few months, Rachel had become such an integral cog in their family life that Kate couldn't imagine life without her. Order, routine and calm were restored and Kate felt like a huge weight had been lifted from her. After weeks, months, maybe years of struggle if she was being honest, she could finally glimpse a sliver of light at the end of the tunnel again.

With more time on her hands and a new zest for life, she had begun to formulate plans of relaunching her career, setting up as a freelancer so that she could work flexibly around family life. Full of renewed vigour, she had started thinking of company names, registering domains and creating social media accounts for her new public relations business. Her head was full of ideas and plans which she had shared with Pete in the evening over dinner and she knew he was thrilled by her enthusiasm and purpose. He'd always told her that one of the things he loved most about her was her drive and determination and she knew she hadn't been showing much of those qualities for a while, when simply getting through the day had been exhausting enough. Finally, the confident, capable Kate he'd fallen in love with was back.

For a few weeks the atmosphere in the house had been charged with energy and optimism for the first time since she'd gone on maternity leave. She couldn't wait for him to come home from work, not so that she could have a break from the children but so she could tell him about what she'd been doing that day to prepare the new business. It felt like the old days again.

But at the point when she had to turn her well-organised plans into reality, she had become gripped by fear and doubt and it suddenly seemed too overwhelming. The first few enthusiastic emails she'd sent out to old work contacts offering her services had been either unanswered or responded to with a friendly but dismissive *no thanks, but we'll certainly keep your details on file*. Each rejection took away a bit more of her confidence. She started to have second thoughts. Her clients would have moved on, she thought, and she hadn't kept in touch with any of her friends from the PR agency. Babies had taken over her life and her ability to maintain old friendships with anyone who didn't have kids themselves. She was too embarrassed to contact them now, out of the blue, to beg for work or contacts. She knew the old Kate would have swallowed her pride, gritted her teeth and pushed herself out of her comfort zone to go after what she wanted. That headstrong, confident, career woman version of herself seemed a distant memory now. The insecurities continued to seep into her already anxious mind – she hadn't worked in years. Would she even be any good anymore? She hadn't kept up with the changes and the industry was so full of young, capable people, who knew the right people in the right places. Why would anyone want her? How could she justify charging clients a fee when she no longer considered herself an expert in her field? She was a bloody fraud, a joke, that's what she was, and everyone would know it.

So, like many great plans, they fell by the wayside. The months went by and Rachel stayed on, outperforming in her own role as their family manager, and leaving Kate oscillating between relief that she had her support, shame that she couldn't manage on her own with the kids or restart her career, irritation with Rachel for being better than her, and annoyance with herself for feeling like that about someone so lovely. It was exhausting, all that self-doubt, and she was just so tired. *One day*, she told herself, *one day soon I'll get it all sorted but just not right now*.

It was around that time she had decided they should move house. They had more money now, thanks to Pete's endless promotions, and a fresh start was just what they all needed. She was going to make their home perfect, she decided – a place where the children's friends always wanted to come over and play and Pete looked forward to coming back to every night. Once they had moved in, she would let Rachel go and take over the running of the family. She would cook homemade meals rather than chicken nuggets and waffles, they would constantly have people round for playdates and lunches and they would be so, so happy. And then once the girls were both at school she'd look into going back to work. *Yes*, she thought, that was the new plan and the idea filled her with energy and enthusiasm again.

The house they eventually bought needed a lot of work and when they moved in, she'd had to focus on the refurbishment. It had been just what she needed, finally something that she was good at again. She told herself it would be easier if Rachel stayed on to help because the house would be full of builders and paint fumes and she would be able to take the girls out while Kate managed the project. Now the refurb was done and dusted save for the garden, both children were at school, project career launch was still on ice and she still hadn't let Rachel go yet. Old habits die hard. But she'd done what she set out to do – the house was absolutely stunning, everyone said so; it looked like something from a magazine centrefold. And the children's bedrooms, with their co-ordinated colour schemes, rocking horses and dolls houses, were like something plucked from a little girl's dream.

With a jolt back to reality, she became aware that Rachel had stopped talking and was looking at her with concern. 'Are you all right, Kate?' she asked. 'You look a little peaky.'

'I'm fine,' she answered automatically. Erin glanced over at her as the lie slipped out, but she didn't feel ready to share her situation with others just yet. She wondered if Erin was doing as she had done just seconds before, wondering whether Rachel was the other woman and coming to her own, similar conclusions.

Sensing the tension in the kitchen Rachel quickly excused herself, chattering about having to put on laundry and tidy bedrooms, and made her escape. *She probably thinks we were having a row*, Kate thought. If only it was that simple.

She looked at the clock again. It was approaching lunchtime and she still hadn't had anything to eat. In a few hours the children would be finishing school and she would have to brush all this aside temporarily and act like everything was fine again. The sound of her phone ringing broke through the silence. She looked down at the screen and her heart sank when she saw the name of the girls' school, which never signalled good news. She picked up the phone.

'Mrs Garland? This is Eileen calling from the school office at Greenway Primary School. I'm afraid Lily's had an accident.'

'What kind of accident?' Kate asked, expecting to hear of projectile vomit, a bloody nose or twisted ankle. This was the last thing she needed right now.

'Lily fell awkwardly during PE and has been unable to put any weight on her leg at all. She's in a lot of pain and we think it might be broken. We've called an ambulance and they're taking her to the Whittington Hospital. Her teacher is with her.'

*Jesus.* Kate's heart was racing as she stood up and started frantically gathering her keys and purse, while Erin looked at her quizzically. 'I'll be there as soon as I can.'

# 4

## PETE

He had noticed Claire immediately. She was sitting at the reception desk, working with an easy confidence which suggested she'd been there all her life when he guessed it was her first day because he'd never seen her before. He was feeling ratty after a crap start to the day, the kids declaring full-on war with each other over a favourite breakfast bowl, which resulted in said bowl being smashed and Kate losing her shit and snapping at everyone.

Months later, Claire had asked him when it was that he realised he was attracted to her. 'The second I saw you,' he replied.

What was not to like? She was undeniably beautiful. But like the many attractive women he had come across in his life up until now, his thoughts hadn't gone beyond this initial, almost subconscious acknowledgement. He gave her a welcoming smile, introduced himself, made the necessary polite conversation and went on his way. By the time he got to his office on the fourteenth floor, he'd forgotten all about her.

In the weeks that followed, their interactions consisted only of a brief hello when he came into work and the odd phone conversation when she called up to tell him someone had arrived for a meeting. By the time he left to go home, she was usually gone. To him, she was no different to any of the other pretty receptionists who had come and gone before her, with their glossy hair and pencil skirts.

But then one day he came into work early so that he could prepare for a big client meeting. He'd hardly spoken to Kate the evening before, she'd been busy looking for new kitchen tiles on Pinterest, and this morning she'd busied herself with the kids and barely said two words to him. That was nothing unusual in their household but for some reason he was brooding over it today. Maybe because the country was in the grip of a late summer heatwave and all he wanted to do was loosen his tie, sit in a beer garden and drink ice-cold lager but instead he was dealing with three grumpy females who acted like they didn't even notice he was there, yet got shitty with him when he wasn't.

As he walked into the foyer, he saw Claire sitting at the reception desk eating her breakfast and looking pristine in a sleeveless silk top, a stark contrast to his crumpled shirt, damp with sweat from the sweltering commute. She looked up at him in surprise, which she quickly transformed into a professional smile and suddenly he had a compulsive urge to talk to her, to have a conversation with someone that wasn't about builders' quotes, parents' evenings or bed wetting.

'You're in early,' she said, looking a bit sheepish. She wasn't supposed to eat while working on the front desk, not that he cared.

'Client meeting, loads to prepare,' he told her. He looked at her croissant. 'That looks good,' he said, and his tummy rumbled as if on cue. She laughed, tore a large piece off and offered it to him, which he took gratefully. The warm, sticky pastry gave him a sudden rush of pleasure and he found he didn't want to leave. He leaned against the desk, propped up by one elbow, and they fell into an easy conversation.

Claire was sharp and funny. She was twenty-seven, lived in Wimbledon and liked to travel as much as possible, she told him. She enjoyed temping because she didn't want to commit to anywhere long term. She particularly liked working on reception because she got to people-watch all day. She was clearly intelligent, the type of person who would probably be good at any job they were given but work to her was simply a means to earn enough money to go on her next adventure. After a decade of toeing the line – working his way up the career ladder, getting married and having kids – he loved her attitude. He didn't think he'd done a single impulsive thing since he bought a last-minute plane ticket to visit Kate in Thailand when she went travelling the summer after they graduated from university. *Christ, how long ago had that been?*

'I'm living vicariously through you,' he told her with a grin when she regaled him with tales of what she'd been up to over the weekend, getting tipsy in the champagne bar at St Pancras Station and jumping on the Eurostar to Paris for a night just for the hell of it. Maybe it was a midlife crisis, sad and stereotypical as it was, but he found himself feeling undeniably envious of her carefree life, so far removed was he from it. Before he knew it, half an hour had passed, and colleagues started trickling into the office. 'Shit,' he said. 'Better go prep for the meeting. Thanks for the croissant.'

'Any time,' she said, smiling at him before returning to her work.

Over the weeks that followed he started stopping by regularly to say hi. Soon he realised that he was looking forward to seeing her. She was an escape from his own mundane life and it was like a breath of fresh air in the stifling heat. He started coming into work early several times a week, telling her – and himself – that it was down to his heavy workload when he knew deep down it was so that he could have some time alone with her in the quiet of the early morning before the masses arrived for work and burst their bubble. It became his favourite part of the day.

One evening he was leaving on time for once and as he came downstairs he saw her applying lipstick, checking herself carefully in a little compact mirror.

'Going anywhere nice?' he asked her.

'Date,' she admitted with a shrug.

He felt a pang of jealousy which surprised him. 'Well, have a great time,' he replied briskly and hurried off before she had a chance to notice his reaction. He had no right to be pissed off but for the rest of the evening he felt inexplicably low. The next morning he didn't come into work until later, giving her what he hoped was a cheery wave as he walked past her in a steady stream of people and headed straight up to his office. He never asked her how it went.

Pete had never cheated on his wife and Christ, he'd been offered it on a plate often enough. He'd had some flirtations over the years, attractive colleagues or clients leaning in close to him at business dinners or corporate events and making their intentions perfectly clear. He'd enjoyed their attention, certainly, and he'd even been tempted once or twice but he hadn't crossed the line. His dad had been a liar and a cheat and he'd always promised that he would be better. Plus, he'd been with Kate since he was nineteen years old and he couldn't imagine life without her. But recently, life with her had become hard.

They'd always been in sync, the two of them, from their student days through their twenties and into their early thirties. She was nothing like any woman he had ever met before and she was everything he had ever wanted – fun, confident and ambitious. But since getting married and having kids, she had completely changed to the point where he felt he barely even knew her. She was withdrawn, always tired and, seemingly, always angry at him for unknown reasons. Whatever lust for life she'd had for all those years had been snuffed out of her. Was she even aware of it, he wondered? He'd tentatively brought it up a few times, suggesting she talk to someone about it, and she'd shot him down so viciously that he'd given up trying. *Perhaps this is just what happens when you have kids*, he thought. He had never given any serious thought to the fact that their marriage might be in trouble, he had simply accepted his lot and got on with life. *It'll get better when the children are older*, he told himself, *that's what everyone says. Those first few years are the hardest.* And anyway, they were perfect for each other, him and Kate, everyone said it.

He still remembered the first time he had met Kate like it was yesterday. Tall, slim and sassy, with long auburn hair and long legs clad in tight jeans, she sauntered into the student bar as if she owned the place and stole his seat. When he returned from the bar and suggested that she sit on his lap, he was half expecting her to be affronted but she simply laughed and replied, 'You're on.' They'd chatted all night and the next day he had looked for her in the canteen, desperate to talk to her again.

She was smart, beautiful and confident, and she seemed so different to Beth, his school sweetheart who had decided to stay at home and apply for local office jobs rather than go to uni. She'd been a sweet girl but she had no ambition at all, a stark contrast to Pete who couldn't wait to go out into the world and make his mark. Their relationship was pretty much doomed from the minute he kissed her goodbye, jumped into his battered Vauxhall Corsa and hit the M1, en route to his new life. Pete wasn't close to his family: his brother was a cocky little shit and his mum, who had raised them both on her own, acted like it was all his fault that their father had left them when he barely even remembered the arsehole. He couldn't wait to get away from them and university was his escape route – his chance of a better life. He only went home at Christmas to break up with Beth. Poor Beth, who had been so loyal and patient during that first term, was heartbroken when he told her that it wasn't going to work, but he'd had no regrets. Now he had no ties to that godforsaken town anymore, no reason to go back at all.

Pete was a man of principles so there was no going near Kate until he was single. After he'd dumped Beth, he couldn't wait to get back to Leeds to see Kate again. She was ambitious and intelligent, a straight A student who liked to work hard and party even harder. One minute she'd be downing shots in the student bar and the next she'd be in the library with a latte, nose in her books, studying hard. She could finish a cryptic crossword while balancing a cigarette in one hand and a bag of Doritos in the other. He was in awe of her.

When they first got together, he couldn't believe how lucky he was. They just clicked from the start, there was no drama, jealousy or stress. While his mates' girlfriends threw their toys out of the pram if they went out late or didn't call, Kate couldn't give a hoot because she was out having fun herself. When girls paid him attention it was of no concern to Kate because boys did the same to her and they both trusted each other.

Then the university bubble burst and they found themselves in the real world. People warned him that there might be some bumps in the road ahead but there really weren't. There was never any doubt that they'd move to London to pursue their careers but they agreed to live apart at first and enjoy the experience of sharing flats with their friends before they settled down. They had plenty of time, they both agreed. He felt so fortunate to have her, this vivacious girl who gave him the space he needed so that he never felt trapped yet was always there to come home to. They both did pretty well in their careers, they made friends – some their own and some joint – went on fun holidays and life was good.

So of course they did what they were supposed to do. The minute they hit thirty, he bought the ring, got down on one knee on a romantic trip to Rome and they set the date for the wedding. Within a year of returning from their honeymoon she was pregnant. They were both excited to start a family although, if he was being honest, she had been more into it than him. The thought of babies and nappies made him feel panicky. While her bump grew and she blossomed, he wondered how he would feel when the baby was born and worried about whether he would love it. *What kind of person worries that they won't love their own kid?* he'd thought. He was relieved when he met a bunch of dads at the local antenatal classes that Kate had signed them up to and it turned out that plenty of people worried about it.

Still, nothing could prepare him for parenthood. All of a sudden the life that he had always known, and was rather partial to, was turned completely upside down. Gone were the late nights drinking wine and putting the world to rights, long lie-ins and lazy Sundays in the pub. Instead, their life became consumed by sleepless nights, colicky babies, dirty nappies and the constant fear that this was their life forever more. He loved Lily, he really loved her, but he didn't really like her all that much to begin with. To be fair, what was to like? She cried constantly, was too young to interact with him, and the only thing that made her happy was being attached to Kate's breasts.

But the biggest change was in Kate. All of a sudden, the confident and capable woman that he had loved for over a decade was replaced by someone he could only describe as a nervous wreck. It's fair to say that motherhood did not come naturally to Kate. She transformed almost overnight into someone who was constantly anxious and tearful, scared to even leave the house sometimes. After a while the tears were replaced by resentment towards the world, and him, but he could never work out why. He knew motherhood was hard but he struggled to understand why she was falling apart so much. All the other new mums were sleep-deprived and exhausted but they seemed to be coping okay, whereas Kate just couldn't seem to adapt at all.

He tried to help her, he really did. He offered to take the baby for a few hours at weekends or to hire a nanny for a while to help her out but she seemed to take both offers as a personal insult, as if he were suggesting that she was incapable of looking after her own baby. Nothing he said was right as far as she was concerned and she seemed permanently cross with him for reasons that he just didn't understand because he'd done absolutely nothing wrong.

One day she called him at work in a panic. 'Lily's got a fever, I don't know what to do,' she cried.

'Calm down, I'm sure it's fairly common in babies,' he replied. 'Have you given her some Calpol?'

'Of course I bloody have! It hasn't made any difference. I've been trying to get through to the doctors for ages but it's constantly engaged. I think I should take her to A&E. It could be meningitis.'

Pete, who had been in the middle of an important meeting when she'd called, sighed. 'I don't think we need to take her to hospital, Kate, she's probably just got a cold. Listen, give her another hour or two and let's see how she is.'

'You don't understand, Pete, an hour could be too late – I'm going right now,' and she hung up. Pete went back to his meeting and when it finished, he texted her to find out how it had gone. She didn't reply so he called her, but it went to voicemail.

Starting to panic, Pete grabbed his things and rushed home to find the house empty. After calling her three more times, he was just about to head to the nearest hospital when Kate appeared around the corner, pushing Lily in the pram.

'Kate, what the hell? I've called you a bunch of times, why didn't you answer? How's Lily?'

'Oh she's fine,' Kate said. 'Her temperature went down as I was getting ready to go to hospital so I didn't bother going in the end. She's sleeping it off now.'

'Why the hell didn't you tell me? I've been worried sick!'

She turned and looked accusingly at him. 'You weren't that bloody worried! You didn't even offer to leave work. I figured you didn't care.'

He stared at her, feeling both hurt and irritated. 'Kate, that's not fair, I was in the middle of a really important meeting and I didn't think it was anything to worry about. But you had no right to ignore my calls. Of course I care.'

'It's fine, Pete. I handled it on my own. I'm getting quite good at that these days.'

It was one of the many barbed comments that she had started throwing his way. He couldn't seem to do anything right – he held Lily wrong, he changed her nappy wrong, he bathed her wrong. He became so anxious of experiencing Kate's wrath that Lily sensed his nerves and wailed every time he picked her up. Long days turned into long weeks which, in turn, turned into long months. Work became his refuge and he found himself staying later and later to avoid returning to a crying baby and a crying mother. He felt terrible about it because he loved them both but he also found himself feeling increasingly resentful towards Kate for creating this toxic environment that he dreaded coming home to.

As time went on, things slowly started to improve. Lily got older and became more interactive and fun, and Kate became a bit less stressy. By the time Lily was a toddler, Kate seemed to have found her stride. She had stopped breastfeeding and her possessiveness over Lily subsided, which meant that he could be more involved in looking after her. She began going for runs, getting her nails done and meeting mum friends for coffee at the weekends. By then Lily was in a bedtime routine and so they had their evenings back and started enjoying takeaways, wine and movie nights again. She even agreed to let her sister Erin babysit once or twice so they could go out for dinner. Life started to go back to normal – not pre-baby normal but a new kind of normal which lay somewhere in between content and discontent. Routine at least, even if things between them weren't like they used to be anymore.

So, when Kate suggested they try for baby number two, his first reaction was dread. He didn't think he could go through all that again and he wasn't sure that their marriage could survive it.

'It'll be different this time,' Kate reassured him. 'I know what I'm doing, I won't be a first-time mum. And if I need help, I'll ask for it, I promise. I won't let what happened the first time happen again. I know it was tough for you, Pete.'

'I don't know, Kate, it was hard, so hard. For you more than anyone, darling. And we're settled now, do you really want to turn our lives upside down again?'

'I don't want Lily to be an only child. And we've always talked about having at least two kids. I know it will be tough in the beginning, but it'll be worth it in the long run, it really will. I promise you. This baby will complete our family.'

So, just a few weeks after they celebrated Lily's first birthday, Kate presented him with two blue lines on a pregnancy test. The reaction was somewhat more subdued the second time around, the celebration slightly muted. He was just as anxious during this pregnancy but for different reasons – he knew what lay ahead this time and he was terrified. Not of the baby but of his wife.

When Maggie made her arrival into the world, things started off much better. Kate seemed calmer and more together. The distraction of having a toddler helped, she said because she didn't have time to dwell on things as much. She agreed to let Pete give Maggie a bottle in the night so she could get some more sleep and to take both girls out to the park on Saturdays to give her a lie in. He began to breathe again, believing that this time it would be okay, that they had escaped the nightmare. So, when the dark times came again, he wasn't expecting it. Maggie was a few months old and in a good routine. She was a happy, fairly uncomplicated baby compared to Lily, with her fussiness and clinginess in the early months. There was no trigger that he could put his finger on but one day, he came home from work on a Friday evening, humming to himself and looking forward to the steak and chips that Kate had said she would make for them. It was gone 7.30pm so he expected the kids to be in bed already, or at least on the final stretch – maybe he'd make it in time for bedtime stories with Lily, he thought. As soon as he walked into the living room, he knew something was very wrong.

Maggie was lying on her playmat wailing, the stench of her soiled nappy almost unbearable. Lily was sitting on the rug watching *EastEnders*, wearing only her pants and a pair of wellington boots, eating ice cream which she proudly told him was her dinner. And Kate was sitting on the floor staring into space with a vacant expression that suggested she had checked out some time ago.

'Kate?' he asked tentatively. She didn't respond. He scooped up Maggie, soothing her with kisses and cuddles and headed upstairs to run the bath. He bathed both children, put them to bed and came back downstairs to find that Kate hadn't moved. She was wearing just a vest and shorts and the chill of the evening had set in, causing her to shiver involuntarily. He reached for the blanket and wrapped it around her. This gentle act of kindness was like a floodgate and suddenly she was crying hysterically, letting out what felt like three years' worth of tears and anguish.

'Talk to me, Kate, tell me what's happened? What can I do?' he'd asked her.

'I don't know,' she just kept saying over and over again. 'I just don't know.'

The next morning, he told her that he thought they should get a nanny. He was expecting her to resist vehemently again, so he was surprised when she agreed without much protest. Within a few weeks they had hired Rachel – one of those capable sorts who you'd never have to worry about fancying, but you instantly have complete faith in – and she restored order and harmony to their home again. This time Kate gave her baby up to the arms of another person almost too gratefully. She started going to the gym, looking for houses to buy – 'a new start for us,' she told him – and even began talking about going back to work.

For a while things started looking up again but it didn't last. Her career ideas never made it off the ground and the short burst of enthusiasm for life that she'd had was soon snuffed out and replaced with a frustrating resignation that this was her lot.

Their marriage continued to deteriorate. It was like they had nothing in common anymore other than their children and they couldn't think of anything else to talk about. Their previously infrequent lovemaking became non-existent. He felt like he had lost the Kate he had known for all those years and he didn't know how to get her back. At the same time he didn't seem to have the energy to do anything about it either. He was constantly exhausted and so was she. Their babies were growing and blossoming into beautiful little girls but their marriage had stagnated. And now, all these years later, not much had changed. They existed together, co-parented together, and actually got on well enough, but the spark had gone.

On the outside they seemed like the perfect family but behind closed doors it was a different story. And Kate didn't even seem to care. As long as everyone else thought they were doing great, it didn't matter to her what was really going on. She was obsessed with making everything look perfect, agonising over fixtures and fittings for the house, outfits for the girls, making sure they got good marks at school. But when it came to Pete, it was like she had no more energy left for him. He felt like he'd been stuck in a rut for so long that this half-life had become normal and he barely even questioned it day to day. But recently he had found himself dreaming of something better and feeling that he deserved better than this. If he was being honest, it had started at around the same time he met Claire.

Looking back, he could pinpoint the exact moment when he realised that this 'thing' with her was different, that it was more than just a harmless attraction and a chit-chat. His company held Free Drinks Friday once a month, to coincide with payday. It was basically an excuse for the staff to get pissed as farts on free booze and while he'd wholeheartedly embraced it when he was younger, he hadn't been to it for years. But one day Claire casually mentioned that she would be going and asked if she'd see him there. His initial reaction was to scoff at the idea but then he found himself reconsidering. He hadn't been out for ages; why not have a few drinks before going home? And if she was going, there was no harm in having a chat with her.

As the day went on, he could feel anticipation building up inside him at the prospect of the evening ahead. But just as he was considering logging off early for once and hitting the bar, he got side-tracked by a minor work crisis and by the time he got downstairs, it was gone 8pm. As he walked out of the lift and into the foyer, excited at the prospect of seeing Claire and having a drink with her, he saw her heading purposefully towards the exit. His heart sank.

'Leaving so soon?' he called out to her, hoping he sounded casual.

She turned around and regarded him with a cool, calm expression. 'Yes, I've got somewhere else to be.' Was it him or did she seem pissed off? Either way, he realised that he didn't want her to go, he was desperate to convince her to stay for a drink. But he found himself tongue-tied and had no idea what to say to her, so he just stood there like an idiot. He could barely conceal his disappointment when she swivelled on her heel and sauntered out, no doubt heading off to meet some twenty-something bloke with no wife and kids at home to worry about.

In the bar, he drowned his sorrows with a lager and made polite conversation with colleagues before excusing himself and heading home. As he sat on the train, he told himself that he was being ridiculous. Of course nothing could happen between them, he was married and she probably wasn't interested anyway.

But at home, as he opened a bottle of red wine and half watched a chick flick that Kate had already started, he found himself thinking about her, the way she'd looked at him, in fact, the way she'd looked full stop – sexy and unobtainable. For the rest of the weekend his mind kept flickering back to her over and over again. By the time Monday rolled around, he couldn't get to the office fast enough. And sure enough, there she was, almost as if she'd been waiting for him the whole time.

'Good weekend?' he asked her.

'Could have been better,' she replied and, although he couldn't be sure what she was referring to, he knew exactly what he hoped it was. And he promised himself that the next time he had an opportunity like that, he wasn't going to fuck it up.

So the following month, when she mentioned that she was going to Free Drinks Friday again, there was no doubt in his mind that he'd be there.

They had sex that night. It was the first time he'd had sex in a very long time and it was quick and over too soon. Afterwards, he felt awful. He left as quickly as possible and got the train home. The heady combination of booze, lust and adrenaline had worn off and he felt tired and empty, like an addict after the hit has passed. By the time he got home Kate was already asleep and he sat in the kitchen with a whisky until 2am, thinking dark, guilty thoughts and eventually drinking himself into oblivion. The next day he woke up with a heavy head and an even heavier heart. Kate turned to face him and gave him an unsympathetic look. 'Late night?' she asked.

'Yeah, I ended up going to that free drinks event they do each month. I had to show a bit of face, rally the troops. There's some redundancies in the pipeline and everyone's feeling a little rattled,' he told her, surprised at himself at how easily the lie rolled off his tongue.

'Well, you're on swimming duty and there's nothing like two overexcited girls, manky changing rooms and a sweltering pool to kill off that hangover,' she said, looking at him almost victoriously, he thought, as she got out of bed and slipped her dressing gown on. He groaned and shoved a pillow over his head.

He wondered what Claire was doing that morning. Not going down to the local swimming pool that looked like it hadn't seen a lick of paint since the 70s, that was for sure. Probably staying in bed until 10am before eventually rousing herself to get ready so she could meet friends for brunch at some trendy café. He briefly felt a pang of resentment at the thought of her commitment-free Saturday and the fact that he couldn't be enjoying it with her. Then he got out of bed, stretched and padded over to the bathroom, turning on the shower and reaching for his toothbrush. 'Just another day in paradise,' he said aloud to himself as he opened the shower door and walked into the hot stream of water, cleansing his sins and transforming him back into the role of doting family man.

On Monday he felt nervous as hell about seeing her again. He'd spent the weekend convincing himself that it was a one-off and that it would never happen again. He didn't want to be disrespectful to her, so he'd planned to go in early as usual, before the crowds arrived, and explain that she was lovely but that his situation was complicated and it wouldn't be right to pursue this any further. It was him, not her, etc. But the minute that he walked into the building and saw her looking directly at him, one eyebrow raised suggestively, all his resolve vanished into thin air.

'Hey you,' she said, looking up at him as he reached the reception desk.

Thank God there was no one else around at this early hour. He could practically see the sexual tension between them. *Get a grip*, he told himself. 'Hey yourself,' he said back, feeling like a nervous teenager with a crush.

'So, it was quite an interesting night on Friday, eh?' she said, avoiding the small talk and cutting straight to the chase. It was typical Claire.

'Um yes, yes you could say that.' He felt embarrassed all of a sudden. He hadn't had the morning-after-the-night-before chat since he was nineteen years old.

'So what happens next? I think we both know that the ball's in your court here, Pete. Whatever you decide is totally cool with me. I'd just like to know either way.'

Her directness threw him for a moment and he didn't know how to respond. He frantically searched his brain, trying to locate the well-rehearsed speech that he'd been planning all weekend, but he couldn't seem to find it. Instead, he heard himself saying, 'Are you free on Wednesday evening?'

She grinned at him. 'I am.'

# 5

# KATE

$K$ ate woke up with a jolt. She'd been lying awake for so long that she hadn't even realised she'd dropped off. She must have only been out of it for half an hour or so. She turned to look at Lily, lying next to her, her leg encased in a cast and propped up by pillows. She was dead to the world, sleeping soundly in a way that only children can.

The previous day had been one horrendousness after the next. One minute she was trying to come to terms with her marriage crisis and the next she was rushing into A&E and being ushered into a cubicle where poor Lily was sitting, her little face pale with shock, tears running down her cheeks. Kate enveloped her into a hug and showered her with kisses, desperate to carry the pain for both of them.

'What on earth happened?' she asked Lily's teacher, Mrs Jones, who was sitting with her, keeping her company until Kate arrived.

'She just slipped and fell,' the poor woman explained, visibly shaken. 'We thought she'd twisted her ankle at first but then it started swelling up like a balloon and she couldn't walk on it at all. She's already had her X-rays and we're waiting for the results.'

'Thanks, I can take it from here,' Kate told her. The teacher stood up, patted Kate's arm and then reached over and gave Lily a hug. 'I hope you feel better soon, Lily. Everyone will be thinking of you and looking forward to seeing you back at school.'

After she left, Kate sat next to her daughter, putting her arm around her and pressing her body close to her. She kept thinking that she needed to call Pete, to tell him what had happened, before remembering that she couldn't. She felt alone in the world. Even if they'd had a row or were cross with each other, she had always known that she could call him if she needed to. Now she was totally on her own and she was terrified. How had it come to this?

A nurse appeared, breaking her out of her thoughts, and told them that the consultant was ready to see them. She helped Lily into a wheelchair and pushed her slowly down the corridor and into a room, where the doctor was waiting. He smiled at them warmly. 'Well, Lily, you've been in the wars, haven't you?' He turned to Kate. 'So Lily has broken her tibia, one of the long bones in her lower leg. The good news is that the bones are still aligned so she doesn't need surgery. However, she'll need to wear a cast for six weeks and she won't be able to put any weight on her leg. She'll need to use crutches.'

He saw the shock on Kate's face and added reassuringly: 'It's a fairly common injury in children, and she'll be running around again before you know it. They tend to cope pretty well with crutches – better than most adults at any rate.' He chuckled and turned to Lily: 'You'll get to wear a lovely cast and all of your friends are going to want to see it. You can even choose what colour you'd like it to be.'

'Pink,' Lily decided immediately, already warming to the

idea of being the centre of attention. The doctor smiled at her. 'Pink it is then.'

They'd managed to get her home in one piece, where Erin was waiting with Maggie to greet them. Lily was shattered and her earlier bravado evaporated as quickly as it had arrived, so Kate had helped her up the stairs and into her nightclothes.

'Where's Daddy?' the little girl had asked, looking at Kate with wide, tearful eyes. 'I want to see Daddy.'

'I know, sweetheart,' Kate told her daughter, 'but Daddy's gone on a business trip.'

'Can we FaceTime him?'

'I'm afraid not, darling, Daddy is working and he won't have his phone on.' God, she felt absolutely awful. How was she going to keep this up? How long would she have to keep it up for? Suddenly she felt a desperate need to compensate for Pete's absence.

'I tell you what, why don't you sleep in Mummy and Daddy's bed tonight?' she suggested. Lily's eyes lit up. The girls were never allowed to sleep in their parents' bed. Kate had helped her into bed and the little girl had been asleep before her head even hit the pillow.

Unfortunately, Kate couldn't say the same for herself and so here she was at 3am, lying next to her sleeping daughter and feeling wretched. Thoughts, fears and anxieties infiltrated her mind from every angle. How was she going to cope without Pete? How was she going to carry on as normal? What on earth was going to happen long term? Why had this happened? Could she have stopped it?

As if yesterday hadn't been awful enough, the accident had totally thrown her. Lily was going to need her parents now more than ever and she didn't know if she had the strength to get through this and act like everything was fine. She just couldn't process all the different emotions that she was feeling –

overwhelming anger at Pete, worry about what lay ahead, and guilt that she was to blame. She was a failure of a wife. At the back of her mind she'd known for a long time that she needed to make more of an effort in their marriage but she simply hadn't been able to find the energy to do anything about it. *Soon*, she'd thought. *I'll fix it soon*. But *soon* never came. Still, until now she hadn't realised things had got this bad.

She was glad when the sun finally started to peek through the cracks in the curtains and Lily stirred. The last two nights had been the longest of her life and although she was exhausted, at least the day took the edge off the demons and dark thoughts that had come out to plague her in the depth of the night.

She turned to her side so that her face was inches away from Lily's. 'Morning, beautiful,' she said. 'How did you sleep?'

'Where's Daddy?' Lily asked, rubbing sleepy eyes with curled up fists.

Kate's heart broke all over again. 'Daddy's away, remember? But Mummy's here and we can have a lovely day at home together. How about I make your special pancakes?'

'With chocolate spread?' Lily's eyes instantly lit up in anticipation.

Kate smiled, relieved at how distractible children were. 'With chocolate spread.'

Getting an impatient, wriggly child with a broken leg up, washed and dressed was, she soon discovered, something of a challenge but she welcomed the distraction. Lily was a trooper, brimming with excitement at the novelty of being off school. 'When can I show my friends my cast?' she kept asking. Kate felt a stab of pride at her little girl for putting on a brave face and wished Pete was here to see it too. Maggie, disgruntled at not being the centre of attention, played up more than usual and Kate was relieved when Rachel arrived to walk her to school.

After settling Lily on to the sofa with some milk, a duvet and a Disney film, Kate reached for her laptop and sat down beside her daughter. She immediately logged on to Facebook, searching for Pete's profile on impulse even though she knew it wouldn't be there. As she checked her email, she suddenly had a thought. Bringing up a new message, she typed Pete's personal email address in and started writing.

```
Pete,

    I don't know if you're checking your
emails. I don't even know where you are.
I don't know what's happened to us. I'm
really angry with you, Pete, I can't
pretend I'm not. You took the coward's
way out, you should have talked to me,
given us an opportunity to fix this first
before you decided to run. You've always
talked about being a man of principles,
of being different from your dad, but
then you go and do this. I don't know
what to think. Was it so bad that you
couldn't tell me how you felt? All these
years we've been together and you
couldn't come to me with this? When did
it all go so horribly wrong between us?
    Lily's broken her leg. She fell at
school. She's been asking after you and I
don't know what to say to her. She wants
to know when you'll be back. What do
I do?
```

She didn't know what else to write, so she pressed send and listened to the whoosh as her message disappeared off into the digital ether. She had so many questions yet in that moment, she couldn't think of anything else to say.

Erin called round later that morning with gifts for Lily and a bottle of gin for Kate. 'I think you're going to need this over the next few weeks,' she told her sister as she hugged her tightly and went to put the kettle on. With their tea they sat down together at the kitchen table.

'Any news?' Erin asked her.

'Nothing,' Kate replied. 'Although I emailed him this morning just in case he's checking them.'

'Have you had a chance to make a plan of action?'

'Not really. I didn't sleep a wink last night. I can't believe Lily's managed to break her bloody leg. I can't work out if it's literally the worst timing ever or if it's a welcome distraction from the rest of the nightmare that is my life at the moment.'

Erin couldn't help but laugh. 'You've got to love kids, haven't you?' She looked at Kate thoughtfully for a few seconds before adding: 'I've been thinking. Maybe you should contact one of his mates from work and see if they know anything. Do you have any of their numbers?'

'I don't think so but I'm friends with a few of them on Facebook. I could send them a message, I guess.'

'You need some answers, Kate. Perhaps they can get a message to him about Lily too. He'd want to know, even if I'm not entirely sure he deserves to.'

'You're right,' Kate said. She reached for her laptop and searched for Dan's profile. Dan was one of Pete's closest mates from work. She'd met him several times and he was a nice bloke. His wife, Laura, was lovely. She began typing a message to him.

Dan,

Hey, it's Kate. I hope you and Laura are good. Look, I'm sorry to bother you, this is really awkward. Pete's gone away and I don't know where he is. Lily's broken her leg and I need to tell him but I've got no way of reaching him. I just wondered if you were in contact with him? Is there any way you can get a message to him for me?

I don't know how much, if anything, you know, but any information you can give me would be really appreciated. I'm just trying to make sense of it all.

Kate xx

She showed the message to Erin who nodded her approval, then Kate hit send. Within a few minutes she could see that Dan had read the message and the little speech bubble appeared, signalling that he was writing a reply. She held her breath as she waited. It took a long time and she could imagine poor Dan, torn between loyalty for his friend and doing the right thing. Finally, the message appeared.

Kate, hi! I'm so sorry to hear about Lily, is she okay? Please send her all our love. Listen, this whole thing with Pete, I'm really sorry. I don't know what to say, to be honest. Last time I saw him was at his leaving do last week, I've not spoken to him since. I take it you've tried his mobile? Is he answering emails? If I can do anything to help at all, just let me know x

Erin, reading the message over Kate's shoulder, exclaimed: 'Leaving do? What leaving do? Has he left his job?'

'I don't know,' Kate spluttered. She immediately hit reply.

What leaving do, Dan? Has he quit his job? He's left his mobile at home, and he's deleted his social media accounts. I don't know what's going on.

The speech bubble appeared again.

I'm sorry, Kate, I thought you knew. Yes, he handed in his notice a couple of months ago and he left last week. Look this is really awkward, you really need to talk to Pete. I'm sure he'll get in contact with you. He'd want to know about Lily. Maybe try email?

*He knows*, Kate realised. *He knows exactly what's going on and he's trying to protect his friend.* She supposed she didn't blame him but now she'd made contact with him, she had to find out the truth. The thought of Pete handing in his notice at work and even attending his own leaving do without telling her made her feel sick. She knew their marriage was hardly the stuff of dreams anymore but what kind of husband makes such a big decision without even discussing it with his own wife?

Erin read the message too. 'This is an early midlife crisis,' she said with conviction. 'He's quit his job, taken up with a younger woman. I'm surprised he hasn't bought a flipping Porsche. What a cliché. You need to probe Dan, get him to spill the beans.' Then she added as an afterthought: 'If he's quit his job, then how is he getting paid? Has he got a new job?'

'I don't know,' Kate added, feeling increasingly panicked. They had plenty of savings, thank goodness, but she was more aware than ever that she was reliant on Pete for everything. She didn't earn a penny.

She composed a reply to Dan.

Look, I don't want to put you in a difficult position but I really need to know what's going on. Can we meet?

He didn't reply for forty-five minutes. It was the longest wait of her life and she wondered if he was going to ignore her message entirely, but he was too nice a guy for that. Eventually, his response popped up.

Please email Pete, I'm sure he'll reply. If you don't hear back from him in a few days then of course we can meet. But I just think it's better coming from him, not me. I'm sure he'll be in touch, he'll want to know how Lily is. I'm sorry but I can't think of any other way of contacting him than by trying his personal email. His work emails are being forwarded to a colleague. Let me know when you hear from him x

That was it then. He wasn't giving anything else away, at least not for now. It was like torture, the knowledge that someone else knew the full story about the breakdown of her marriage and she didn't. Just as she was trying to decide what to do next, her phone pinged with a message.

Hey gorgeous! SO sorry to hear about Lily. Is she okay? Everyone is asking after her. Are you still free for a coffee this afternoon? 2pm? I can come to you? xx

Oh God, Nadia. She'd totally forgotten that she'd arranged to meet her for a coffee. Nadia's children went to the same school as Lily and Maggie but they had first met at antenatal classes years ago when Kate was pregnant with Lily. Five women with nothing in common, brought together purely by baby bumps, while their other halves stood around awkwardly making jokes about swapping beer for baby bottles. They all lived in Muswell Hill apart from Kate and Pete who were still down the road in the somewhat less salubrious Turnpike Lane at the time. Nadia soon established herself as the unofficial leader of this new friendship group, setting up group chats and arranging pregnancy yoga sessions and lunches in the trendy cafés along the Broadway. When the babies started coming, one by one, the meet-ups were replaced by pram power walks in the park and desperately needed coffees in whatever café was most welcoming to breastfeeders. They'd lost touch with one of the couples after a few years but the other four had remained in fairly close contact.

Nadia was one of those friends who you knew wasn't any good for your mental health but you just couldn't shake off. She had sailed effortlessly through parenthood, always looking perfect with her glossy activewear and dark silky hair tied neatly into a ponytail as the group marched en masse around the park with their babes in prams. Of course Nadia's baby would be sleeping peacefully, no dummy needed, while Lily wailed and wailed and Kate reddened with the shame of being unable to comfort her own child and avoided eye contact with any passers-by, convinced they were all judging her substandard mothering abilities.

Nadia was the type who always made you feel inadequate in any situation, even if she didn't actually mean to. Of course, at the end of her maternity leave she had negotiated part-time hours with her employer and seemed to juggle her successful career and being a homemaker effortlessly. She was the one who always brought beautiful home-made cupcakes to the school bake sale and cheerfully manned a stall for the duration while Kate either sent Rachel or rushed in at the last minute, clutching armfuls of cookies she'd panic bought from Waitrose and getting the hell out of the chaotic, overcrowded hall as soon as physically possible.

Nadia wasn't a nasty person really but she did love a good gossip and Kate realised that once she had hold of this new information, the secret would not be hidden for long. The news would travel through the school and parenting community of Muswell Hill until everyone knew about it.

*Poor Kate, ditched by her husband for a younger model*, that's what they'd all say.

*And they had seemed so perfect. Guess you never know what happens behind closed doors.*

*She didn't work, had a nanny to look after her children and still she couldn't keep her husband happy*, that would be the insinuation.

Playground gossip was the least of her worries at the moment but Kate still couldn't bear the thought of people talking about her and knowing that she was a big, fat, utter failure.

'Nadia's messaged,' she told Erin. 'She wants to come over for coffee.'

'That two-faced yummy mummy? No way,' came her sister's reply. Erin did not care for Nadia. Her friends were all salt of the earth types who'd lie down in traffic for each other and never seemed to have a nasty thing to say about anyone. 'Tree huggers', that's what Pete had called them, but Kate thought they were just genuinely nice people who had found the elusive secret to life – simply being content with what they had. It was certainly something that Kate hadn't managed to find.

'I've got to face the vultures sooner or later,' she told her sister. 'I can't hide the fact forever. He's gone, Erin, and people are going to notice sooner or later.'

'Yes, but give yourself some time, Kate. Hunker down, get your head straight and make your plan. There's no rush. Let people find out on your terms.'

She was right of course, but Kate was never any good at saying no to Nadia. So, despite her sister's advice and her own inner voice screaming at her not to do it, she quickly typed out a reply:

Sure! See you at 2pm x

As soon as she knew Nadia was coming over Erin scarpered,

with promises to call Kate later. Nadia arrived bang on time, clutching home-made cupcakes for Lily and a beautiful bunch of flowers that definitely weren't from a petrol station for Kate. 'Oh my goodness,' she gushed, when she saw Lily's leg propped up by cushions. 'You poor little thing. Sadie and George are asking after you, they send their love. Everyone misses you at school. You'll be better before you know it!'

Once Lily had been left to indulge in an age-inappropriate amount of cake, the women went into the kitchen and Nadia turned to Kate, studying her face carefully. 'You look awful,' she told her. 'Is it just Lily, or something else too?'

*How does she do it?* Kate wondered. *No one can be that perceptive. Has she had CCTV secretly installed in our house? Or do I really look that shit?* She assessed her options and decided that lying to Nadia was a bad idea. When she eventually found out, she'd be peeved. So, she came clean. 'Things haven't been too great between me and Pete recently,' she admitted. 'He's gone away to clear his head and I don't know if or when he's coming back. The kids don't know and it needs to stay that way, okay?'

Nadia stared at her in shock, mouth open, no doubt wondering how soon she could share this most exciting gossip with the other mums. She was probably already deciding which WhatsApp groups to post it to while she was still sitting with Kate. 'Oh my goodness, Kate, I'm so sorry. I'm completely flabbergasted because I had no idea there were any issues at all. You seemed like such a solid couple, so happy. How long has this been going on for?'

'If I'm honest, things haven't been great for a while. I mean, we don't really argue but we don't really talk much either, I guess.' She smiled self-consciously. 'We've kind of just been living our own lives – you know what it's like when you have kids, you forget each other and everything is about them. You stop taking time for yourselves and your marriage.'

Nadia looked like she wanted to disagree with that statement but then, in fairness to her, thought better of it. Even she knew that now was not the time to divulge the details of all the different ways that she and her husband made time for themselves and each other.

'It's just a glitch,' she assured Kate, proffering a cupcake at her. 'It happens to lots of couples. Maybe you both need some time to realise how much you love each other. And then your marriage will be better than ever. I know a great marriage counsellor, a good friend of mine had issues,' she lowered her tone, 'he was having an affair, you see, someone from work, and said this woman was amazing. Here, let me get you her details, you should call her.'

Kate almost snorted out her coffee. 'I think both parties need to be present for a marriage counsellor,' she reminded Nadia. 'I'm a man down.'

'Yes I know, but he'll be back soon, you mark my word. You and the girls, you're amazing and no man in his right mind would leave that behind. You belong together, I just know it. This isn't permanent, Kate, remember that. You'll be making a call to that marriage counsellor to book an appointment before you know it.'

But, although Kate took the number from Nadia and made a show of saving it to her phone, she already knew, despite her sleep-deprived, brain-addled and distressed state, that she wouldn't be calling any marriage counsellor.

## 6

## PETE

The second time they had sex it was much better. They'd gone straight back to her flat after work, picked up a bottle of wine on the way home and made it through less than half a glass before he was on top of her on the sofa, practically ripping her clothes off. God it was so good to feel desire after all this time. It had lasted longer and he'd made her climax, something which he knew he hadn't done the first time.

Afterwards, instead of making his excuses and getting out of there as quickly as possible, he'd stayed for a short while, lying on the sofa with his arms wrapped around her and staring up at the ceiling. They didn't talk much but it didn't feel awkward either. He allowed himself half an hour of guilt-free bliss, just to lie there and enjoy the moment, before gathering his things and preparing to leave. To be fair to her, she didn't give him a hard time about it. She helped him find his missing shoe under the sofa and then walked him to the door, giving him a kiss.

'See you at work, Pete,' she said, and she had already turned her back on him and walked back into the flat before he'd even shut the door.

After that, they started meeting regularly. The meetings were always instigated by him and they never communicated by work email. Instead, he would send her a brief WhatsApp message – nothing romantic, just a few words to make arrangements – and she would respond with one word, *yes*. She rarely said no. He was very careful but he changed the password on his phone anyway just in case Kate or one of the girls picked it up and started messing around with it, and he tried not to leave it lying around the house either.

He was acutely aware that this was turning into something more than a minor indiscretion, it was now bordering on an actual affair, yet he was powerless to prevent it from happening. He was like a giddy child on a rollercoaster, soaring down the rails after years of uphill climb with such a rush of adrenaline and a deeply thrilling feeling in his stomach that nothing could stop him.

It wasn't just the sex, although that was fantastic. He fancied her more than he'd ever fancied anyone in his life, even Kate. From the beginning, he'd been in awe of Kate and had thought she was an incredible person. But this sexual chemistry with Claire was something else. She oozed confidence in bed, was totally uninhibited and they were undeniably compatible, as she liked to tell him afterwards when they lay exhausted in post-coital bliss. 'You're the best I've ever had, Pete.'

But there was more to it than that. She'd made it clear that she enjoyed his company but she didn't demand anything from him. She had her own life and her own things going on and her lack of reliance on him was liberating. He found himself wanting to confide in her, to talk to her about everything and she listened – actually listened to him. She was genuinely interested in him and what he had to say. It was nice to have someone pay attention to you again, he thought.

Instead of leaving straight after sex, he found himself staying longer and longer, leaving it as late as he could get away with before he had to go home to his other life, as he had started to think of it. He never talked about his family but found that he had plenty of other things to talk about instead. They would open a bottle of wine and get stuck into all sorts of topics, from which bridge in London was their favourite to the intricacies of British politics. She was frighteningly clever, Claire, and wasted on her temp jobs but when he told her that she just laughed and shrugged. She didn't care what people thought. It felt like they would never run out of things to say to each other, no matter how long they were together.

It was almost too easy to hide the affair from Kate. She was so used to him working late and having business dinners that she didn't bat an eyelid when he came home at antisocial hours. To be honest, he wasn't sure she cared whether he was there or not. His presence in the house seemed more of an inconvenience than a pleasure. For years they'd cherished each other's company and he had always looked forward to seeing her. Now he felt that she looked forward to seeing the builder more than him. He'd even wondered if she was having an affair herself once or twice, but he'd always dismissed it. He didn't think she could be bothered.

One evening, after they'd been meeting at Claire's flat pretty much every week for a couple of months, they were lying in bed together and he was stroking her thigh distractedly, when he found himself blurting out, 'I really bloody hate my job.'

'Well quit then,' came her reply, as he had expected it would.

'It's not as easy as that though, is it?'

'Why not? You're talented, you're successful. You'd get another job easily. So decide what you want to do, then go and get it. Life's too short to spend it doing a job you hate – but you've got to make the change, it's not going to happen on its own.'

He left her flat feeling optimistic about his future for the first time in ages. She was absolutely right, the world was his oyster. Why had he been working for the same company for over ten years, dealing with the same old shit over and over again? He'd been too scared to rock the boat, that's why. It was easier to stay where he was, doing a job he could do with his eyes closed. He'd been playing it safe for years, in his job, in his life. At work he exuded authority but inside he was losing a bit of his soul every day and Claire had finally made him face up to the truth.

Why hadn't he talked to Kate about it? He had been feeling this way for years, but he hadn't said a word to her. Yet he'd known Claire for just weeks and he was already confiding in her. Kate would have been instantly dismissive, he thought. *She would tell me to suck it up and get on with it, like everyone else has to.* All she cared about was the job security, paycheque and annual bonus. Yet she didn't work. She stayed at home spending his money. The bloody nanny that he'd suggested to help her out for a few months when Maggie was a baby was still there five years later and what was Kate doing? Redesigning their kitchen and having coffee with friends. Not taking care of their children, anyway. Anger bubbled up inside him, like a beast that had been sleeping for years finally waking up. *This is just as much her fault as mine*, he told himself. *She's driven me to this.*

But the feelings dissolved again as soon as he got home and were replaced with guilt at the inevitable knowledge that no matter how he packaged it, this deception was his and his alone. When he was with Claire, he had trained himself to ignore it, to lose himself in the moment and forget about everything else, but at home he would battle with it constantly. The way that the girls leapt up at him when they saw him, screaming 'Daddy, Daddy, Daddy' and smothering him with kisses made his heart break. Even Kate, despite her usual indifference towards him, could make him feel like crap. Every so often she would make a wry joke or throw her head back and laugh at something with such carefree abandon that it would transport him back to their happy, early years together. And he would look at her, study her, and wonder if she was still there, buried inside this new, impenetrable version of his wife.

One Friday evening after a few glasses of wine, he was well on the way to being tipsy and he got a wave of nostalgia. They'd decided to sit at the kitchen table together for once, instead of automatically going to the living room, switching on the TV and sitting in silence, playing with their phones and living their lives through social media rather than each other. He opened another bottle of red wine while she took the lids off the Indian takeaway they'd ordered. Sitting opposite each other, munching away with a candle between them, it felt comforting and companionable.

'Tell me about your day,' he said.

'Oh, not much to report really,' she replied. 'Lily got full marks in her spelling test and Maggie's teacher said she did really well with her reading today.'

A typical Kate answer, focusing only on the children and their achievements. But he put his negative thoughts aside and probed further. 'And what about you? What did you do?'

'Not much. I met the antenatal mums for coffee in the morning, then I went to Brent Cross and took that lamp back that didn't look right in the sitting room.'

'How *are* the ladies?'

'Oh fine,' Kate said, before chuckling to herself. 'Anna said that she and her old uni mates went back to Newcastle for a reunion at the weekend. She said it looked nothing like it did when they were students – and although they'd talked about having a mad night out, they were all in bed by 11pm! It got me thinking about Leeds.'

'Oh, those were the days,' Pete said wistfully. 'Maybe we need to organise a reunion weekend ourselves. I haven't spoken to any of the old gang in ages. I wonder what they're all up to? Do you think they'd be up for it?'

'I'm sure they would. I haven't spoken to them in ages either but I have all their numbers so we could set up a group, put the feelers out and see what they say. I'm sure Erin wouldn't mind having the girls for a night or two.'

They looked at each other and grinned, their enthusiasm growing for the idea. They had so much shared history together, the two of them, so many fun times under their belt. *We could get our mojo back*, he thought, *we just need to try a bit harder, to talk a bit more.*

Later that night, when they were in bed and she was lying on her side, facing away from him while reading a book, he curled up against her, stroking her arm before moving his hand towards her breasts. He hadn't made any moves for so long he felt nervous about how she would react. He'd become scared of rejection from his own wife. But she gently put her book down on the bedside table and turned around to face him, putting her arms around him and starting to kiss him.

He kissed her back, slowly at first and then with increased enthusiasm. For a minute, he felt twenty years old again, lying in bed with the woman of his dreams. *This is it*, he thought, *this is the moment that will change everything, that will put our marriage back on track.* She pushed her body up against him and he felt the familiar stirrings of lust building up inside him. He helped her out of her nightdress and urgently pulled her on top of him, excited and aroused. But then, out of nowhere an image of Claire popped into his head. He tried to push it out of his conscience or at least to the very back of his mind but it wouldn't go away.

*Focus*, he urged himself, *focus on the moment.* But he already knew that the moment had gone as quickly as it had arrived and he wasn't going to get it back. The spell had been broken. She sensed it too, the subtle pulling away from her, the slight turn of his head and the inevitable loss of his erection. She looked down at him and he saw the hurt and confusion in her eyes for a second before they were replaced by something else he had come to know well. Resignation. Without saying a word she stood up, walked into the bathroom and slammed the door behind her.

The next morning, he woke up with a splitting headache and regretted opening that second bottle of wine. The events of the previous evening came flooding back to him and he groaned inwardly before rolling over to look at Kate. *Might as well face the music*, he thought. But the bed was empty. He lay there for a few minutes, contemplating his options. It was entirely his fault, he knew, but he still couldn't bear the thought of going down the stairs and seeing her hostile expression. All of a sudden, he had an urge to talk to Claire. Before he could overthink it, he reached for his phone and typed out a message to her.

Hey you. Lying in bed thinking of you. What are you up to today?

It was the first time he'd sent her a message that didn't just contain dates and times. He knew he was breaking his own rules but he was craving the thrill of communicating with her. He saw the two blue ticks appear, signalling that she had read the message, followed by the notification that she was typing. He waited for her response, feeling the familiar sense of anticipation building inside of him at the very thought of talking to Claire. Finally, her message appeared.

Hey yourself. Also lying in bed. Wishing you were here with me. No great plans today, the weather is rubbish so I'm going to hibernate with M&S supplies and some box sets. Later I'm going out x

Going out? Going out where? With who? He found himself wondering if Claire was seeing other people. They'd never discussed it and of course he could hardly tell her she wasn't allowed – he was, after all, a married man. Still, the thought of her going on a date with someone else made him feel irrationally jealous. *She's mine*, he thought, *I want her all to myself*. But he couldn't tell her that because at best he'd look possessive and at worst he'd look like a complete psycho. Either way she'd probably run for the hills so instead, he composed a more measured response.

Going out, lucky you! Anywhere nice?

Her response came quickly.

A birthday thing for a friend at a new restaurant in Mayfair. What are you up to?

The truth was most likely soft-play hell, followed by a child's birthday party later, followed by a tense evening with Kate while he watched Netflix, she played on her laptop in the kitchen and they both ignored what had happened the previous night – and each other. He realised he'd rather be anywhere else but here. Before he'd had a chance to think it through, he typed:

Fancy some company?

Her response was instant:

On a Saturday? Well that's a treat. Sure, come on over.

He was up and in the shower within seconds, humming to himself as he lathered up and planned what he would say to

Kate to explain his absence on a weekend. The familiar feeling of guilt and shame niggled him, a voice inside him warning him: *you've taken it a step too far, you've let it encroach on family time, you're being careless, you need to stop this*, but he turned his mind away from it, refusing to acknowledge it and instead allowing himself to get lost in the pure excitement at the thought of getting out of this house and being with Claire in the next couple of hours. It was amazing how easy it was becoming to banish those guilty thoughts. By the time he got downstairs, he was fully prepared.

'I'm so sorry, love, Angela from work has just called. There's been some crisis with a client and it's all hands on deck. I've got to go in for a few hours, I'll be back this afternoon, okay?'

She didn't even turn around. 'Fine,' she said.

# 7

# KATE

Within forty-five minutes of Nadia's departure, Kate's phone started beeping with messages. All in the same vein – *So sorry to hear about Pete! How are you doing? I can't believe it, do you need anything?* She ignored them all. But now that word was out, Nadia and some of the others would probably be gossiping about it at the school gates and when Rachel returned, she knew immediately from the look on her nanny's face that she'd overheard something. Sending Maggie into the living room to play with Lily, she sat down at the kitchen table and gestured for Rachel to join her.

'I'm sure you've heard the gossip,' she began. Rachel interjected at once: 'I don't listen to gossip, Kate, your personal life is your own and you don't need to tell me anything. Just let me know what I can do to help.'

Kate's eyes filled with tears at Rachel's lovely response and before she knew it, she was sobbing uncontrollably. It was the first time she had cried since this whole sorry situation kicked off and once she started, she couldn't seem to stop. Rachel, who it seemed was not even fazed by hysterical jilted wives, enveloped her in a big hug and held her tightly, allowing Kate to cry as much as she wanted. When the tears finally slowed down she sat back and wiped her eyes, looking quickly at the door to make sure that the girls were still in the other room.

'Thanks,' she said, 'I needed that.' She took a deep breath and started talking, filling Rachel in on the events of the last forty-eight hours.

When she was finished, Rachel gave her another hug. 'It's going to be tough for you, Kate, but you're a strong, capable woman and you'll get through this. And whatever you need, you let me know, I'm here to help.'

Rachel to the rescue again, picking her up when she was down, stepping in to save the day. It was just like when Kate had first met her, she'd been a nervous wreck then too. BC, as she liked to call it – before children – she loved her job at a big PR agency. Imposter syndrome was not a concept that Kate was even aware of in those days. She worked around the clock, always the last one standing at work socials and the first one in the office with a bacon sandwich and a coffee the next day. She'd loved her job and had known she was pretty damn good at it. So, she had assumed that she'd be pretty damn good at parenting too and it came as quite a shock to her when she wasn't. Having children was always on the cards for them and as soon as they hit their thirties it was operation conceive. They'd had plenty of fun in their twenties but she'd started to feel the biological clock ticking and knew it was time to start the next chapter in their life. They were fortunate, within a few months of trying the two blue lines appeared before them as they sat together in the bathroom, holding hands and waiting in anticipation for the results. They'd both grinned at each other, giddy.

'I think it's a girl,' Pete had said. 'I'm getting girl vibes.'

Kate had giggled, caught up in this special, shared moment. 'Me too, definitely girl vibes. I wonder what cravings I'll have.

Marmite on marshmallows anyone? Oh, Pete, we did it! We're having a baby!'

Kate had stroked her stomach as she envisaged the next nine months – a life-defining time as she wore floaty maternity dresses, bonded with the baby growing inside her and glowed with the joy of pregnancy. The reality was somewhat different.

Pregnancy was boring. She knew how lucky she was to be carrying a healthy child and she was grateful for it, but she couldn't help but feel resentment when Pete continued to live his old life, going out for client weekends away and Christmas parties, coming home full of booze and stories, while she stayed at home feeling knackered, bloated, nauseous and left out. She knew she was being selfish, but she just couldn't shake off the feeling that she was making all the sacrifices, not him. *It'll be different when the baby comes*, she told herself. *Then Pete will be able to bond with it and our parenthood journey will really begin, together.*

After a twenty-seven-hour labour and emergency caesarean, Lily arrived in the world and shattered all of Kate's preconceived ideas about being a mum. She loved Lily with every ounce of her being from the minute she was born but she didn't understand her at all. Gazing into her daughter's beautiful eyes she thought, *How on earth am I going to look after you? I have absolutely no idea what I'm doing.* She couldn't stop crying and although everyone reassured that this was normal, the baby blues that every new mum got, this loss of control over her emotions completely floored her.

She was sleep-deprived, anxious and desperate to please this tiny little person who seemed furious about her lot. The more she tried to get it right, the more she got it wrong. Pete seemed so confident, handling Lily with ease, cooing at her and suggesting pub lunches and meeting up with friends but she was terrified to go out in case she couldn't stop her crying or she had a nappy explosion and there was nowhere to change her. Breastfeeding was a nightmare but she was so worried that people would judge her for bottle feeding – or that she wasn't giving her baby the best start in life – she persevered through the pain and frustration, crying every time Lily latched on and sobbing that she couldn't even feed her baby properly. Whenever Pete suggested a bottle, she shot him down immediately.

One day she was out walking in the park with two of the antenatal mums, Nadia and Abi, and they were discussing the joys of parenthood.

'It's SUCH hard work, but isn't it just SO rewarding,' Nadia enthused.

Abi nodded. 'I know, I just can't stop staring at his gorgeous little face. I could sit there for hours just staring at him. I don't even mind the middle of the night wake-ups as it's just another opportunity to hold him and give him a cuddle.'

They had looked at Kate expectantly, waiting for her to agree. But she was too tired to play along. 'It's fucking hard,' she said. 'Way fucking harder than I thought it would be. Sometimes I really hate it.'

Nadia and Abi had stared at her, speechless, eyes wide in shock, and she had immediately regretted her honesty. Quickly she added: 'But it's the most amazing thing I've ever done, of course.' The two women smiled and nodded, and they carried on their way. Kate never spoke of her true feelings again.

But the reality was that she felt overwhelmed and incompetent at the biggest job of her life. Her parents, who had moved to Devon a few years previously to enjoy their retirement, visited a few times but seemed genuinely terrified at the prospect of looking after a baby again so they were of little help, except to look away nervously whenever she got a boob out or to enquire as to what their daughter – messy-haired, bleary-eyed and covered in baby vomit – would be preparing for their dinner that evening. She had never felt more alone and out of her depth but no one seemed to get it. Her only beacon of hope throughout those first few months was Erin. But as lovely and supportive as she was, she didn't have children of her own and didn't really understand what it was like. And she worked full-time anyway, so she was never around during the long, lonely weeks when everyone else was at work.

Pete tried, he really did, but he didn't get it either. He seemed to think maternity leave was a holiday. As she insisted on exclusively breastfeeding, she was the one who had to keep getting up in the night. At first, he would get up too, keeping her company and trying to help soothe a fussy, writhing Lily back to sleep. But when he returned to work after two weeks' paternity leave, he was shattered and the cracks were beginning to show, so she suggested that he move into the spare room, just for a few weeks, so that he could get a good night's sleep and be refreshed for work. He took her up on the offer gratefully. Weeks turned into months and those long, dark, lonely nights on her own were the worst of her life.

The days weren't a great deal better either. Lily grew into a clingy baby who cried when anyone else held her but Kate. If she put her down, even for a minute, she would wail and kick her little legs in frustration. It was relentless and Kate had no idea how to soothe her. As her anxiety worsened, so did Lily's tears. Kate became convinced that everyone thought she was a terrible mother, and her fears were made worse when she met up with the other new mums and they all seemed to be doing a brilliant job. They'd talk about adventures they'd been on at the weekend – popping their offspring into a sling and getting the Tube into town for a day of culture or going away for a couple of nights with a big group of friends – when the idea of simply going to the local park brought Kate out in a cold sweat. Each day felt like a new battle and over time, she became less and less able to face it.

She knew she was hard to live with in those days. Pete would return from work and offer to have Lily for a while but the minute he took her she'd find some fault – he was holding her wrong, or he was making her overexcited and she'd never sleep, or how dare he suggest giving her a bottle? She sounded neurotic, she knew, and she hated herself for it afterwards, but she couldn't seem to stop herself.

Looking back, it was obvious now that it was far more than 'just the baby blues', which is what she called it when Pete had gently suggested that she seek some help. She'd clearly had postnatal depression but she'd never allowed herself to admit it as it seemed like another admission of failure. If only she had, she might have got some much-needed help and found a way to navigate through the long, dark, lonely tunnel of hopelessness.

She did eventually find her way out on her own, when Lily was a toddler, but by then the damage had been done to their marriage. Pete was coming home later and later, claiming that things at work were crazy when she knew it was because he wanted to avoid being around her. The tiny little seed of resentment that had been planted inside her during those first few months of pregnancy, that she had been left to go through all of this while he still got to live his life almost as normal, had been growing. Some days she'd have killed to sleep in the spare room and get a full eight hours, or to go to work and leave him at home with the baby but he simply didn't understand that.

To him, as he once joked before seeing the murderous look on her face and quickly trying to backtrack, maternity leave was made up of going for long, lazy walks in the park, watching box sets and meeting other mums for cappuccinos and gossip. And although he tried to be understanding and sympathetic about how she was feeling, she sensed at the back of his mind he was really thinking, *Why is she finding this such a struggle when everyone else seems to manage just fine? She's hardly the first woman in the world to have had a baby.*

As the end of her maternity leave loomed ever closer, Kate got in touch with her boss about returning to work. As much as she'd fantasised about slipping back into her old life and going back full-time, she knew deep down that she didn't really want to go back to fifty-hour weeks and never being there to put her own daughter to bed.

'You don't have to go back at all,' Pete had told her. 'You had to work some pretty long hours and go to so many evening events, it's not compatible with our lives anymore. With my promotion, we can afford for you to stay at home.'

But she'd been desperate to go back to the job that she'd excelled at, to get her identity back for just a few hours a week, and so she'd applied to return part-time. She was absolutely certain they'd say yes, after all she'd been there for years and she was one of their top performers. She'd already started ordering new work outfits online with a growing sense of anticipation, knowing full well there was no way she'd be squeezing into her old ones any time soon, when she got the email from her boss, declining her application. It was full-time or no time.

'At least the decision's been taken out of your hands,' Pete told her. 'The short-sighted pricks can't even be flexible for one of their most loyal employees. You wouldn't want to work at a place like that now you're a mum anyway, they'd make your life a misery, making you work full-time hours for part-time pay. Tell them to stuff it, and apply for jobs at smaller, more family-friendly agencies.'

And so she'd handed in her notice and the final connection to her previous life was severed just like that. She didn't even bother having a leaving do, so unceremonious was resignation from a place that she had given her all to for nearly a decade. They sent her a gift voucher in the post and a card signed by some of her old team with the usual messages, expressing their devastation that she was leaving and promises to keep in touch. She never heard from any of them again.

She had cancelled the nursery place that she had secured for Lily. 'I'll keep her at home with me for the time being,' she told Pete. 'There's no point her being at nursery if I'm not working. As soon as I get a job, I'll enrol her again.'

But after scouring job listings every week, she soon discovered that part-time jobs in PR were pretty hard to come by. And anyway, who the hell had time to write a CV and pithy covering letters when they were also looking after a toddler? Each day Kate told herself that she'd spend Lily's nap time on job hunting but then something would distract her – the online grocery shop or an email from her mum that she hadn't replied to – and she never quite got around to it. Before she knew it, months had passed and she'd started to think about baby number two. *There's no point getting a job now*, she thought, *best wait until I've had the second baby and then I can really get stuck back into my career knowing that the pregnancy and baby days are behind me.* And then of course Maggie had arrived, along with another onslaught of postnatal depression, and blown away the last shred of confidence she had. By the time Rachel arrived on the scene Kate didn't really know who she was anymore, and was too exhausted to figure it out. Now here she was five years later, still being looked after by Rachel, and not a great deal had changed except that she thought she'd got a lot better at hiding how she felt and acting like everything was fine. But now she was beginning to realise that she'd been wrong this whole time.

Rachel stood up to start making the girls' dinner and Kate went to help her, the two women working next to each other in companionable silence. Once the girls were at the table eating, Rachel said goodbye and slipped out, leaving Kate alone with them. She looked at them both and felt that familiar rush of love for them. For years now she'd struggled with motherhood, compared herself to others and concluded each time that the girls deserved better than her. But here they were, two beautiful, happy little girls who loved and laughed without a care in the world. In a fleeting moment of clarity, she thought *I've got this, I can do this*. She smiled at them both as they munched on their pasta. 'Who's up for a game of snap after dinner?'

# 8

## PETE

He wasn't supposed to spill the beans but it just came tumbling out, like most secrets tend to do in the end. He'd gone for a pint with Dan after work and as they sat down, drinking with relish after a long day of meetings, Dan had looked at him thoughtfully. 'What gives, mate?'

The suddenness of the question had startled Pete but before he could stop himself a wry grin had escaped involuntarily. 'What do you mean?'

'You're like the cat that's got the cream. I haven't seen you this chirpy for ages, it's like you're a new man. So, what gives?'

Pete quickly weighed up his options. They had agreed to tell no one about the affair, even close friends. It had been his idea but Claire hadn't seemed to mind. She wasn't an over-sharer, like most other women he knew, and she told him she preferred to keep her private life to herself. So he fully believed that she hadn't told a soul. Yet here he was, the one with the most to lose, and he simply couldn't keep it in any longer. 'So, I've actually met someone,' he said slowly, observing Dan to see his reaction.

Across the table Dan raised his eyebrows but said nothing.

'I know it's terrible, I'm a massive shithead, etc., etc., but things between me and Kate haven't been good for a long time, mate. And I wasn't looking for anything but then it came along and I couldn't stop it and now, well, now I think I might be a bit smitten.' It was the first time he had admitted how he felt but he'd been thinking it for a while now. Saying the words only confirmed his feelings, and the pint he was necking at a significant rate definitely helped. He was mad for this girl.

'Bloody hell, Pete, how long has this been going on for?'

'A few months,' he admitted.

'Who is it?'

'It's, erm, well it's Claire from work.'

Dan's brow furrowed as he mentally worked his way through the people at work, looking for a Claire. His eyes widened as he hit the jackpot. 'Claire from reception?'

Now Pete was properly grinning, despite the inappropriateness of it all. 'Yep.'

'I don't know what to say, mate. I mean fair play, she's hot, but what the fuck, Pete?' He held his hands up. 'I'm not judging – it's clear that you're really happy – but this is a big deal, you know that, right? What are you planning to do about it?'

He'd thought about it of course, although he and Claire hadn't discussed it. After that minor slip when he'd gone to see her on a Saturday, he'd felt so uncomfortable for the rest of the weekend that he'd promised himself he wouldn't do it again. But they were still meeting after work every week.

Earlier this week he'd got an email from HR to say he'd been given an extra two days' annual leave for his low absence rate and he'd immediately hatched a plan to spend it with Claire. Kate managed his usual annual leave allowance like the Gestapo, each day accounted for with holidays, long weekends or childcare responsibilities. But these two were all his, and he had already started researching out-of-town options where he and Claire would be safe from prying eyes. Perhaps they could even make a mini-break of it – he could tell Kate he was taking clients away for a night. He did it fairly often so she wouldn't be suspicious. The thought had made him tense with excitement. But they were still very much living in the moment, both refusing to acknowledge the reality that it probably couldn't go on as it was forever. At some point, Pete would need to make a decision either way.

'I really don't know,' he admitted to Dan. 'It was never meant to come to this. I've literally never cheated on Kate before. When it happened, I thought it was a one-off but then it just kept happening and before I knew it, I was really into her.'

'Do you feel guilty? About Kate and the kids?'

'Of course I bloody do. Especially with the kids. With Kate it's really complicated. I do feel guilty but I also feel like she's partly to blame. The way she is with me, she's really off, mate. It's like all she cares about is maintaining this image of the perfect life; she's obsessed with people thinking that we're this happy family but she doesn't seem to care what actually happens on the inside. And we've really drifted apart. She's not the person I met, or the person I married.'

'What about marriage counselling?' Dan asked.

'For marriage counselling we'd have to admit our marriage is in trouble and we haven't even done that,' Pete replied. 'It's like we're both in denial and we don't want to rock the sinking boat. I thought this was just what life was like when you settled down and had kids but now I'm not sure. What about you and Laura?'

Dan considered the question carefully. 'It's hard, having young children. You're so busy running around all day that it's easy to forget to look after yourselves. Most evenings we're so exhausted we collapse into bed soon after the kids. And arranging to go out together, just the two of us, is like planning a military operation. But if you're asking if I'm happy then the answer is yes. Do I still love Laura? Definitely yes.'

'That's the thing,' Pete replied. 'I'm not happy and I can't really remember the last time that I was. I've just been so tired of life, of everything, for so long and then when Claire came along I suddenly felt like myself again.'

'I get it, Pete, I do. Marriage is hard. Raising a family is relentless and exhausting. Sure there have been times when I've wanted to run away from it all and become a scuba diving instructor in Thailand.' They both grinned in acknowledgement at the fantasy. 'But at the end of the day, you're in it together with your partner, you're a team. And if that team isn't working anymore, then you need to look at why. Either way, you have to face reality, Pete, you can't go on like this forever.'

Pete sighed heavily. 'It's not as simple as that though, is it. The decision isn't between two women, it's between two life choices. And there's the kids to think of.'

'Yes, but the kids aren't going to be happy if their parents are unhappy. You need to confront this situation head-on. You either fight for your marriage, work hard to fix it and find happiness again, or you walk away and make a clean break. I know people stay together for the kids but personally I think that's a bad idea. Kids aren't stupid, they can sense when things aren't right.'

It was all starting to feel a bit too real now. The buzz of confessing his secret had worn off and now he was regretting telling Dan. He wasn't ready to confront all of this yet. Of course it was playing on his mind, forever lurking in the background, but he was pretty good at shoving it into a dark corner and ignoring it. He wanted to live in his little bubble of denial for a bit longer. Was he trying to have his cake and eat it? Probably, but bloody hell he was having a good time. And he deserved a good time.

'Look, Dan, I totally get everything that you're saying,' he told his friend. 'And believe me I know that this situation is less than ideal. I'm going to sort it, I promise.'

He quickly moved the conversation on to a drama at work and Dan happily took the bait, probably as relieved as he was to get off the topic. They didn't mention it for the rest of the evening. But by telling him, he had a feeling that something had changed. He had opened the can of worms. It wasn't a secret anymore and now he was, in some way, accountable for his actions.

# 9

## KATE

Pete, what the hell? It's been over a
week and I haven't heard from you. At
least let me know where you are. You
can't just vanish like this, it's really
unfair. I have no idea what to say to the
girls. Lily is asking after you all the
time, she keeps wanting to FaceTime you
and I'm running out of excuses. Maybe you
don't love me anymore but surely you
still love them? If you get this email
please at least do me the courtesy of
responding. Kate.

The train pulled into Farringdon Station and Kate stepped
off and made her way up the stairs to the street. Looking
around her she felt that instant rush of excitement at being in
the hustle and bustle of central London. God, she loved this city.
It had been so long since she'd been in town, she'd forgotten
what it felt like to be surrounded by hundreds of people,
dashing this way and that way to offices, meetings, coffee shops

and restaurants. She spent pretty much all day and every day trapped in suburbia, where the highlight of the day was a trip to the park.

It had been ten days since Pete had vanished and Dan had agreed to meet her. She'd spent the last few days contacting his friends to ask them if he'd been in touch. Some had simply replied to say he hadn't, not interested in prying further, others had called her to ask what was going on. They'd all been shocked to hear what had happened and she believed them. They didn't know anything.

As a last resort, she'd called his mum, Karen. Pete wasn't close with his mum at all and Kate didn't really know her that well. A single mum, she had raised Pete and his brother David on her own and Kate knew from what little Pete had told her that they didn't have much money growing up. He didn't talk fondly of his childhood. David had apparently never been interested in school or making much out of his life, whereas Pete had been the complete opposite – driven to the point of obsession, as if he had something to prove. He never spoke about his family and although he had often stayed with Kate at her parents' house in the university holidays, whenever she suggested that she visit him at his mum's he'd always made an excuse.

She met his mum for the first time at graduation and the minute the ceremony was over, he'd practically manhandled Karen away from Kate and her family, saying that they were going out for lunch together before she got the train home. She'd always felt that Pete was ashamed of his family but whenever she brought it up with him, he refused to discuss it. In the end she'd given up trying. The years had gone by and she'd all but forgotten he even had a family because they had never been in their lives. When Lily was born and she became a mother herself, she had felt a new, overwhelming sadness for

Karen. The poor woman had all but lost her son and wasn't being given the opportunity to be in her granddaughter's life either. Whatever had happened between Pete and his mother, surely it wasn't completely insurmountable? So she had suggested that Pete get in touch with her and arrange for her to meet the baby but he'd frowned and told her that it wasn't going to happen. When she'd probed, he'd got angry and ordered her to leave it and that was the last time she ever brought it up.

She'd had to dig Pete's phone out and look through his contacts to find the number. As she dialled from the home phone, she realised that she was terrified of speaking to her and when the phone started ringing she nearly hung up. But before she could change her mind, Karen picked up.

'Karen, hi, it's Kate. Pete's wife.'

The silence that followed went on for so long that she wasn't even sure if Karen was still there but eventually she answered. 'What's happened?'

Her response threw Kate and for a second she couldn't find the words to reply. How had his mum known something was wrong straightaway? But then she realised that there was no other reason why her daughter-in-law would be calling her out of the blue after so many years.

'It's Pete, he's– erm, well I just wondered if you'd heard from him at all?'

Karen laughed so hard that she started coughing. 'Love, I'm the last person to have heard from Pete. He hasn't done a runner has he?'

This whole conversation was making her feel extremely uneasy and she wanted to finish it as soon as possible. It had been a stupid idea to call. Of all the places where Pete might have gone, it was never going to have been his mum's.

For want of anything better to say she replied with the same frankness. 'Yes, he has.'

'I'm sorry to hear it, I know you've got young children too, but what can I say? He's always been a selfish one him. Like father like son.'

She knew there was no love lost between them and it was clear she wasn't going to get much further with his mum. 'Okay, well thanks anyway, Karen, I'm sorry to have bothered you.'

The older women relented a bit. 'Look, give me your number and if I hear from him, I'll let you know.'

She read out her number and hung up. It wasn't until later that she realised Karen hadn't even asked after her grandchildren.

After a few days of trying other avenues, and her emails to Pete still unanswered, she had got back in contact with Dan and told him that she'd exhausted all her other options and he was the last one left – it was time for him to talk. They had arranged to meet for coffee at a place in the City, near his work. She felt a mixture of anticipation and fear about what she was going to hear. She was desperate to know the whole truth, yet she knew that she would hate it. She found the café immediately and paused for a second before she went in, steeling herself. Dan was inside waiting for her. He stood up and gave her an awkward hug and as they both sat down, he glanced at her nervously. This was just as hard for him and she knew she was putting him in a difficult situation, but she hadn't been left with much choice.

They made small talk until the waitress came over to take their order, with Dan asking after the girls and Kate enquiring about his family. As soon as the waitress had gone, Kate went straight to the point. 'Dan, thanks for arranging to meet me, I know this is difficult for you but I need you to tell me what you know.'

He nodded, already resigned to his fate. He'd obviously decided to tell her everything and she was grateful to him for it, he was a decent guy. Perhaps he'd discussed it with Laura, Kate thought, and she had urged him to do the right thing. Despite the fact that she hated everyone knowing about their personal life, she had to get to the truth.

'Her name is Claire. She worked on reception for a few months. I don't know much about her, she kept herself to herself and didn't socialise much. I've asked around in the office to see if anyone is still in touch with her but no one is. As far as anyone else knows, she was a temp and she left.'

He paused for a minute as their drinks arrived before continuing. 'Pete told me about the affair a few months ago. I think it had been going on for a while by then. He told me that he'd decided to quit his job and move to France with her. I told him he was making a mistake, but he wouldn't listen. The last time I saw him was at his leaving do a couple of weeks ago. He told me that he was going to tell you everything before he left so I am as shocked as you are that he didn't.'

And there it was. The truth. She realised her hands were shaking and she wrapped them around her coffee cup to steady them.

'Who else knew about this?' she asked.

'Only one other person, Carl from work,' Dan replied. 'There were rumours about Pete and Claire flying around the office but no one knew anything for sure. When they both left at the same time, people gossiped but Claire was a pretty private person and no one could get any information out of her.'

'Do you know Claire's full name? Or anything about where she lived?'

'Her last name is Robinson. I think she lived in south London but that's all I know.'

*Claire Robinson.* Not a particularly unusual name, there was no way she'd be able to find the right one on social media, she thought.

'Are you friends with her on Facebook or anything?'

'No, I'm sorry, I'm not. I didn't know her well. None of us did, she wasn't there very long and like I said, she kept herself to herself. I could find out the name of the temp agency she came from if you like, although I'm not sure if they'd tell you anything. I know HR won't give me her details, they run the department like Fort Knox.'

'Thanks, Dan, that would be helpful if you don't mind. I'm not sure yet if I'll do anything with it but it would be good to have it nevertheless. Do you know where in France they were going to?'

'No, he didn't give me any details. He just said it was a property that Claire's family had owned, somewhere rural. He was going to work remotely but he said he'd come back to London regularly for meetings and to see the girls.'

'Did he tell you where his new job was?'

'He might have done at some point but I can't remember. I'm sorry. It was a tech firm, I think.'

Now that she had the answers she'd been looking for, Kate realised that she didn't want to stay any longer. There was no point prolonging the agony for them both. She drained her coffee and stood up. 'Listen, Dan, thank you for your honesty, I really appreciate it. If you hear from him, will you let me know?'

'Of course,' he said, standing up to give her another hug. 'And if you need anything at all, Kate, you or the girls, please let me know.'

'Thanks, Dan, I will.' She smiled sadly at him one last time and left.

Outside she checked her phone and saw a message from Nadia inviting her to lunch with the ladies. It was, quite literally, the last thing she wanted to do. They had all been lovely, the others, but she knew that they were probably talking about her behind her back and it made her feel sick. It was at times like this that you realised who your real friends were, she thought, not the ones who send sympathetic text messages and then bitch about the state of your relationship with other people over coffee, but the ones who genuinely offer to help. And, apart from Erin who had been amazing, there didn't seem to be too many of them left anymore. When had she lost touch with all her real friends, the ones who really cared about her?

At university she had attracted friends like magnets. The girls she'd lived with during her three years in Leeds had become like sisters to her and they had stayed in touch throughout their twenties. Some were living in London like Kate and Pete, others had moved to different cities or countries, but they always made an effort to meet up regularly. She'd also made some good friends in her job, although looking back now they were good-time friends – great fun for work drinks on a Friday night or a hungover brunch the next day, but not ones to come flocking in a crisis. And when everyone hit their thirties and started having babies, things changed. Even her beloved uni girls drifted away – the non-baby ones having amazing adventures in far-flung places or working their way up the career ladder and the baby ones so absorbed in the daily challenge of parenting tiny people that they didn't have the time to keep up with old friendships anymore.

Perhaps if she'd got more involved in the children's school lives she'd have made more friends but Rachel did most of the school runs so she'd never really had the chance to mingle, other than with the antenatal mums who she already knew. They must all think she was a terrible snob, she thought, the mum who doesn't work but still has a nanny. No wonder she didn't have any bloody friends. Unless you counted Nadia and the others but she wouldn't exactly call them close. Pete had never liked them that much but they all adored him. At Sunday lunches in the local pub or occasional dinner parties, all arranged by Nadia, they had cooed over him, enthralled by his sharp wit and easy banter. Oh, he could put the charm on when he wanted to and they'd all fallen for it.

'Pete is SO lovely,' Nadia had gushed to him on one of their meet-ups in the park. 'Such a doting father. And you two are just, like, the perfect match.'

And despite how she was feeling on the inside, Kate had loved it. The idea that everyone thought they were this amazing couple, the epitome of family life: it was all she had ever wanted and if it couldn't be real it was a close second that at least it looked like that to the outside world. Looking back now, she realised how shallow and ridiculous that was. What did it matter what everyone else thought when your husband was having an affair with another woman and doing everything he could to avoid coming home to his family? If she'd worked harder on their marriage and less on making the house, the children, everything look so perfect they probably wouldn't be in this situation.

Still, Pete wasn't here and Nadia was and she needed all the friends she could get, so she replied to say she'd be there and headed back to the station, pausing for one last minute to savour the bustling anonymity of the City before reluctantly getting on the train that would take her back to reality.

## 10

# PETE

Pete jumped off the Tube at Paddington Station and headed towards the coffee shop where they had arranged to meet. A little frisson of excitement ran through him. Today, instead of going to work, he and Claire were going away together. It was only for one night but he felt like a kid breaking up for the summer, as if time stretched endlessly ahead of him, with nothing but fun and carefree abandonment to enjoy.

He'd booked them into a trendy inn in Oxfordshire, one with a Michelin-starred chef, so they could go for country walks, eat and drink fine food and hopefully have lots of sex in a boho chic room. He'd felt under pressure to organise something trendy for Claire, she was that type of girl. He'd spent hours on the internet at work, when he was supposed to be doing the budget for next year, researching suitable venues. According to *The Sunday Times* this was one of the hippest mini-break destinations of the year and judging by how much it cost, it better be bloody exceptional. Thank God he had an Amex card that Kate didn't have access to.

The train was leaving in fifteen minutes, so he ordered a

couple of coffees to go and stood outside the café, waiting for Claire.

A couple of minutes later she rocked up, looking unhurried and effortlessly sexy as she always did, wearing her signature oversized sunglasses and clutching a small holdall. Her face lit up when she saw him and she walked over to give him a kiss. 'I'm so excited, Pete,' she said with a grin.

He grinned back. 'Me too.'

It was the first time they'd been on a proper date, if you could call it that. It was a bit of a risk which was why he'd decided to go out of town, to a county where they didn't know anyone. The chances of bumping into another mini-breaking Londoner on a Tuesday during term time were slim to none. They headed for the platform, instinctively staying apart from each other while London rules still applied. On the carriage he looked around furtively, making sure that they didn't know anyone, before sitting down next to her.

As the train pulled out he felt himself relaxing and he reached towards her and kissed her. 'I've been looking forward to doing that for days,' he said.

'I hope it was worth the wait.'

'You're always worth the wait, Claire.'

They regarded each other for a minute, the tension building between them, and she looked pointedly at the toilets and back at him. Was she suggesting what he thought she was suggesting? Train toilets were bloody disgusting. And there was always someone waiting outside, making you feel like you had to pee as quickly as possible. But already the thought was beginning to turn him on. This girl was something else. He nodded and they stood up silently and made their way to the toilet.

Inside, he locked the door and pushed her up against the tiny little sink. It was early enough in the journey that it didn't smell of piss yet but Christ there was barely enough room for one person, let alone two. This was not going to be the most comfortable sex he'd ever had. Yet the sheer recklessness of what they were doing almost overwhelmed him and after only a few seconds of kissing he was shoving her underwear to one side, using his fingers until she shuddered with pleasure before pulling down his flies and pushing himself into her with such urgency that he thought he was going to explode. It was quick, it was dirty and it was amazing.

Afterwards they made their way sheepishly back to their seats, avoiding eye contact with everyone else in the carriage.

'Well, that was a first,' he whispered to her after they'd sat back down.

'Me too.'

'Possibly a last too,' he added with a laugh. 'Not the most luxurious experience of my life.'

'But pretty hot, right?' she replied, raising her eyebrows at him.

'Pretty hot,' he agreed.

The rest of the journey was somewhat less eventful. They bought another coffee and did a crossword together. When they got to their stop they jumped into a taxi and arrived at the hotel with a couple of hours to kill before lunch. Donning their wellies and waterproofs they prepared to go out for a walk.

'Jesus, we look like a right pair of Londoners on a day out in the country,' he said with a laugh, observing their pristine Barbour coats and Joules wellies in the mirror before they went out. Without warning he had a flashback to the first country weekend away he'd been on with Kate. They'd been skint students at the time so they'd stayed in the cheapest B&B they could find. It was the ugliest room they'd ever seen and the en suite they'd been promised had turned out to be a toilet in a cupboard and a shower cubicle in the actual bedroom. They'd laughed so hard they'd been rolling around on the floor crying.

But they didn't need fancy bedding and expensive toiletries to have a good time back then: all they needed was each other. They'd gone for a long, lazy walk, broken up by pints in the pub, until they were so pissed that Kate had fallen over on the way home and ended up head to toe in mud. Then she'd had to wash it all off in the 'en suite' while Pete sat on the bed, merely inches away, laughing so hysterically that he had almost wet himself. It had been one of the best weekends of his life. How long had it been since they'd laughed like that? It seemed like a whole lifetime ago.

Banishing the thoughts to the back of his mind, he took Claire by the hand and shut the door behind him. *Time to focus on the now*, he told himself.

'Tell me about your children?' Claire asked him. They were sitting opposite each other in the inn's restaurant having just eaten one of the best meals of his life. He felt full and happy as they drank the remainder of the red wine they'd ordered with dinner and the question threw him. He raised his eyebrows at her.

'There's no point pretending they don't exist, Pete. They're a big part of your life and I want to know about the things that matter to you.'

'Well Lily is seven, Maggie is five,' he began. 'They're like chalk and cheese, the pair of them. Lily is the serious one, very conscientious at school and a heart of gold. Maggie is a cheeky little mare but she doesn't half make me laugh.'

'Did you always want children?'

He considered the question for a moment. 'I guess it was just something that we always assumed we'd do. It's not like I had a burning desire to be a dad but it was the standard pathway, you know? Not that I'm saying I don't like being a dad, I love my girls, but it wasn't something I'd dreamed of all my life, if that makes sense.'

'Are you close to your own family?'

He shook his head. 'Not at all. My dad left when I was young and I have no idea where he is. I don't want to know either. I never really got on with my mum. She's the sort of person who always has a chip on her shoulder. Not the most supportive mother in the world. When I told her I wanted to go to university she just didn't get it at all. "Why don't you just get a job like everyone else?" she asked me. I think she was expecting me to contribute financially rather than swan off for another three years of studying. I couldn't wait to get away. How about you?'

'The total opposite,' she said with a wistful smile. 'My mum was my best friend. When she died it hit me really hard. But me and my dad, we got through it together and it made us closer than ever. When he died, I felt totally on my own for the first time in my life. It was hard.' She paused to sip some of her wine.

'I've not been back to my dad's house in France since he died. I just couldn't bring myself to do it. But recently I've found myself thinking about it more and more. Maybe it's time to go back. Perhaps you could come with me?'

'I'd like that,' he said, already mentally calculating how it would be possible to get away for a few days. He could easily fabricate a business trip. 'I'd like that a lot.'

Afterwards they went back to their room. Lying next to Claire in post-coital bliss, a nightcap glass of whisky in his hand, he allowed the warming effect of the drink to overcome him and he drifted off into a contented sleep.

The next morning she was already in the shower when he woke up. She came out, rubbing her wet hair with a towel and perched on the bed next to him.

'Morning, sleepyhead,' she said, giving him a kiss.

'What time is it?' he asked her.

'Just gone nine thirty.'

*Bloody hell, I haven't slept that late since...* he couldn't even remember when. 'I slept like a log,' he said, stretching and sitting up.

'Nothing like a bit of country fresh air for a good night's sleep,' she said. She smiled at him but she seemed a bit distracted.

'Are you okay?'

'I'm fine, just a bit sad that it's all over and we have to go home. I've had such a glorious time.'

'Me too,' he said, reaching out to pull her towards him. But she resisted.

'I'm sorry, Pete, it's just, oh I don't know, most of the time I'm absolutely fine with the fact that you have this whole other life. I knew what I was getting myself into. But sometimes I just wish that it could be something more.'

*Oh shit.* His heart sank. This was the first time she'd brought it up after months of their no-ties agreement. He'd been lulled into a false sense of security that she was totally, 100 per cent fine with the arrangement. She'd been so cool and undemanding about it up until now. Had he been naïve? She was a woman after all, emotions always came into it in the end. He thought back to the conversation he'd had with Dan at the pub, when he had told him about the affair. He'd told his friend he was smitten with Claire. Did he mean it or did he just say it in the heat of the moment? *You have to make a decision*, Dan had said. He just wasn't ready yet. Why was she bringing it up now? They'd had the most amazing day and night and now she was totally ruining the vibe.

As if she could read his mind, she immediately leant in to

kiss him. 'Oh, just ignore me, Pete, I'm only being silly. Forget I said anything. Now, where were we?'

She dropped her towel and crawled into bed with him, pushing her warm body up against him. He relaxed and reached for her, running his hands up and down her body and allowing himself to get lost in the moment again. But her words stayed with him for the remainder of the trip.

# 11

## KATE

Pete, it's me, again. I don't know why I keep emailing you, it's clear that you're either not checking your messages or that you don't want to respond. But I can hardly just forget about you and pretend you never existed. Is that what you want me to do? I keep waiting for you to get back into contact. Every day I wait for a call, a text, anything that tells me that you're okay, that you're thinking of us, that you're coming back.

I'm still finding it hard to comprehend that you just upped and left us in limbo like this and I've been thinking about what made you do this. I can't stop thinking about it. I know things weren't great between us and hadn't been for a long time but was I that much of an ogre that you couldn't talk to me about it? I would have understood.

    I accept that our marriage is in trouble, maybe it's even over, I don't know. But I do know that we need to talk. And we've got stuff to sort out. You can't just walk away from us. Surely you know that? Please contact me. Please, Pete.

K ate sprinted across the hallway to answer the phone. She'd been sitting at the table doing the household accounts when it started ringing. Pete had been gone for over a month now but while her world stood still, trapped in this strange, surreal nightmare, the rest of life went on as usual. The outgoings continued to disappear from their account like nothing had happened, yet the income was zero. Since they'd had children, she'd taken his income for granted but she couldn't live off their savings forever. Whatever happened in the future, she would need to start standing on her own two feet again. It was terrifying but at the same time, she found it strangely motivating. Looking at the Excel spreadsheet that she'd created on her laptop she was feeling more proactive than she had done in weeks.

The doctor had prescribed some sleeping pills, which had taken the edge off the insomnia and made her feel more human again. Unfortunately, with sleep came nightmares. There was a recurring one she had where Pete was hanging off the edge of a cliff and she was lying on her front, holding on to him and trying to pull him back. But she knew that she wasn't strong enough. If she stayed holding on to him, she would eventually be pulled down with him. If she let go, he would plunge to his death, but she would save herself. In the end she always let go, and immediately after she would wake up in a clammy sweat, her heart racing. She would turn to look at the empty space in bed where he used to sleep before closing her eyes and breathe slowly to calm herself down. After a few minutes, she would come back to herself although she knew she wouldn't sleep again that night. In the morning, the nightmares would be banished and she would put on her make-up and face the day. She was living a life of two halves – trying to pretend that everything was okay during the day and admitting that it was far from it at night.

She grabbed the receiver just before it stopped ringing. 'Hello?'

'Kate, hi, it's Karen.' Pete's mum.

'Oh, hi, Karen.' She was the last person Kate had expected to hear from.

'Look, I know I was short on the phone the other week. I've not been able to stop thinking about it. It's just, it was a bit of a shock hearing from you after all this time.'

Kate was so surprised by the call she didn't know how to respond at first. Finally, she replied, 'Please don't worry, I totally understand. I'm sorry to have bothered you.'

'No, it's not that. I'm glad you called. It's just, well, it's been hard for me, not being a part of Pete's life, and the girls. But I always thought, as long as you're all happy that's what matters. So when you said he'd left, I was thrown. And bloody furious with him. You know his dad left me when my boys were young?'

'I do.'

'So I never thought Pete would do anything like that. He always acted like he was better than us all. But it turns out he's not. And that, well, that was a shock.'

This was the longest conversation Kate had ever had with Karen. The call, and her honesty, had totally taken her aback.

She felt herself welling up and hurriedly tried to compose herself.

'Have you heard from him yet?' Karen asked.

'No, I'm afraid not.'

'I'm sorry to hear that, Kate, I really am. How are the girls?'

The girls had asked about Pete almost constantly in the first few weeks – *when will Daddy be back? Can we call him? Why isn't he home yet?* Each time she'd found an excuse. It was absolutely exhausting, and heart-breaking. But then something strange had happened. A few days ago, they'd stopped asking. It was as if they'd accepted that he wasn't around and that was that. Children were so adaptable it was terrifying. Yet she was on constant alert, waiting for the inevitable questions to come again, trying to plan her response. At some point the business trip excuse wouldn't wash anymore. She was going to have to tell them something else and she wasn't quite ready for it yet.

'The girls are okay. Well, Lily broke her leg, but to be honest she's been absolutely loving it. She sits on the sofa, being waited on hand and foot, while friends come round with presents and cake. I'm sending her back to school on Monday: she's a dab hand with those crutches.'

'Oh poor love,' Karen replied. 'Pete broke his arm when he was a kid. Fell awkwardly during a football tackle. He was a right drama queen about it.'

Both women laughed.

'How's Maggie?'

'Oh she's fine, a bit of a green-eyed monster over the fact that Lily's getting all the attention but other than that she's her usual mischievous self.'

'I was thinking,' Karen said. She sounded nervous. 'Well, I'd really love to see them. I know you're not keen and I understand why. I wasn't the best mother to Pete, I get that. But, well, they're my grandchildren and I've changed, I really have. I guess age does that to you.'

Karen thought it was Kate who didn't want to see her? Where did she get that idea from? 'Karen, I'd love for you to meet the children. I've suggested it to Pete more than once. What made you think I wasn't keen?'

'Pete told me. He said that you didn't want me to be in their lives.'

*Fucking Pete.* She felt another rush of anger towards him. What was he playing at, making her the baddie? It had all been him, not her. But inviting Karen into their lives now, wasn't that a mistake? Surely the last thing she needed right now was a reminder of Pete in her life. And what would the girls say? Wouldn't it confuse them and make them miss their dad even more? The whole thing seemed like a bad idea. She should just make the right noises about how lovely that would be and end the call without actually making any concrete plans.

But then, on a strange impulse she found herself saying, 'I never said that, Karen. I'm so very sorry that you thought that. How about next weekend?'

After she had hung up the phone, she sat on the hallway floor for a minute, wondering what the hell she'd just done. Karen had been really pleased by the invitation and, after asking what kind of toys the girls were into at the moment, she'd hung up cheerily, telling Kate she couldn't wait to see them all. What kind of idiot invites the estranged mother of their estranged husband to their home? Yet, despite how furious she was with Pete, the truth was that she wasn't ready to let go of him and talking to his mum had made her feel connected to him. It had brought a strange and unexpected comfort and she realised that she still craved a link to Pete in her life. *What a tangled web.* She needed some wine.

Pouring herself a glass, she sat back down at the kitchen

table and turned her attention to the spreadsheet again to distract herself. The girls would be back from Erin's house, where they'd spent the afternoon, in an hour or so. Looking at the outgoings again, she kept focusing on Rachel's salary. It was ridiculous to be paying that much for a nanny when she didn't even work. The time had come to face reality: she didn't need Rachel anymore. She'd been foolish to keep her on for so long as it was, she should have let her go years ago. But could she cope on her own with the children? The idea brought back the familiar feelings of fear and doubt. What would she do to entertain them? What would she cook for them every night? Would she be enough for them? She was a terrible mum, she was incompetent, she couldn't handle the children on her own. It would be a disaster. She took another gulp of wine.

But then another, stronger voice entered her head. *What is wrong with you? You love your children and they love you. What are you so afraid of?* It was time to stop this bullshit. She'd been hiding from reality for so long that she barely knew herself anymore. *Enough*, she told herself. *Enough*.

On Monday, Rachel arrived at the usual time like clockwork.

'Rachel, hi,' Kate said from the kitchen, where she was making toast. 'Lily is going to school today so I'm going to drive. Even Little Miss Crutch Champion probably won't make the journey on foot. And perhaps we can have a coffee afterwards?'

'Sure,' Rachel said amenably as she started looking around for school bags, shoes and packed lunches.

'All done and by the front door,' Kate called out.

'Impressive,' Rachel replied with a laugh.

Together, the two women helped Lily into the car and drove the short journey to school. In the playground Lily's friends flocked around her, oohing and aahing over her cast. Lily beamed and Kate felt a surge of pride. Her little girl was going to be just fine. She got back into the car with Rachel and they returned home, where Kate made them both a coffee. Sitting down at the kitchen table, she was feeling shaky with nerves but she might as well rip the plaster off.

'Rachel, you know how much we all love you. Christ, you pretty much saved us when you came into our lives all those years ago.'

Rachel started to object but Kate held up her hand to stop her. 'You know you did. And we will forever be grateful to you. I hope you know how important you are to us. But the fact is that things have changed a lot since then. And it's not even about Pete. My girls aren't babies anymore, they're at school and let's face it, I don't even have a job. It's time for me to finally accept a truth I should have accepted long ago. We love you but you're a luxury that we simply can't justify. I'm so sorry.'

She wasn't sure what to expect from Rachel – anger, tears maybe – and she braced herself for the inevitable. Rachel had every right to be disappointed.

But instead she simply nodded and took Kate's hand in her own. 'I completely understand, Kate, and I'm not surprised. To be honest, I've been expecting it for a long time. It's been a privilege to be a part of your family and I'm going to miss you and the girls so much but it's time for me to move on.'

'What will you do?' Kate asked, feeling a wave of relief. She'd done it, it was over. And Rachel's reaction had been much better than she'd expected.

'I've had a family trying to poach me for months. One of the mums at the girls' school. She works full-time and has had a succession of unreliable nannies. Every time she sees me at the school gates, she offers me a job. It's a decent gig, and it means

I'll still get to see Lily and Maggie. I'll give her a call now and see if she wants to make it official.'

The two women hugged and Rachel left to make the call. Ten minutes later she was back. 'She wants me to start immediately. I've told her that I have to give you at least one month's notice...'

'It's fine,' Kate interrupted. 'It's absolutely fine if you want to start straight away, Rachel, honestly.'

'But what about Lily and her leg? I feel awful for leaving you in the lurch like this. I could at least wait until the cast is off and she's walking again?'

But Kate just stood up and gave Rachel another hug. 'It's okay, Rachel, I've got this.' And for the first time in a long time, she thought she might actually believe herself.

The girls were gutted about Rachel at first. What with their dad suddenly disappearing from their lives, then Rachel, the timing couldn't have been much worse and she felt awful about causing so much disruption to them in such a short space of time. But then, as only children can, they'd rallied within minutes.

'Who will take us to school?' Lily asked, wiping her tear-stained cheeks.

'I will, darling.'

'Every day?'

'Yes, every day. And I'll pick you up. And we can go to the park or have tea at a café. It'll be fun.'

'Yay, Mummy is going to take us to school every day,' Maggie started chanting, jumping up and down on the sofa. 'Mummy is taking us to school, Mummy is taking us to school!'

'And you'll still see Rachel all the time,' Kate added. 'She'll be working for another family whose children go to your school and she can't wait to see you every day. And she'll still come to your birthday parties and so on. She'll always be in our lives.'

Kate gestured to Rachel, who had been lurking outside the door, waiting for her cue. She came in and gave both the girls a big hug. 'Your mum's right,' she said. 'You can't get rid of me that easily, I'll be seeing you all the time,' and she tickled them both until they were wriggling around and shrieking with delight. Once the girls were immersed in a game of doll's hospital the two women went back into the kitchen for a cup of tea.

'Have you heard from Pete?' Rachel asked her.

'No, not a thing. I'm starting to think he's not coming back at all.'

'Of course he is,' Rachel replied. 'He wouldn't just disappear like this, without a trace. He loves you and the kids.'

'I thought so too but I just don't know anymore. You know I spoke to his mum the other day. She told me that Pete had told her I didn't want her in our lives. She'd stayed away all these years because of me. But it couldn't have been further from the truth. I wanted her to meet the girls and to spend time with us, but every time I brought it up, Pete would get angry and tell me to leave it. I've been with him for so many years but maybe I didn't know him at all.'

'I'm sure he had his reasons,' Rachel said, as always trying to find the best in people. 'He must have thought it was the right thing to do, for you and the girls.'

'Maybe,' Kate conceded. 'Or maybe he's just a manipulative, lying bastard.'

Rachel's eyes widened.

'Sorry, Rach,' Kate said hurriedly. 'Not appropriate at all, it must be because you're leaving us, I've gone all unprofessional on you.'

'Not at all,' Rachel said. 'If my husband had left me and my kids without a word, I'd be calling him a lot worse than a bastard. It would start with a C and end with a T.'

Kate snorted with laughter. This new dynamic between

them felt comfortable, as if she was in the company of a friend. 'We must keep in touch, Rachel, we really must.'

'Of course we will,' Rachel replied confidently. 'What are you going to do if he doesn't come back?'

'Rage, cry, rage a bit more and get on with my life, I suppose,' she replied. 'I've already started to accept that our marriage is probably over. It can't survive something like this, I'll never forgive him for what he's done. And it's more than that anyway. Things haven't been good between us for so long and I knew it but I didn't do anything about it. I've been in a weird state of denial for so long, letting life pass me by, too afraid to wake up and face the truth.'

'And now?'

'I don't know, I'm still fragile, I'm still angry, upset, anxious, afraid of what the future holds. But I've been forced to wake up. I've been left on my own to deal with stuff and I've had to get on with it. So I have. Not always well, but at least I'm trying. As each day goes by I feel a little braver, a little more capable.'

'Are you okay for money?'

'Right now, yes, but it has made me realise how much I've relied on Pete for everything. And that's not going to wash in the future, no matter what happens. I'm going to start looking for some freelance work again and I mean properly looking, not just designing a pretty website but never actually getting any clients. I need to start standing on my own two feet again.'

'You'll do it,' Rachel said firmly.

'I wish I had your confidence.'

'Oh you do, Kate, you do. You just don't know it yet.'

*Would Pete be proud of me?* Kate wondered, lying in bed that night and staring at the empty space next to her. Would he be impressed with how she was handling herself? At the worst possible point of her life she was finally starting to feel like herself again which made no sense to her at all. Perhaps none of this was real and she was just in survival mode which would make her crash and burn when the adrenaline wore off. She hoped not, she had to keep it together. Perhaps she should see a counsellor to work through some of her baggage. If she had got help earlier and started to build herself back up again would this have happened? She couldn't have stopped him meeting this woman but perhaps he wouldn't have been tempted by her if things were happier at home. Or perhaps it would have happened anyway – maybe their marriage had simply run its course.

While she was still furious and hurt at the way Pete had betrayed her, she realised that she didn't feel jealous of this other woman anymore. She had at first, she'd felt it with an animal-like rage, but now she'd had time to calm down she was, in an odd way, pleased that Pete had found someone who made him happy. Clearly she didn't anymore and he certainly hadn't made her happy for a long time. They hadn't had sex in what felt like years and they didn't enjoy being around each other that much either. She loved him, yes, but not in the way she should. Had they just stayed together out of habit because they couldn't remember any different?

*If only we could have talked about it*, she thought, *perhaps I could have had time to calm down and we could have parted friends.* Or perhaps not. She would have given him a hard time, she knew it. Maybe that's why he'd decided to leave the way he did and the knowledge that it was her doing was a guilt she'd have to live with for the rest of her life. The saddest thing was, it was the children who were going to suffer from her mistakes. But she was going to make damn sure that she made it up to them, and that meant being the best mum they could ever have.

## 12

## PETE

Pete inhaled deeply on his e-cigarette and leaned back against the headboard, watching the tiny, pathetic little wisp of vapour waft up to the ceiling. It was nowhere near as good as the real thing but he still enjoyed the occasional hit of nicotine and he was no longer in his carefree, invincible twenties when smoking a pack of Marlboro Lights on a night out and reeking of fags was acceptable. And anyway, post-coital indulgences were restricted to devices that didn't set off smoke alarms now. Even his vices had become boring, what a depressing thought.

He turned to look at Claire, who was lying on her side, propped up on her elbow, watching him with an indulgent look. She was one vice that was definitely not boring. Christ, he'd missed that look. The last time he'd had sex with Kate, however long ago that was, she was sitting up and reading her Kindle within seconds of him pulling out. He couldn't believe that their affair had already been going on for six months, yet at the same time it had become a way of life for him and he could barely remember what it had been like before. He knew he should feel bad about it and some days he did but today wasn't one of them.

After a difficult day in the office, followed by a series of passive aggressive texts from Kate about forgetting to put the bins out and generally being a terrible husband, he needed something to cheer himself up.

Despite his sneaking around, he had managed to avoid arousing any suspicion in Kate. He and Claire never called each other, they weren't friends on social media and he checked his clothes meticulously for lipstick or the scent of perfume every time he left her. They left work separately, only meeting again when they got to Claire's flat and other than that cheeky night away last month they never went out, instead holing themselves up in the flat, eating deli food or takeaways, drinking wine, chatting, having sex. And life was good.

He still knew deep down that it was wrong – all the time at first and then more intermittently as time went on – but he was starting to think that this was actually a good thing. Kate wasn't interested in having sex with him but she was very interested in him being a good husband. And he was actually a BETTER husband now. He was happier, more attentive to her, eager to talk about the banality of her boring day every evening and taking the kids to their weekend classes and activities without complaint. He even made it through a dinner party with that ghastly woman Nadia and her boring-as-fuck husband, cooking some delicious steaks, charming them with his wit and acting every inch the perfect husband. He knew Kate had been pleased because afterwards she had come up behind him as he was doing the washing up and wrapped her arms around him, merry on wine and a successful evening of hosting. *Yes*, he told himself, *this is actually a good thing, everyone is happy, I'm doing no harm. I love two women but I'm only in love with one.* And if life had continued like that, who knows how long it could have gone on for.

But after Oxfordshire his and Claire's relationship had

shifted slightly. Since they got back from their night away, she had begun making noises about how lovely it would be if they could go out for dinner together, hang out with friends, or even go on holiday. She never dwelled on it for too long and she quickly changed the subject when she saw that he wasn't ready to discuss it but she had planted the seed of a new future in his mind and it was starting to grow, causing his imagination to wander down a different life path and see what was there. He imagined them down the local pub on a Saturday, a big table full of friends laughing and joking, before popping into to the chippy for a cheeky post-drink supper and then home for lazy sex. He saw them jumping on a flight to Ibiza, sitting side by side on sun loungers, uninterrupted by the noise of tantrummy children and demands for ice cream and the cold, disapproving silence of his wife, with the day stretching ahead of them, full of possibility and opportunity. He envisioned glorious weekends with the children, the four of them on day trips to London Zoo, or eating ice cream on Hampstead Heath, looking out over London. In his visions the children were clutching on to Claire's hand and looking up at her adoringly as she laughed and cuddled them. Perhaps he was almost ready to discuss it seriously with Claire, maybe he just needed a few more months to get used to the idea. He was grateful she didn't nag him at least.

But in all his fantasies, they lived in London – perhaps south London, far enough away from the memories of Muswell Hill, but easily accessible to the children. So when Claire brought up France, it was quite a bolt from the blue.

'Pete, I've been thinking,' she said, intertwining her legs with his.

'Mmm?' he asked, still watching the vapour from his e-cigarette as it disappeared into the air.

'Remember my dad's house in France – the gorgeous one near that quaint little village?'

*Here we go*, he thought, *she's going to ask me to go on holiday with her*. Already he was making mental calculations of how he could get away with it, how it would work logistically and how many days he could manage without Kate getting suspicious.

'I've been thinking about restoring it. Doing a bit of a *Grand Designs* job on it, making it amazing. A bit rural chic. It's a lovely space, I think it could be amazing. I could even convert the outbuildings into gîtes and rent them out to tourists, turn it into a little boutique B&B business.'

He hadn't been expecting that. His mind whirred with a thousand questions – *was she moving to France? Was she ending their relationship? Or was she just thinking it would be a side hustle? And where the fuck had he heard the term 'rural chic' before?* 'Okaaaay,' he said slowly. 'It's certainly an interesting plan but what's the aim? Would you sell it? Or would you be planning to run this business?'

'So I was thinking that I would run it. From France. As in, live in France.'

It hit him like a blow to the stomach. She couldn't leave him, she was his lifeline, his breath of fresh air, his glimmer of hope in his otherwise dull existence. Without her his life would continue to be boring, grey, devoid of any colour or excitement. In an instant he realised how much he had come to depend on her for his happiness. He sat up straight and looked at her, not even trying to hide his alarm now.

'As in MOVE to France? What the hell, Claire? You live in London, your whole life is in London. And, well I hate to be arrogant and all, but I'm kind of in London too.'

'Yes, that's true, but it doesn't have to be.'

'What do you mean?'

'Well, you could come too.'

'To France?'

'Yes, Pete, to France.'

She'd clearly lost the plot. There was no way in the world that he could move to France. He wasn't even sure if he was going to leave his wife yet, let alone leave the country. Why oh why did she have to rock the boat? Things had been so perfect and now she was throwing a totally unnecessary curveball. *Perhaps it's just a fantasy*, he thought, *something that she talks about but will never do.* But he had come to know Claire pretty well over the last few months and when she set her mind to something, it usually happened no matter what anyone else thought.

'Why would I want to move to France?' he asked her.

'Why wouldn't you? You're always complaining about how much you hate your job and London – well this is your chance to escape it all. Just imagine, you and me in a beautiful French gîte, walking to the local bakery each morning for *pains au chocolat* and fresh bread.'

'It's a sweet idea, Claire, but that's all it is, just a fantasy. You have to see that there's no way it could actually happen. If you want to go to France then that's your decision, though of course I'd be absolutely gutted. But there's no way that I can do it, no matter how delightful it sounds. Now, do you fancy a Chinese?'

She regarded him for a second, probably wondering if she should push it further before seeming to think better of it. 'Sure,' she replied, reaching for her phone.

And just like that, the conversation was over. But as they ate their vegetable spring rolls and chicken satay he couldn't help but think about what she'd said. It was a totally ridiculous idea that would never happen, he knew that, but just for a second he closed his eyes and allowed himself to indulge in the daydream. When he opened them again Claire was looking at him with an expression that he couldn't read but he had a sudden and horrible thought that it was disappointment. He'd let her down by dismissing her idea so quickly. And although he knew she'd been totally unrealistic to suggest it and that he had every right to tell her so, the thought of him being a disappointment to her and the prospect of her leaving him and going to France anyway, without him, absolutely terrified him. He swallowed hard and the spring roll which had tasted so amazing just a few seconds ago now caught in his throat.

# 13

## KATE

Hi, Pete. Your mum is coming to visit us today. If that doesn't shock you into getting in touch, I don't know what will. The girls are really excited, they can't wait to meet her.

Lily is getting her cast off next week, she can't wait. She'll have to wear one of those space boots for a couple of weeks and then she should be as good as new. We are going to McDonald's to celebrate after the hospital appointment. Lily's request of course. Maggie is delighted that her sister will no longer be a celebrity.

I let Rachel go this week. I should have done it years ago, but then you already knew that didn't you? So, I'm finally taking control again and standing on my own two feet and I'm actually feeling really good about it, a little

more like the old me again. Are you proud
of me?

Where are you, Pete? And when are you
coming home?

The knock on the door made Kate jump out of her skin, even though she'd been expecting it. The girls leapt up from the sofa where they'd been looking out of the window for the last twenty minutes and clamoured for the door, as excited as if it was Christmas Day. Today, for the first time, they were meeting their granny.

She opened the door and Karen stood in front of them, clutching bags and looking nervous. Despite being desperately excited all morning the girls suddenly became shy at the sight of her and retreated behind the safety of their mother's legs.

'Karen, hi! Lovely to see you, come in, come in.' Kate bustled her in through the door and took her coat before ushering her into the living room. 'Can I get you a drink? Tea? Coffee?'

'Cup of tea would be nice, thanks, love,' said Karen, looking around uncomfortably before perching on the edge of the grey sofa. The poor woman looked terrified but then so was Kate. She'd been up most of the night the previous evening panicking about the visit and wondering what on earth had possessed her to invite Karen into their lives. The girls had been confused when she'd told them that Karen was coming.

'Will Daddy be there?' Lily had asked.

'No, darling, Daddy is still away at the moment,' she'd replied.

'But when is he coming home?'

It was the first time she'd asked about Pete for a few days and, not for the first time, Kate fretted that she'd opened up a giant can of worms by inviting Karen to visit. As she had lain in bed in the early hours, plagued by her usual fears and worries, she had wondered if she would ever sleep properly again. She had stopped taking the sleeping pills because she couldn't handle the nightmares; and insomnia had become such a part of her life now that she could barely remember a time when it was normal to get a good night's sleep. In the morning she had studied her tired, wrinkled face in the mirror and thought, *I look like I've aged five years in the last five weeks.* Yet despite the fact that she was running on empty during the day she still found herself feeling energised by this new, proactive version of herself, one who was starting to run her own family again and make decisions.

As Kate busied herself making drinks in the kitchen the children milled around her, not sure what to do with themselves. 'Go and see your granny,' she told them. They looked doubtful. 'She's brought presents.'

That did it, they were in the living room before she'd even boiled the kettle. As she made tea she could hear their quiet little 'thank yous' as Karen passed them gifts, followed by shrieks of delight as they opened them, their shyness forgotten. By the time she arrived in the room carrying mugs of tea and a packet of biscuits under her arm the children were climbing all over Karen, despite Lily's broken leg.

'Oh gosh I'm sorry, Karen. Girls get off her!'

'Oh it's no bother,' Karen said, laughing with delight. 'No bother at all.'

Karen was amazing with the girls. She got down on the floor with them, playing with them, asking them questions about school and films they liked watching. She seemed to be enjoying the games just as much as the girls. Lily and Maggie loved Kate's parents, Nana and Gramps, but they weren't very hands-on with them like Karen was. It was like they'd forgotten how to be around children. Kate watched Karen and thought, *Why did Pete keep her away from us for so long?*

After Lily and Maggie got bored of adult company and retreated to their bedrooms to play with their new toys, Kate found herself alone with Karen and the nerves returned. But her mother-in-law simply took her by the hand, looked at her with concern, and asked: 'How are you?'

'I'm fine, I'm fine,' Kate immediately replied, her stock response to anyone who asked except Erin.

'I've been there, remember. I know what it's like being on your own with two young children, wondering if you'll ever see their father again. I know it's a lot. You're angry, you're frightened, you're angry all over again. I get it.'

'I'm so angry!' Kate blurted out. 'I'm sorry, Karen, I know he's your son but I'm so bloody angry! And I'm terrified. And I'm worried. And I'm wondering how much longer I can hold it all together. I feel like the seams could burst at any given minute and to be honest I have no idea how they haven't already.'

Karen nodded. 'I understand,' she repeated.

'And sometimes I have moments where I think it's all going to be okay. And for a few minutes, I feel fine, optimistic even. I have moments where I actually think this whole disaster has made me stronger and more capable. But then it all comes flooding back and I think that I'll never be okay again.'

'But you will. You will be okay, Kate.' Karen clutched Kate's hand tighter. 'When Pete's dad left me I was livid, with myself as much as him. I knew he was no good but I fell madly in love with him anyway, let him get me pregnant even though I was only nineteen. And I blamed Pete. It's painful to admit that, Kate, I'm not proud of it at all but I was young, stupid and heartbroken. I thought, *If only he wasn't so difficult, so hard to live with – always demanding things, having tantrums, not giving us a minute's peace. That's what drove Ian away, not me. If only I hadn't had a baby, none of this would have happened.*'

Karen paused for a minute to wipe her eyes and compose

herself. 'I was angry with Pete for a long time which is something I'll regret for my whole life. Of course it wasn't his fault, his dad was a total waste of space who only thought about himself. Ian left a few months after Pete's brother came along. My family had given up on me ages ago, and I was so overwhelmed with having two young children I just didn't have anything left to give to anyone. I don't blame Pete for walking out as soon as he was old enough and not wanting to have anything to do with me. I drove him away.'

It all made sense now, Kate realised. Pete's animosity towards his mum, his reluctance to have her in their lives. His memory of his mother was of a cold, unloving woman who made him feel responsible for his father abandoning them. She suddenly felt acutely sorry for Pete and wished she could tell him that she understood. The pain of realising that she couldn't hit her like a fresh blow.

'It's not lost on me that Pete has done the exact same thing to you,' Karen said. 'And I can't help blaming myself. If I'd been a better mother...'

'Stop,' Kate interrupted her. 'I understand now why Pete felt the way that he did about you but I don't blame you. Jesus, Karen, I was over ten years older than you when I had Lily and I was in a happy, secure marriage but I still felt completely out of my depth. There were times when I was angry at everyone – angry at Lily for being so demanding, angry at Pete for not understanding how hard it was for me, but mainly angry at myself for not being able to cope with it. You were on your own, without any support. I get it.'

The two women looked at each other, bonded in their shared knowledge of their mistakes.

'You're nothing like I thought you'd be,' Karen said, blowing her nose.

'Oh no?' Kate asked, curious.

'I guess because Pete told me that you didn't want to have anything to do with me, I built up a picture of you in my mind. But you're lovely, Kate, and so are your children. They are such beautiful, happy little girls. You've done a great job, you really have.'

Kate felt the rush of maternal pride at being complimented about her children. Yet taking praise from Pete's mum made her feel awful. The tears that she'd managed to keep down until now spilled over. 'I'm sorry, Karen, I'm so sorry.'

'Don't be sorry, darling, don't be sorry, you've nothing to be sorry about.'

'I just feel so guilty. It's my fault, it's all my fault.'

'What are you talking about?'

This was the moment, the moment when she should have let it all out, all the insecurities that had been running around her mind for the last five weeks. She had been craving the release, the opportunity to finally be rid of it from her conscience. It was her fault Pete wasn't here. She'd been pretending that she was fine but she wasn't. She hadn't been for years. She'd been floating around like one of those dementors in the Harry Potter books – barely alive, sucking the joy out of anyone who came near her, lost in her own misery. Depressed, that's what she was, and she had been for years but she'd been too proud to get any help. She had driven him to this and she had ended any hope they had of a future together. But just as she was about to start talking, her self-preservation kicked in. The dark thoughts were for her only, no one needed to hear them, least of all Pete's own mother.

'Oh don't mind me, I'm just feeling a bit emotional,' Kate said before changing the subject. 'Karen, thanks so much for coming. The girls have loved seeing you.'

'I've loved seeing them. And you have a lovely house, Kate, just lovely. Thanks for inviting me, I've really enjoyed myself.

And if you ever want to talk, I'm here. Now how about we gather up those two lovely girls of yours and play a game?'

After Karen had left and the girls had gone to bed, Kate sat down on the sofa and reflected on the day. They had hugged when she left, with promises to keep in touch and see each other again. It had been such a surreal experience, sharing so much about herself with a woman she had barely met before. How funny that she should bond with Pete's mum now, after all these years, when he wasn't around to see it. Would he be furious with her, she wondered, if he knew what had happened? Or would he be able to forgive his mum after all these years? Karen had acknowledged that she'd made mistakes and she wanted to make amends. She was a different person to the one she'd been all those years ago, abandoned, alone and afraid in her early twenties.

Kate had no idea if there was a place for Karen in their lives, it all felt horribly complicated. But she had enjoyed the afternoon and so had the girls.

To distract herself, she logged on to her website. She'd built it herself a few years ago when she'd decided to start freelancing but she hadn't touched it since, except to renew the domains every year, promising herself that when the time was right, she'd have another attempt at starting up her business. Right now the time couldn't be worse – Rachel had left, her husband was AWOL and she was struggling to keep control, proactive and positive one minute and bereft the next. Yet she had to be realistic about her future and the fact that she couldn't rely on Pete anymore. She needed to start earning an income again. Did she have it in her to go back into PR? She had no idea but she couldn't think of anything else she was qualified to do and she had absolutely loved her job for years. She thought about the things she'd enjoyed about it – the writing, the pitching ideas, the hit of adrenaline when a story she'd worked on appeared in a prominent newspaper. She couldn't go back to the cut-throat nature of a large PR agency but perhaps she could start small, offering her services to local organisations, charging a lower fee to get her confidence back and build her portfolio. Right now, she just needed to get back on the horse.

She scanned the website – it actually looked pretty good. She'd worked hard on it. Logging in, she started tweaking bits of the site, updating information and content. Pouring herself another glass of wine, she became so absorbed in it that she was shocked when she looked at the time and saw that it was gone eleven o'clock. She'd been working on it for over two hours. Closing her laptop, she headed upstairs and climbed into bed, suddenly feeling so exhausted that she didn't even have the energy to brush her teeth. She was asleep within minutes and slept for six hours straight for the first time in weeks.

## 14

## PETE

'Same time next week?' Pete asked Claire as he got dressed and prepared to leave.

'I can't do next week, I'm going away,' Claire replied.

'Going away where?'

'To France, to my dad's house.'

It was the first time she'd mentioned it and his heart started to pound. It had been a few weeks since she'd brought up the idea of moving to France and they hadn't discussed it since. He'd begun to relax again, assuming she'd realised that the idea was absurd and let it go. He still knew there was no way that he would ever move to France but he hated the idea of her going without him.

'You never mentioned it before. Is it just for a holiday? Who are you going with?'

Claire looked at him with sleepy eyes and smiled. She was clearly enjoying the fact that he was getting a little riled. 'I'm going with my friend Michael. He's an architect and he's going to look at the house and the outbuildings and see what the potential is to do them up in exchange for a free holiday and lots of cheese and wine.'

Pete knew from what Claire had told him about her friends that Michael was gay so he wasn't threatened by him but the fact that she was thinking seriously about sprucing up the place surprised him. 'How long will you be gone for?' he asked.

'About a week,' she replied. 'Don't worry, I've already booked the time off at work.'

He didn't give one shit about her bloody annual leave allocation. But he suddenly had a sinking feeling that this new life he had become accustomed to, no matter how precarious and dangerous it was, was about to change again and he didn't like it. 'So you're seriously thinking about this whole move to France, then?'

'Yes, Pete, I told you so a few weeks ago.'

'Well, you mentioned it in passing but you haven't said anything since. I didn't realise it was still on your mind.'

'Well, it is.'

He felt himself getting cross. This was the closest they'd come to an argument since they'd been seeing each other. 'It would have been nice if you'd kept me in the loop.'

Claire unfurled her legs and sat up, looking at him square on. 'Look, Pete, your situation is complicated, I get it. But mine isn't complicated. I'm fed up of London, of temping, of living in a rented flat. I fancy a change. Nothing is set in stone yet but I'm going with Michael to do a recce and I'll take it from there. I don't even know how I'll feel about it all because I haven't been to my dad's house in years. I might go and decide it's a terrible idea but there's only one way to find out.'

Looking at the anguish on his face, Claire softened a bit. 'Pete, I adore you. You know I do. There is nothing I would love more in the world than for you to be going on this journey with me but that's up to you. I know you would have to make a lot of sacrifices but I still think it could work for you, for your family and for us. In fact, I think it could be amazing. But as I said, that's your decision, not mine.'

On the way home, he replayed the conversation over again in his head. He'd assumed that if he wasn't up for the whole idea that she wouldn't be either. Clearly he'd been wrong. But he didn't want her to go: the thought of losing her absolutely terrified him. Once again he realised how far he'd let this go – she'd gone from being the other woman to potentially the love of his life. Because that's honestly how he felt about her now, that she was the only person in the world who truly understood him.

But there was no way he could move to France. He knew that his marriage was in trouble and he had known all along that he would have to do something about that – either fix it or end it – but his whole life was in London, his children, his job, his friends. He couldn't give all that up and she shouldn't expect him to.

Perhaps if he pretended to toe the line a bit she might ease up on the whole idea, he thought. He could act like he was actually considering the idea, pretend to do a bit of research and then tell her that it just wasn't possible but that he adored her and didn't want her to go without him. And she might relent because she knew that he had done his best to try and make it work. Yes, that's what he'd do. Reaching for his phone, he sent her a quick message.

Tell me again how you think the whole France thing could work
for us.

Her reply came as he was waiting to get the bus home from the Tube station.

You'd start by applying for new jobs that offered remote working.

Then once that was secured you could look for a nice two-bed flat to
rent, near the girls, so you had a London base. We'd start work on
the house and could move by autumn xxx

He was still humouring her but he typed out a quick reply.

OK, I'll look into it.

Then he opened up his BBC app and turned to the sports
headlines.

That weekend, he was in a bit of a funk. Claire was going to be
away all of next week and he was already annoyed at the
prospect of not seeing her. He was standing in the playground
with Kate while the girls hurtled down the slide, sipping a coffee
and stewing in his own bad mood when she said: 'I've been
thinking about the summer holidays. We haven't booked
anything yet. How about France?'

He almost spat out his coffee. Taking a minute to compose
himself, he said: 'I don't fancy France, actually.'

'Why not?'

'Can't guarantee the weather. Why not somewhere like
Greece or Italy?'

'Okay, I suppose,' she said. 'Shall I go ahead and look into it?'

'Sure.' It felt weird talking about booking a holiday with her.
But trying to dissuade her from doing so would certainly arouse
suspicion. Better to act normally, he thought. He had an image
of them sitting by a poolside, sipping gin and tonics and
watching the sun go down. Perhaps this could be a make-or-
break holiday? The more he thought about it, the more he liked
the idea. Maybe what they needed was some time away together,

away from the everyday stress and strain of life and they'd either come back stronger than ever or he'd know for sure that their marriage was over. Either way, it put off the decision for a couple of months.

'Tell you what, why don't we have a look together tonight?' he said.

Her eyes lit up. He normally left that kind of thing to her, telling her to just put the dates in their shared diary.

'I'd like that,' she said, smiling at him.

He felt a pang of guilt that she was so pleased by the prospect of them doing something together, even though it only involved staring at a computer screen. For the first time he considered the thought that it wasn't just her who had stopped making an effort. 'And do you know what?' he said. 'Let's really push the boat out, book something amazing. I think we all need a good holiday.'

That night she cooked his favourite dinner, steak and chips, and they sat down together, scrolling through the endless holiday options before deciding on a five-star hotel in mainland Greece. Paying the deposit and booking the flights, she turned to him and grinned excitedly. 'I can already feel the sunshine on my skin,' she said. He grinned back. 'I'm already there drinking a gin and tonic in the pool bar.'

'I'll order us a guidebook to Greece,' she said, 'so we can go on a few day trips. Teach the girls a bit of history that doesn't involve a water park.'

'Not too much history,' he groaned.

She laughed – it was just like the old days when they used to go away together in their twenties. She was always looking for a museum or art gallery to visit while he just wanted to sit in a piazza somewhere soaking in the atmosphere and drinking a cold beer. 'You don't need to stare at a piece of art to understand the culture of a place,' he would tell her. 'You just need to sit in the right place, with a local tipple in hand, and watch the world go by.'

That night when they went to bed, he'd thought she was asleep so when she spoke, it startled him. 'I know things have been a bit tough lately, Pete. But maybe this holiday is just what we need.'

She reached for his hand and he squeezed hers back. 'Maybe it is,' he replied.

The conversation seemed to break a barrier between them in the days that followed. They were a little bit kinder to each other, more considerate. With Claire being away and no client engagements that week he had no reason to stay out late and so he was home in time for the girls' bedtime every night. For the first time in a long time they did the routine together, smiling as Lily and Maggie giggled and splashed each other in the bath. He felt a little better about himself then.

If he was being honest a part of him was still annoyed with Claire for pursuing this whole France idea, and for going off on holiday without giving him much notice too, and perhaps his revenge was to be a bit more attentive to his wife. Either way, it felt nice. He didn't message Claire once during the week and she didn't message him either. Whether it was an unspoken agreement between them or one was just waiting for the other to initiate contact he didn't know. He tried not to think about it. The girls seemed to sense the harmony in the house and were absolute delights all week. And Kate didn't even have a go when he forgot to buy milk on the way home, despite not being able to have her evening cup of tea. By the following weekend, he was almost feeling good about family life.

'Why don't I take the girls to the park this morning?' he told Kate when they woke up on Saturday. 'You could have a nice long bath or go and get your nails done, and then we can meet at the usual café for brunch together.'

'That would be lovely,' she said. 'Thanks, Pete.'

In the playground he watched as the two girls ran around together, racing over the equipment and flying down the slides on their bellies. He looked around at all the other dads who were on Saturday morning parent duty while their wives did chores, worked or met with friends. He was one of them too, he realised, and it really wasn't that bad. So, he didn't have sex with his wife anymore, but all couples struggled with that after kids. They just needed to start making an effort again and this week had proven that they could still get along and enjoy each other's company with a bit of effort. It had to stop now, he decided, he'd had his fun and now it was time to concentrate on his marriage. He had too much to lose.

As he was pushing Lily and Maggie on the swings, his phone beeped. He pulled it out of his pocket and read the WhatsApp message.

Bonjour stranger. I'm back from France and I can't wait to see you. Wednesday? Xx

He quickly pocketed the phone and concentrated on pushing the girls. But already he was imagining being in Claire's flat and the need to see her was instant. Feeling all his resolve from just minutes ago dissolving he tried to ignore the urge to reply.

'Come on, girls,' he said. 'Time to go and meet Mummy for brunch.'

That evening, as he was reading a bedtime story to Maggie, he heard his phone beep again in his pocket. Kissing his daughter goodnight, he stepped out of the room and scanned the message.

You okay? Xx

Once again he put the phone back in his pocket and went downstairs to help Kate make dinner. He could feel it burning a hole in his jeans and he desperately tried to forget about it. 'Shall we watch a film on Netflix tonight?' he asked Kate.

'Sounds good,' she replied.

'And maybe an early night?' he ventured, raising his eyebrows at her suggestively.

'Not tonight, Pete,' she said without hesitation. Then looking at him she added: 'Wrong time of the month.'

'Fair enough,' he replied. 'Netflix it is.'

By Monday he still hadn't replied to Claire. She had sent him one more message on Sunday.

Pete, I'm worried now, is everything okay?

He knew he couldn't ignore her forever, he would have to face up to it sooner or later and it should probably be sooner in case she did something stupid like try to call him when Kate was around. On his way into work he typed out a quick message to her.

Sorry, Claire, busy weekend. Are you free this evening? We need to talk.

Her reply came quickly.

Sounds ominous. Okay, see you later.

The day dragged on and on and he struggled to concentrate on anything else. By the time he was ready to leave for Claire's flat he was feeling nervous but resigned. He knew what he had to do. Taking a deep breath, he knocked on the door of her flat. She answered in a silk dressing gown, despite only having been home for twenty minutes herself. 'Hi, Pete, I was just about to take a bath, fancy joining me?'

She wasn't going to make this easy for him. 'No thanks, Claire, can we go and sit down?'

'Sure,' she replied. She curled up on the sofa, wrapping her long legs underneath her and looked at him expectantly.

'How was France?' he asked, putting off the inevitable for a few more minutes.

'Oh it was glorious,' she said, her face lighting up. 'I was nervous about going to my dad's house but with Michael with me it gave me the strength I needed to rip off the plaster and open that front door. And when I was in there I felt... I don't know... sad of course but also excited. Michael was excited too, he said the place had so much potential. And of course we spent lots of time drinking wine, eating far too much bread and cheese and coming up with ideas for the house. It was lovely.'

'Great,' he said, feeling anything but great.

'How about you? Good week?' she asked.

'Yes, fine thanks. Look, Claire, I've been thinking. What I'm doing... it's wrong and it's unfair to my family. Clearly Kate and I have our issues – this whole thing wouldn't have started if we didn't – but I've had time to think while you've been away and we need to stop this. I adore you, you know I do, you're an amazing woman and if I'd met you in another lifetime, things would be different. I'm sorry.'

'Okay.' She shrugged.

He wasn't sure what he'd been expecting but it wasn't this. 'Are you okay?' he asked.

'Sure, Pete, I'm fine,' she said and smiled at him. Why wasn't she more pissed off? Shouldn't she be crying or raging at him? She seemed so cool with it.

'So, I'll see you at work?' he asked.

'Yep, see you at work. I'm off for my bath, you can let yourself out.'

And with that she stood up, gave him a kiss on the cheek and walked into the bathroom, closing the door softly behind her and leaving him alone on the sofa wondering what the hell had just happened.

## 15

## KATE

Pete. Lily's finally walking around normally again. Or should I say strutting! She asked me to send you a video, which I've attached. I sat the girls down for a chat at the weekend. I told them you'd gone away and that I didn't know when you'd be coming home. They had a lot of questions which I tried to answer as best I could. I told them that you loved them very, very much but that you'd been feeling sad for a long time and you had gone somewhere that made you feel happy. They wanted to come of course but I told them that it was very far away and that we couldn't go. I have no idea if it was the right thing to say but I didn't have many options. I think they might think that you've gone to the place where the My Little Ponies live.

They were both upset and asked if it

was their fault. I assured them that it was absolutely, in no way, their fault. I think they believed me but they don't really understand it. It was absolutely horrible but I had to do something. You've been gone for three months, even children know that business trips don't go on for that long.

It's Christmas in a couple of weeks. We went to get the tree yesterday and decorated it. The girls are super excited about the school fair and guess what — I'm manning a stall! Yes, you heard me correctly, I'm like a proper 'school mum' now. Since I've been doing the school runs every day I've got chatting to a few new parents and they're lovely. I've started organising playdates and going for coffee with them after drop-off on Fridays and when they asked me if I wanted to join the Christmas fair committee I thought, why not? I've even been doing some PR for them!

I've started seeing a therapist too. It still feels strange and uncomfortable talking to a total stranger but it's helping. Like letting Rachel go, it's one of the things I should have done years ago. Perhaps if I had done, you'd still be here with us now.

I'm still hurt and I think I always will be. But I admit that I'm as much to blame as you are and I'm sorry, I really am. I've been a terrible wife to you over the last few years. I refused to give you the love and attention you deserved and I drove you away. If it helps, I refused to give myself the love and attention I deserved too. We're both paying the price.

I'm not going to ask you if you're coming back anymore. In fact, this is the last email I'm going to send you. You know where we are. Our marriage is over, that much is clear to me now, but there is still a place for you in the children's lives. Don't leave it too long, Pete.

Kate applied another layer of mascara and stood back to look at her reflection in the mirror. She didn't look too bad, actually. The daily school runs and running around after the girls had given her a bit of an outdoorsy glow, plus she was a few pounds lighter than she'd been in years. *That's what post-traumatic stress disorder in the wake of your life being turned upside down does to you*, she thought wryly, *it's the ideal diet plan*. She felt the familiar clutch of fear in her stomach before pushing it away and focusing on her reflection again.

Erin was on her way over to babysit and she was going out for the first time in months. A few of the mums from Maggie's class had asked her along to their end-of-term dinner. It was the first time she'd been invited out with them and she was feeling nervous. She'd been doing the daily school runs ever since Rachel left and now she wondered why she'd avoided it for so long. When Lily started school she'd gone to the new reception parents drinks and stood around nervously making small talk with the other mums and dads but it hadn't been a particularly sociable class. Nadia, whose daughter was in the other reception class, had of course instantly made friends with the other mums and formed a little gang. She'd always invited Kate along to things and she sometimes went but she never felt truly part of it. When Maggie had started the previous year, she hadn't even bothered going to the welcome drinks.

She had been afraid of all the other school mums. They all seemed so together and she felt like an absolute joke in comparison. On the rare occasions that she'd talked to them in the past she always came away feeling that she had put her foot in it in some way, saying something stupid or stuck-up when she didn't mean to. She would analyse the conversation for the rest of the day, berating herself for opening her mouth at all. In the end it was easier just to let Rachel do the majority of the school runs and after-school playdates and make a quick getaway on the days that she did do them. But with Rachel gone, she'd had no choice but to get over her fears.

On only her third morning on school run duty she'd caught the eye of a couple of mums who had children in Maggie's class and they'd smiled warmly at her before making their way over.

'Hi, Kate isn't it?' one of the women, who introduced herself as Lottie, asked. 'My daughter Ava is in Maggie's class and she never stops talking about her. We'd love to have you over for a playdate some time.'

'That would be great.' Kate had smiled back. Then, on impulse, she added: 'How about next week? Would you like to come to ours?'

'Lovely,' Lottie replied. 'Fridays are good for me, I work Monday to Thursday.'

'Friday's great.'

The following week, while Maggie had been overjoyed at the prospect of having Ava over to play, Kate was full of nerves.

She'd had playdates before of course, with Nadia and the others in the antenatal gang, but this felt different. This was a new friend and she was as nervous as if it was her first day at school. As she scooped crisps into bowls and made carrot batons, she realised how annoyed she was with herself for being so worried about this. She used to pride herself on being able to negotiate with difficult, high-profile journalists to secure articles in major publications for clients without breaking a sweat. Yet here she was getting clammy about a sodding playdate. Taking a deep breath she slowly put the carrot peeler down, wiped her hands, and got ready to go and meet Lottie and Ava at the school gates.

The girls bundled out of school together, high as kites at the prospect of the afternoon ahead. Lottie smiled at Kate and they made their way back to the house together, Lily, Maggie and Ava skipping ahead while the mums hung back. Once they were home, Kate offered Lottie a drink: 'Tea, coffee, squash?'

'I'd love a glass of wine,' Lottie replied. Kate grinned, her nerves starting to disappear. 'On it!' she replied, reaching for the white wine in the fridge.

Over a drink, Lottie told Kate about herself. She was originally from Oxford but had lived in London for years. She worked part-time for a charity. As the wine flowed the conversation became easier and more open.

'We wanted a second child after Ava,' Lottie told her. 'But it just didn't happen for us. It was hard to come to terms with but in the end we had to move on. It was consuming our lives, ruining our relationship and preventing us from enjoying parenthood with the one beautiful, amazing child we did have.'

Kate nodded sympathetically. 'It's amazing that you were able to move past it. I know of other couples who haven't been able to. It eats them up.'

'What about you?' Lottie asked. 'Do you work?'

It was the first time she'd been asked the question in that

way. She normally got: 'What do you do?' and had the embarrassment of having to reply, 'nothing'.

'Not at the moment,' she began, before adding, 'not at all if I'm being honest. I used to work in PR many moons ago but haven't been back to it since I had kids.'

'Would you like to? Or are you happy being at home?' The question came without any judgement, just curiosity. It made Kate feel a bit braver.

'To be honest, I'm not sure I have a choice anymore. Obviously you know about me and Pete?'

Lottie looked bewildered. 'Is Pete your husband?'

*Christ, she doesn't know.* Kate had assumed the whole school was gossiping about her but it was clear that Lottie had no idea what she was talking about. 'Yes he, erm, he left me three months ago.'

Lottie put her hand to her mouth. 'Oh gosh, I'm so sorry, Kate, that's awful. How are you coping?'

'Not great at first,' Kate admitted. 'Still not brilliant, obviously, but getting better. That's the one thing about kids isn't it, you can't just sit around feeling sorry for yourself – you've got to plough on.'

'Is he still seeing Lily and Maggie regularly?'

'Well, that's the thing.' Kate realised that she was feeling a bit light-headed from the wine and the pleasure of an understanding ear, and in danger of oversharing. 'I haven't heard from him since he left.'

Lottie gasped. 'That's terrible. Do you know where he is?'

'Nope.'

'Did he give you an explanation at all before he left?'

'Just a note saying he'd met someone else. He left his phone behind, quit his job, deleted his social media accounts and I have no way of contacting him.'

'What a bastard!' Lottie was aghast. 'Kate, I am so sorry that this has happened to you. I wish I'd known, I would have been in touch sooner, but I had absolutely no idea.' She reached for Kate's hand and squeezed it.

'I thought the whole school was gossiping about it,' Kate admitted.

Lottie shrugged. 'Not that I know of. I mean I only really know the parents in Maggie's class but none of them have mentioned it. How are you coping?'

'We're getting used to life without him, slowly. It's forcing me to confront some issues that I've been burying for a long time. Our marriage clearly wasn't a happy one but I refused to admit it, and I've been feeling pretty low for a few years now and it can't go on any longer. It's already cost me my marriage and I can't let it affect the girls too. I'm seeing a therapist which is helping and I'm hoping to start doing some freelance work too so I can earn my own income. Obviously I let Rachel go.'

'Rachel?' Lottie looked at her quizzically.

'Our nanny?'

'Oh, yes, I think I've seen her.'

Kate couldn't believe it. All this time she had thought that the other parents judged her, her glaring absence from school, but now she was starting to realise that most of them hadn't even given it a thought. They were all just busy getting on with their own lives.

'Anyway, I'm slowly starting to stand on my own two feet. And you know what? It feels good. Scary, but good.'

'Good for you,' Lottie said, smiling. 'Good for you.'

After Lottie and Ava left, Kate felt the familiar fears and doubts surfacing, as they did most days. Did she say too much? Did she sound like an idiot? She should never have had that glass of wine. But then she started doing the breathing exercises that her therapist had recommended and slowly calmed herself back down. She'd had a great time and so had the girls. As she left, Lottie had invited them to her house the following Friday so it can't have gone that badly. When Kate had replied that they'd love to, she realised that she actually meant it.

After the girls had gone to bed, she had sat down with her laptop to check her emails. She hadn't looked at them all day and as she scrolled through the endless junk, she spotted one from Jenny, an old client she used to work with. The previous week she'd started sending out emails again to some of her old contacts, letting them know that she was looking for work. She had spruced up her website and LinkedIn and spent hours reading up on the latest industry news. She'd also joined a couple of groups for freelance PR professionals. She quickly opened the email.

Kate, hi!

How ARE you? It's so lovely to hear from you. And your message couldn't come at a better time. We're launching a new campaign in the spring and we really need some PR support. From what I remember about your work, it's right up your street. We're closing down for Christmas soon but are you free to meet for coffee in the New Year? Maybe first week of Jan? We need to get the ball rolling.

Looking forward to working with you again! Jen x

Kate felt a shiver of excitement. Her first possible piece of work! She quickly typed a reply to Jenny to suggest some dates and then sat back to consider the prospect of working again. It would be a shock to the system, no doubt, but a good way to ease herself back in – working with a client who she knew well already. And once she had a recent campaign under her belt, she could add it to her portfolio and make herself more appealing to other potential clients. It felt like the first step on the ladder. She wasn't as scared as she thought she'd be, perhaps it was because the meeting wasn't for a few weeks yet – or could it just possibly be because she was feeling stronger? Pete's betrayal had changed a lot of things and one of them was making her stand on her own two feet again. She'd relied on him for too long.

The knock on the door brought Kate back to the present. Erin had arrived. When she opened the door, her sister looked her up and down and whistled.

'Looking good there, sis. Hot!'

'Oh don't, it's only a drink with the school mums, Erin!'

'Just the mums? No sexy single dads?'

'Ha ha, very funny. Strictly mums only.'

'Well I've heard how crazy nights out with the school mums can get. You never know!'

Kate picked up her bag and coat and gave her sister a kiss. 'I'll be back by eleven.'

At the restaurant she was relieved when she got a seat next to Lottie. There were eight of them out for dinner in total and she didn't know the others that well. But after a few drinks the conversation was flowing and everyone was having fun.

'What do you do?' asked one of the other mums, who introduced herself as Lisa.

It was a question Kate knew all too well. But this time, she said proudly, 'Actually I've just started my own PR consultancy. I worked in the industry for years but stopped when I had the children. I've decided to ease myself back in.'

'What kind of PR?' Lisa asked.

Kate filled her in on her background.

Lisa said, 'I work for a local college and we're desperate to get some positive stories about ourselves out there. Would you be interested? Our budget won't be anything like what you're used to but if you fancy having a chat, let me know.'

'I'd love to!' Kate replied, her eyes lighting up, before adding, 'I really need to build up my portfolio so I'd be happy to offer a discounted rate in exchange for some recent work and a testimonial.'

'Let's swap details,' Lisa said, pulling out her phone. 'Maybe we can meet for coffee in the New Year?'

On the way home, Kate tottered along the pavement in her heels feeling slightly tipsy and more than slightly happy. She'd had a great night and for once she didn't feel like she'd said anything stupid, plus she'd potentially got some more work lined up for next year. At once the thought of Pete entered her head, as it always did when she felt even the tiniest glimmer of hope. It would keep happening, she knew, for a long time, probably even forever. But what had happened had happened and now she had two choices – to live in the past or to live in the present. And at that particular moment she chose the present.

Letting herself back into the house she walked into the living room where Erin was watching a film. 'Good night?' her sister asked, looking up.

'Fabulous,' Kate said, sinking down on to the sofa and peeling off her shoes.

'Good for you, you deserve it. The girls went to bed with no bother. I haven't heard a peep out of them since.'

'Thanks for babysitting, Erin.'

'Any time, love.'

After Erin left, Kate got a glass of water from the kitchen and made her way upstairs. Peering into the girls' rooms she saw they were both fast asleep. She felt a rush of love for them. Her beautiful, brave little girls. Would she be enough for them? She'd have to be, she had no choice. As she went to her own bedroom all her earlier happiness dissolved and she let the dark thoughts consume her again. Those poor girls, missing their father. Would it be like this forever, she wondered? Fleeting moments of happiness replaced by loss and sadness again? All of a sudden, she felt exhausted. Without even taking her clothes off she climbed into bed, turned off the light and waited for sleep to come.

## 16

## PETE

The urge to see Claire came on without any warning. There was no trigger, no fight with Kate, just a sudden, overwhelming desire for something exciting to break up the dull monotony of his existence again. It had been three weeks since he'd called things off with her and he'd been proud of himself for finally putting an end to the whole thing. Now he could focus on getting his marriage back on track and being a good father.

Except nothing had really changed. He and Kate were still being nicer to each other and he didn't feel like he was constantly treading on eggshells but ultimately his life was still the same. Boring, boring, boring. Work was boring, his marriage was boring. And so, he started having cravings for a release again. And Claire, beautiful, uncomplicated, sexy, clever, uninhibited Claire, was his release. He was getting a sandwich from the Pret near work at lunchtime when the desire to contact her appeared, out of the blue, and hijacked his mind until he simply couldn't focus on anything else. Finding a bench, he sat down and typed out a quick message before he could overthink it.

Hey you, can we meet? Tonight?

He saw that she'd read the message. Would she torture him by not responding for hours? No, she couldn't be bothered with game playing, it was one of the things he loved about her. Her reply came seconds later.

This is a surprise. Is it for another fun 'chat' or something else?

He grinned.

Definitely something else.

Well then, come on over.

He stood up, feeling giddy. She'd let him off lightly and it was probably more than he deserved but he didn't care. He was going to see her tonight and he couldn't be more excited. He quickly typed out a message to Kate.

Hey, got to work late tonight, don't wait up, kiss the girls from me, see you tomorrow x

Back at the office he tried to concentrate on work but he kept looking at the clock, willing the minutes to tick by as quickly as possible. Every second was agony. Finally, at 5pm, he switched off his computer, grabbed his jacket and practically sprinted out of the office. He arrived at her flat just minutes after her and she opened the door and let him in with an expression that he couldn't quite read. He didn't care, he was there and she had let him in. That was what mattered.

'Glass of wine?' she offered.

'Please.'

146

She walked into the little kitchen and emerged a couple of minutes later with two full glasses. 'Cheers,' she said, clinking glasses with him before sitting down and observing him coolly. 'So, Pete, it was quite a surprise to hear from you.'

He nodded. The last few weeks had been difficult at work. He was used to stopping by her desk for a chat most mornings but instead he'd been giving her a smile, not wanting to seem rude, and heading straight up to his office. If she'd been hurt, she certainly hadn't shown it, but he knew he had some serious making up to do.

'I know and I'm sorry, Claire,' he began. 'The last thing I want to do is to mess you around, you don't deserve it. It's just been hard for me. I'm married, I have children, it's complicated, you know?'

She nodded at him to continue.

'I've been pushing the feelings of guilt to the back of my mind for so long that I thought I'd nailed it. But when you were in France it all came flooding back – how I was hurting my family, what I could be throwing away.'

She raised an eyebrow at him, but he felt that honesty was the best policy right now.

'I love my children, Claire, and I love my wife – not in the way I should anymore, probably more out of habit, but I do love her. And what I'm doing to her isn't right.'

'So why are you here, Pete?' Claire was looking a bit pissed off now.

'Because I love you.' It was the first time that he'd said those words to her and as they came out, he realised how true they were. Even Claire looked taken aback.

'Christ, Pete, I thought you were just coming over for a quickie. I didn't think you were going to drop the L-bomb on me.'

They both laughed. 'Sorry, Claire, I didn't mean to go all heavy on you.'

'No, it's fine, I appreciate your honesty. I think you know how I feel about you, Pete, but the question is, what happens now?'

'I don't know. I need a little bit more time. Not much but maybe a few weeks to sort my head out. I know it's a lot to ask, too much really, but can you give me that?'

She looked at him for a long time before standing up and going to sit next to him. 'Yes, Pete, I can give you some time. But not too much time, okay?'

He nodded. 'I promise.'

After they'd had pretty amazing make-up sex, they lay intertwined in Claire's bed. How could he feel so wrong and so right at the same time? He watched her, as she lay there, and thought, *I have literally never felt this way about anyone before.*

'I'm going back to France in a couple of weeks,' Claire said. His heart sank.

'Okay.'

'Just for a long weekend with some friends. Ever since I went there a few weeks ago I've been desperate to go back.'

'Are you still thinking about moving there?' He really didn't want to know the answer but he had to ask.

'Yes and no,' she admitted, turning on to her side to look at him. 'I'd love to but, well, there's someone here who I'm rather fond of. And I've stupidly agreed to give him some time.'

In that moment, he would have done anything to please her. So he found himself saying: 'I'm open to the France idea. I'm not saying that I'm going to do it, just that I am happy for us to look into it. A little bit. But it has to work with me seeing the kids.'

Claire shrieked with excitement, leapt up and straddled him, showering him with kisses. 'Thank you, Pete, oh thank you, you won't regret this.'

Saying things in the heat of the moment when the woman that you're mad crazy about is naked next to you is one thing, but in the cold light of day a week later it was quite another. So, when Claire presented him with printouts less than five minutes after he arrived at her flat the next time they met up, he was caught totally off guard.

'What are these?' he asked her, glancing down at the pages.

'Jobs. For you.'

'What kind of jobs?'

'Senior manager jobs that can be done remotely. There's more out there than you'd think. More and more companies are becoming flexible in their hiring.'

He scanned the listings. Some of them weren't suitable but there were one or two that looked pretty interesting. He hadn't looked for a new job for years and this was actually quite fun. He began to feel himself getting excited. He still thought the whole France idea was a bust but even so, a new job could be just the thing. The beginning of a whole new start and a new chapter in his life, whatever happened.

'Thanks, Claire – really, thank you. These look great,' he said, giving her a kiss. She beamed.

'Promise me you'll give them a good look over and apply to any that sound good?'

'Absolutely.' And he meant it. That evening on the way home he read the job descriptions in detail and got increasingly excited as he realised that not only did one or two of the companies sound really interesting, but that he fit most of the criteria. They were well-paid jobs too, more than he was earning now. By the time he got home he'd decided to apply for two of them. But just before he got in, he folded up the papers and stuffed them into his pocket. *Best not discuss this with Kate*, he thought, *it could lead to too many questions.*

'How was your evening?' Kate asked as he slumped down on the sofa and took his shoes off.

'Oh, you know, same old. Entertaining clients, convincing them to give us their business. How are things here?'

'Oh, you know, same old,' she replied. 'I had a couple of landscape gardeners round to give us a quote for the garden. We really need to sort it out.'

'Sure, sure,' Pete replied, feeling distracted, his mind on the job listings he'd seen. He was wondering how much work his CV needed when he noticed that Kate was watching him.

'Are you okay, Pete?' she asked. 'You look like you've got something on your mind.'

'Oh, just work, don't mind me. Actually, I think I'll go to bed. Early start tomorrow.' With that he stood up and headed to the kitchen to get a glass of water. On the way upstairs he glanced back into the living room and saw that Kate was still watching TV, some trashy soap that he hated. 'Night, Kate,' he said. She glanced up at him and gave him a small smile. 'Night, Pete.'

The next day, in the office, he opened his CV. He hadn't looked at it in years and it needed a lot of work. Instead of preparing for a client meeting, which is what he should have been doing, he spent an hour and a half polishing his CV and making himself sound suitably impressive. Finally, when he was done, he rushed into the meeting, totally unprepared and not even caring.

That evening, Kate was out at the cinema with Erin and after he'd put the girls to bed, he started writing covering letters. By the time she came home, weepy from the tear-jerker she'd been to see, he'd applied to both roles. He quickly closed the laptop.

'What are you up to?' she asked.

'Just a bit of work, can't switch off, you know me,' he said.

She nodded and walked into the kitchen. 'Cuppa?' she called. 'Please,' he replied. She made the teas and came back in. 'I'm going to take mine up to bed,' she told him as she padded up the stairs.

'I'll be up in a few minutes.' Opening his laptop he checked his emails and saw a couple of automatic replies that his application had been received. Feeling excited, he closed it and went to bed.

A couple of weeks went by and he didn't hear anything. He'd almost forgotten about it all until one morning, as he was sipping his coffee and checking his emails, one arrived in his inbox inviting him to an interview. After scanning the message he quickly pulled out his phone and messaged Claire.

Need to speak to you!

She immediately replied.

Pret in five minutes?

By the time he got there, she'd ordered two coffees to go. It was risky, meeting up in public like this but he had to talk to her and didn't want to send the news in a message. He told her about the interview and her eyes lit up with pleasure.

'That's amazing, well done, Pete! Want to do some interview prep one night this week?'

He doubted much interview prep would get done but he grinned at her. 'Sure, how about Thursday?'

'Perfect,' she replied. They quickly parted ways and he traipsed back to his office. Now that he'd actually got an interview he started to panic. He'd kind of done it all on a bit of a whim but now shit was getting real. Did he actually want to leave his job? Did Claire think this meant he was going to

France? *Slow down*, he told himself, *one step at a time, it's only an interview, no need to freak out. No one needs to know.*

By the time he got home that evening he had convinced himself that it was nothing to stress about. He was just having a chat with another company, to see what his options were, but it didn't have to mean anything.

∼

Dear Mr Garland,

As per our conversation on the phone, we are delighted to offer you the position of Chief Operations Officer at Cyberd, subject to satisfactory references. The role will be full-time, 35 hours a week, based remotely with an expectation that you will be available to attend meetings at our London hub two days a month. Your start date will be September 28.

We will email the contract over to you by the end of this week. Please can you sign and return it at your earliest opportunity.

If you have any questions, please don't hesitate to contact me. We very much look forward to having you on our team.

Best wishes,
Gillian Jones
Head of People Development, Cyberd.

Pete read and re-read the email before grabbing his e-cigarette which he kept stashed in his drawer for emergencies and heading for the door. Outside, he inhaled deeply and tried to calm the butterflies that were fluttering around his stomach.

He didn't know why but he hadn't been expecting the call. Maybe because it was the first interview he'd had in years or maybe it was because he was still in denial about the whole thing. It had all seemed fun and exciting a few weeks ago but now it was very, very real and it was terrifying. The first interview had gone fairly well and he'd been invited back for a day of further interviews and aptitude tests the following week. Then this morning, they'd called to offer him the job. He'd liked the people and the salary they'd offered was higher than what he earned now but he knew deep down that this was about more than just a new job. It was about starting a new life.

The first person he should have called when he got offered a new job was his wife but she didn't even know that he'd applied for the role. He wanted to tell Claire but he knew she'd think it was a sign that he was up for moving to France and he needed some time to himself to think on that. It would soon be crunch time.

Did he want to leave his wife? Did he want to be with Claire – actually, properly with her? Yes, he thought, he did. He loved her and she loved him. And if loving her meant moving to France, maybe he should just do it. Perhaps a totally fresh start, in a place where no one knew them and their history would be better, as long as he could still see the girls regularly. With the money he was earning and the fact that they'd be living mortgage-free in France he could afford to rent a small place in London and support Kate and the girls.

Bloody hell, he'd have to tell Kate, that would be horrendous. And the girls, would they forgive him? Would Kate turn them against him? No, he didn't think she'd be that cruel.

She'd be incandescent with rage but she wasn't a bad person, not at all. They'd just fallen out of love and she'd come to understand that eventually, when she'd had time to calm down. Perhaps they could even be friends? Or at least civil for the girls. Yes, it could work.

He messaged Claire:

Need to speak to you, can I come over tonight?

Then he headed back into the building, nodding briefly at Claire who was on the phone and went back up to his office to await her reply, which came quickly as it always did.

Yes.

He just about made it through the day and was out of the door at bang on 5pm. He was leaving early more and more now. It was a good thing he was thinking about quitting his job otherwise his boss might have something to say about his new work ethic. As soon as he arrived at Claire's flat, he told her about the job. After congratulating him, she went straight to the point, as she always did.

'So does this mean that you're definitely up for the whole France thing?'

'In theory, yes, but I want to go there first, to check out the house and see how I feel. Is that okay?'

'Yes, of course! I'd love to show you the place. Can you get the time away?'

'I think so, there's a media conference I usually go to every year in York in a few weeks' time but after I've handed in my notice, I doubt they'll want me to go. So we could go then – Kate is expecting me to be away anyway.'

'So are you definitely going to hand in your notice?'

'Yes, I think so, it's a great role and whatever happens with France I think it's time for a change.'

She looked at him. 'A job change or a total change?'

'A total change. But baby steps, please, Claire. I'm pretty freaked out about all this.'

'I understand. Let's just book the trip and take it from there. No pressure.'

He smiled at her before reaching over to kiss her. 'Thank you for understanding. You're amazing, you really are.'

'Yes, I am, and don't you forget it, Pete Garland. Don't you ever forget it.'

By the time he got home that evening it was still warm outside. Kate was upstairs already and he grabbed a cold drink from the fridge and went outside to sit on the patio for a few minutes before going to bed.

The garden was still a total tip. When they had moved in there had been two small, deep ponds which were most definitely not child friendly. They had drained and covered them with tarpaulin so that the kids didn't fall in but they needed filling properly and the rest of the garden was in desperate need of some TLC. There were piles of junk left at the end by the old owners and the old patio was cracked and filthy. It was in stark contrast to the rest of their immaculately designed house and was the final part of the property to be refurbished – the last vestiges of the old, unloved house they had bought all those years ago.

*Were we happy back then?* he wondered, thinking back to the day when they had moved into the house. Kate had been ridiculously stressed in the run-up to the move but he had a vivid memory of her beaming smile when they walked into their new home for the first time – a brief moment of calm together before the storm of removal men and children.

'This is it, Pete, a proper family home!' she had said,

swinging her arms around in a circle. Caught up in her excitement he'd copied her and for a few minutes they had spun round and round, laughing. He remembered thinking, *I've missed that smile* and having a flash of hope that this move was just what they needed after all. *A new start*, he had thought, *a new future.* But in the end it hadn't materialised, it had ended up being the same old.

*Would this time be different?* he wondered. *Is this the new start I've been hoping for after all these years?*

## 17

### KATE

Kate tapped the table, playing imaginary scales with her fingers as she nervously read the press release for the thirteenth time before attaching it to the email and hitting send. Then she sat back and exhaled. It was the first piece of official work she'd done in years and she was terrified at sending it to her new client for approval only for them to tell her that it was a pile of crap. But she was also feeling proud of herself. She'd really enjoyed the work so far and after initially staring at the screen for fifteen minutes paralysed by the inability to write, she'd finally started typing. After that it had all come naturally and she could feel her old confidence creeping back in. *It's just like riding a bike after all*, she thought.

Her New Year's resolution had been to let go of the past and look to the future – to forget about surviving and start actually living. Christmas had been hard. She'd spent so many Christmases with Pete and his absence had been even more poignant. *If I could just talk to him*, she thought, *then everything might be okay*. But it was impossible and the reality of that was a constant pain that she didn't think would ever go away. She wasn't even angry with him anymore. The warning signs had been there but she had ignored them. If it was just her to think about, she probably would have gone to bed and hidden under the duvet for the entire Christmas period but her girls, her beautiful little girls, were so excited about the festivities and she had to make it special for them. So, she had done the exact opposite – she had gone into Christmas overload and made a huge effort. And through their excitement she had felt a trickle of it herself because their joy was infectious.

She wanted to spend Christmas Day just the three of them but she'd invited Karen over on Christmas Eve. They'd hugged each other warmly when she arrived and had spent a lovely afternoon opening presents and listening to Christmas songs. She still didn't know whether inviting Karen into their lives was a sensible idea and she knew it was probably unhealthy to cling on to a part of Pete – but it was done now and she really liked the woman. She was honest, open and non-judgemental in a way that only someone who has made their own mistakes in life can be. Kate loved her parents but they were very reserved people and the warmth and love that radiated from Karen was like a tonic. It was a stark contrast to the woman that Pete had known as a child. Kate wished that he were here to see it.

After Karen had left, Erin had come over with a bottle of bubbles and they'd staged an impromptu Christmas party in the living room, dancing around like loons until Lily and Maggie were so exhausted that they'd had to carry them up to their beds. The two girls were asleep before their heads had even hit the pillows.

Back downstairs, the sisters clinked glasses.

'How are you doing? I mean REALLY doing?' Erin asked.

'I don't know, Erin. One minute I'm absolutely fine, good even, and then the next it hits me like a ton of bricks again. I guess it'll be like that for some time. I've spent weeks, months, analysing our marriage and I accept that we fell out of love with each other ages ago. I've made peace with that. But the way it ended was just so cruel. It didn't need to be that way, it could have been different and that's what torments me.'

'I get it,' Erin nodded. 'He could have handled it so much better. There is absolutely no excuse whatsoever for what he did. I still can't believe it myself – all these months and he hasn't got in touch. It beggars belief, it really does. I'll never understand it.'

'We both could have handled it better,' Kate replied.

'What do you mean?'

'I was a terrible wife, Erin. No, don't try to defend me, I was. Somewhere along the way I just lost myself. I had postnatal depression but I refused to admit it and the longer it went on, the less I wanted to deal with it. But I should have got help rather than glide along through life under a cloud of grey. It's only now I realise that and I'm furious with myself for throwing away so many years of my life – and Pete's. He did try to help me but I wouldn't let him.'

Erin said, 'Look, I've always been fond of Pete but I don't think he was there for you when you needed him, I really don't. He just wanted you to be fine, like everyone else, he didn't want to accept that you weren't. He should have tried harder to help you. We all should have done. I feel absolutely horrendous that I didn't do more, too.'

Kate was shocked to see that her sister was crying. 'Erin, this is not your fault!'

'This is all of our faults. Everyone who ever loved you. We should have been there for you more and I'm sorry, I'm so sorry.'

'Oh, Erin, you daft cow.' Kate embraced her sister and allowed her own tears to come too, until they were both weeping and laughing at each other. 'This is no one's fault but mine, do you understand me? No one's but mine.'

A thought came to her, something buried in her mind from a few months previously. 'Erin, there's something I've been meaning to ask you. When I told you Pete had left, I had a feeling that you weren't that shocked really. Am I right?'

Erin regarded her sister for a moment. 'I'd suspected for a long time that things weren't great between you and Pete. Whenever I saw you together you seemed like polite strangers, like you were co-existing but the love had gone. I don't think anyone else noticed but I'm your sister and I know when things aren't right. But whenever I tried to bring it up you always shut me down so I figured you didn't want to talk about it. I just hoped that you guys would sort it out between you eventually.'

Erin paused, took a deep breath and then continued. 'But in the months before he left, he seemed different. I don't know, happier, more perky is the only way I can describe it. Like he had a new zest for life. But you didn't. If anything you seemed more withdrawn. So I began to suspect he was seeing someone else.'

'Why didn't you tell me?' Kate was shocked.

'Because I had absolutely no proof whatsoever, Kate. It was a hunch, that was all. And I hoped to God that I was wrong. I feel terrible now, believe me.'

Kate's outrage subsided as quickly as it had arrived. This was hardly her sister's fault. 'The stupid thing is that I didn't suspect it. It's so obvious now looking back that something was going on. He was staying out later and later on "client dinners", disappearing off with his phone sometimes, and he could barely touch me. I remember one time we tried to have sex for the first time in ages and he couldn't even get it up. Yet I just ignored it all. I didn't want to know, to be honest. It's only now that I see it.'

'You look bloody good on it though,' Erin replied, and Kate

snorted in response. 'I'm serious, Kate, you've been through hell and back over the last few months but look at you! You've taken control of your life – you've finally told Rachel to move on, become a super-mum, you're seeing a therapist, you're going back to work. I think you're amazing. If this is what Pete going AWOL does to you then I'm all for it!'

Only her sister could get away with saying something like that. 'Like I said, Erin, our marriage was already over and I'm much happier now that I've accepted that and started standing on my own two feet again. I can't believe how insecure I had become. Do you know, I was terrified of spending time alone with my girls? I was terrified because I didn't know how to be around them. It was so much easier with Rachel, it all just came naturally to her and I envied that so much. I've felt like the worst mother in the world for so many years that I had no idea what it was like to not feel that way.'

'And now?'

'I understand now that all I need to do is just be with them, that's all. It doesn't need to be great adventures or grand plans all the time, just be with them, that's all they want really. And actually, I've loved them since the day they were born and although I've not always been the greatest mother, they've turned out pretty good.'

'If you ever need a break, you know I'm here for you, right?'

'Thanks, Erin, but I've had enough breaks. I've sat at home on my sorry arse missing too much as it is. I want to spend as much time with them as possible.'

And on Christmas Day, that's what she'd done. They'd spent the whole day cocooned in their house together, their new little gang, the three amigos, opening and playing with presents, cooking a turkey with all the trimmings and collapsing on the sofa to watch a Disney film. And although the girls still asked if Daddy was coming home, and although Kate felt horrific gently telling them no, Daddy was not coming home but he loved them so very much, they had a good day.

In the New Year, she'd started Operation Back To Work with a vengeance and within a few weeks she'd agreed terms with her old client and had started working on her first campaign in over seven years. The thought of actually asking someone to pay her for her expertise was still daunting but she knew it would get easier. She just had to take it one step at a time and today's step was sending that press release off to her client. Looking at the clock she realised that she had to pick the girls up from school in fifteen minutes. Grabbing her keys and trainers, she legged it for the door and began power walking up the street. On the way to school, she saw Nadia.

'Well hello, stranger!' Nadia said, crossing the road to walk with Kate. 'We haven't seen you for ages.'

'Yes, I'm sorry, I've been so busy. I'm working again and it's taking up a lot of my time.'

'That's wonderful, Kate, good for you!' Nadia smiled warmly. Kate felt bad about the fact that she'd been avoiding her. She wasn't a bad person really.

'Listen, we're having the usual gang over for dinner on Saturday, we'd love for you to join us. Do you think Erin would babysit?'

The last thing she wanted to do on Saturday night was to be surrounded by happy couples, all watching her closely for signs of a mental breakdown.

'Thanks for the invite, Nadia, I really appreciate it, but we're actually going away this weekend.'

'Ooh, anywhere nice?'

Kate had no idea, she'd just thought of it on the spot. Impulsively, she replied, 'I'm taking the girls down to see their granny.'

'Your mum?'

'Actually, no, Pete's mum.'

Nadia raised her eyebrows. 'Pete's mum?'

'Yes, we're back in touch. She's really lovely, actually, we've seen her a couple of times. The girls adore her.'

'What do you think Pete would say about that?' Nadia knew from past dinner party conversations that Pete didn't have a good relationship with his mother.

'Quite frankly, Nadia, Pete isn't here so he can fuck right off.'

Nadia looked taken aback. 'I'm sorry, Kate, I didn't mean to offend you.'

'Oh no, don't worry, you didn't.' Kate smiled sweetly back at her. 'You didn't at all.'

In the playground she bumped into Lottie. 'Hey, I was hoping to see you,' she told her. 'Would you and Ava like to come over after school next Friday?'

'We'd love to,' Lottie said.

The girls ran out of school and launched themselves at her. Laughing, she hugged them both before unearthing the snacks that she'd brought with her. As the girls played with their friends for a few moments, she pulled out her phone and typed a quick text message to Karen.

Fancy some visitors this weekend?

Her mother-in-law called her back on the way home. 'Hi, Kate, what a lovely surprise to hear from you. I'd love that. When were you thinking of coming?'

After making the arrangements Kate hung up and told the girls that they were going to Granny's on Saturday.

'Will Daddy be there?' Maggie asked. The question instantly killed her buzz. They asked about him less frequently now, so she'd stopped being on constant alert for it. Before she had a chance to reply, Lily piped up, 'No, Maggie, remember, Daddy isn't here anymore. He's gone away to be happy.'

She wanted to cry. Instead, she put her arms around her eldest daughter, gave her a squeeze and said, 'Who fancies pizza for dinner?'

# 18

## PETE

Pete looked at the rolling French countryside stretching out before him and felt at once both utter contentment and nagging guilt over what he was doing. Leafing through the photos of Claire's dad's house which she'd put on the little table between them, he closed his eyes and tried to push all his fears and worries out of his mind and focus on the job at hand. What did he want to do with his life?

They'd gone to France together for a few days to do a recce. And he had to admit, he liked what he saw. Claire's dad's house was in a bit of a state, but he could see the potential. And the whole area was just stunning. He could feel the stress and tension of London life ease away with every hour he spent there.

He had accepted the job and handed in his notice at work the previous week. He had six weeks to decide what to do next. He knew he could still just tell Kate he had got a new job and carry on with his life. She'd be confused as to why he hadn't told her about the interviews but he was sure he could fudge it somehow and tell her that he didn't think he'd have a chance of getting it and he hadn't wanted to tempt fate.

Accepting the job was not, on its own, confirmation that he

was going to leave her as far as he was concerned. Coming to France with his lover to consider the possibility of moving there permanently was quite another matter. All he wanted to do right now was to sit back, relax and enjoy the time away with Claire but he knew that she had other things on her mind. Inevitably, discussions would need to be had about their future.

He was so confused. Every time he decided that he was definitely going to leave Kate, something would happen that would change his mind. He oscillated back and forth, sometimes within minutes. He wasn't stupid, he knew what he was throwing away and the hurt that he would cause to his wife and children but on the other hand, he deserved to be happy. He had every damn right to be happy. And being with Claire made him so blissfully happy in a way that he hadn't felt with Kate for years. He honestly didn't think he'd ever find it again with Kate and it was unfair to her for him to stay when he felt like that. She deserved better too and with a bit of time, he was sure that she'd realise it was for the best. Perhaps she'd meet someone – someone who did a better job of making her happy than he had. Because one thing he knew for sure, she'd been bloody miserable for years. Still, it didn't make the whole thing any easier.

That evening, over dinner at the new restaurant in the village, Claire asked her first gently probing question. 'So, Pete, what do you think?'

'I love it,' he replied honestly. 'I love the house, I love the village and I love the whole laid-back vibe.'

'Enough to live here?'

He thought very carefully about his answer. Right now, feeling pleasurably mellow on a few glasses of excellent red wine after a blissful afternoon, he literally couldn't think of anywhere else he'd rather be. So he spoke the words that he was feeling, even though he knew that in the cold light of day he might regret them. 'Enough to live here, yes.'

She squealed and reached for both his hands. 'Oh, Pete, I'm so excited!'

He smiled at her. 'Me too.'

'It'll be amazing, I'm telling you. You won't regret it. We are going to have the best life here and I am going to make you one very happy man.'

There were so many things that they needed to talk about if they were going to have a future together. He'd never spoken to her about kids – did she like them? Did she want any of her own? There was no way he was having any more children, he was done with nappies and sleepless nights. But what if she did? And how much effort was she prepared to make with Lily and Maggie? They would always be in his life and it was important to him that she understood that. Did she expect them to get married at some point? He wasn't sure he had it in him for another wedding. These were fundamental questions, he knew, but right now he wasn't sure he wanted to know the answers. All he wanted to do was drink wine, eat glorious food and have a wonderful evening with the woman he loved. The rest could wait for now.

But he didn't change his mind after all. Even when he woke up the next day with a slight red wine hangover, he'd turned to look at Claire, sleeping soundly next to him and he still felt the same. He wanted to move to France with her and have a new, better life. And now that he'd decided he could relax, enjoy the next couple of days and put off dealing with the reality of it all until he got back home.

But time always flies when you're having fun and within

what felt like seconds, he was in a taxi on his way home from the airport. His bubble of bliss had burst, sending him back down to the real world with a resounding thump. As they said goodbye, he had kissed Claire deeply and told her that he was going to set the wheels in motion immediately. She had looked at him with such delight that he could still picture her face now. But as soon as he put his key in the lock and the children rushed up to him, shouting 'Daddy, Daddy, Daddy,' he knew that now wasn't the right time. He enveloped them in a hug before looking up to greet Kate, who had emerged from the kitchen and was leaning up against the bannister.

'Good trip?' she asked him.

'It was all right, you know how these things are. A bit dull and a lot of schmoozing people but it has to be done.'

'Well, welcome home,' she said, smiling at him.

'How have things been here?'

'Oh fine, nothing to report, same old,' she replied. 'I'll carry on with dinner.' And with that she turned and walked back into the kitchen. He was hardly expecting balloons and a welcome back banner but her dismissiveness of him strengthened his resolve. *This is the right decision*, he thought. *There's no love or affection here anymore.* But then he looked down at his two daughters, gazing up at him adoringly and fighting for his attention and he felt awful all over again. This was exhausting. He peeled the children off him and followed them into the living room, collapsing on to the sofa and staring at the TV, which was halfway through a My Little Pony film. They both jumped up next to him and snuggled down. He closed his eyes, just for a second, and before he knew it he was fast asleep.

The next day, Claire messaged him to tell him that she had given notice on the flat and told the temp agency that she was leaving. It was so easy for her, she had no real responsibilities at home. But he had to decide how to end his marriage and in the meantime, he had to act totally normally around his family. And to make matters worse, they had that bloody holiday to Greece coming up and he couldn't think of a way out of it. He was dreading telling Claire about it.

'Why can't you just leave her now? You've made up your mind, so there's no point prolonging the agony.' Claire had said when they met up a few days later. 'Just do it now and come and live with me in the flat until we move in a few weeks.'

'It's tempting, Claire, it is, but I have some things I need to sort out, loose ends to tie up. Look, I know it's hard for you but we're doing this, we're moving to France so bear with me for a little bit longer and it will all be worth it, I promise.'

He didn't mention Greece. In truth, the reason he hadn't done it yet was because he was terrified. Terrified of telling Kate, of seeing the hurt in his children's eyes as he tried to explain that Daddy was moving away, and terrified that he was making a colossal mistake. Sometimes he felt so overwhelmingly certain that this was the right thing to do and other times he literally thought that he was going to have a panic attack about it all. Often it just felt surreal, like he was dreaming and at some point he'd wake up and realise that none of this was actually happening to him. As days turned into weeks and the moving date inched ever closer, he still failed to tell Kate he was leaving her and the children started chattering excitedly about the upcoming holiday. They were due to fly the following week.

Over drinks with Dan in the pub one evening after work, he confessed his predicament. He'd already told Dan and Carl about the possible move to France but this was the first time he'd admitted to anyone that it was actually happening.

'Jesus, Pete, what are you playing at?' Dan asked. 'You're talking about moving to another country with another woman and you still haven't told your wife? I'm sorry, mate, but that's not on at all. You need to deal with it. Stop being a dick.'

The truth hurt but Pete knew his friend was right. 'I know, I know,' he replied.

'And what about the kids?' Dan asked.

'I'll still see them all the time,' Pete insisted. 'We've planned it all out. I'm going to rent a flat in London and come back twice a month, so they'll stay with me then and they'll come to France for holidays.'

'Do you really think Kate is going to allow that?'

'She wouldn't dare to stop me from seeing my kids. I have rights.'

'I'm not sure how many rights you have if you leave the bloody country to live with another woman. Have you even looked into it?'

He hadn't but he didn't want to admit that to Dan. 'Look, I'm not saying it's going to be easy but we'll make it work. Kate won't stand in the way of me having a relationship with the girls, she's not like that.'

'She'll be angry, Pete, angry and humiliated. And even if she does agree to it, are you really okay with not being a part of their day-to-day lives?'

Dan was a family man, the idea of being away from his children even for a night or two distressed him but Pete was different. He loved his girls, he adored them, but he missed his pre-kids life. And this way, it meant that he would enjoy them even more when he did see them. But he could never admit that to Dan because even he knew it sounded fairly horrific, so instead he said: 'Of course not, but even if I lived in London I still wouldn't see them every day. At least this way they can come and stay with me for weeks on end. And they'll love it, Dan, the place is amazing.'

But there was no convincing Dan. He disapproved and nothing Pete said would change his mind. His friend's reaction hadn't been a massive surprise but it had fed the niggling monster of doubt still lurking in the depths of his mind. Was Dan right? Was this all a massive early midlife crisis that had gone too far and he'd come to regret? Did he just need some time away to clear his head?

He thought about the upcoming holiday to Greece again. He'd go, he decided, he'd go along and see what happened. There was nothing to lose at this stage.

## 19

## KATE

Valentine's Day was coming up. The children had come home from school clutching home-made cards for her. *To Mummy, Happy Valentine's Day, I love you xxx*

Pete had proposed to Kate on Valentine's Day. They were on a romantic trip to Italy and the whole thing was as cheesy as it could get, but she'd absolutely loved it. He'd got down on one knee in a beautiful piazza after they emerged from an amazing dinner and told her that he wanted her to be his wife. Right then, looking into the eyes of the man who had been by her side for a decade, she had never felt happier in her life. After that, Valentine's Day had been a bit of a special thing for them and even after they stopped going out each year to celebrate, he'd always come home with some flowers and chocolates and cook her a lovely meal. They'd stay up and talk for hours, reminiscing about their past and talking about their future and she'd go to bed thinking about how lucky she was to have him.

Eventually his gestures slowly dwindled down to a card and some petrol station flowers and she could hardly blame him – the year Maggie was born she'd completely forgotten what day it was and hadn't even wished him a Happy Valentine's until he got home from work proffering a hastily bought card that he'd picked up in Sainsbury's. They'd been in bed by 8pm. The day lost all of its former glory and became just like any other, so it felt strange that, despite the circumstances, she was actually looking forward to it for the first time in years.

They were holding a Valentine's Disco at the girls' school and Kate had been involved in the planning. She had helped the parent organisers out with the promotion for the event and all the tickets had sold out within the first two hours – a new record. Parents and teachers kept coming up to her in the playground to congratulate her and she felt a warm rush of pride each time. Lily and Maggie were beside themselves with excitement – more about the fact that there would be bags of sweets to buy than the actual dance itself – and she, Lottie and a few of the gang from Maggie's class were going out for pizza afterwards.

Nadia was baking some of her famous cupcakes and cookies in heart shapes and Kate had been relieved that no one expected her to contribute too. Not only was she useless at baking, she was absolutely rushed off her feet with work at the moment. Her first client had given her another campaign to work on and she'd taken on two new projects since. Trying to fit all the work into school hours was proving to be a bit of a challenge but she was absolutely buzzing. She was earning her own income for the first time in ages and she felt great. Each time she didn't have to withdraw money from the savings account to pay for things she felt a rush of satisfaction. Her self-confidence was coming back and the daily doses of panic and anxiety were easing off. She knew they'd probably always be there lurking in the background ready to pounce, but she was learning to control them.

It had been five months since she had last seen or spoken to

Pete. They had been the hardest and most challenging months of her life but they had also been surprising. Despite the heartbreak and humiliation, she finally felt more like herself than she had done in years. It had taken an event so completely horrendous and out of her control to shock her back to reality and make her regain control of her own life. Sometimes distress would still overcome her, without any warning, about what he had done and how it had all been left but it was quickly replaced with sorrow for what he was missing as a result. She got to be here with their beautiful children, watching them grow, but he didn't. And whose fault was that? Was it his for deciding to abandon them? Or was it hers? The truth lay somewhere between the two. But she knew that she had got the better deal.

And honestly? She didn't really miss him that much at all anymore. Once she had got out of the habit of having him around, she found that she liked herself far better now that he was gone. It wasn't his fault, he hadn't been a terrible husband, but they had drifted apart so long ago and had reached the point where they had brought out the worst in each other, not the best. Late at night she would still find herself thinking, *what would Pete say if he could see me now? What would he think?* She still craved his approval, even after all this. *He'd be pleased*, she thought. *Pissed off as hell that I waited until he'd gone to finally sort my life out, but proud.* But then maybe he'd had to go for her to change her outlook on life. Perhaps she never would have done it if he were still there. His mere presence had become a barrier, hiding her and trapping her at the same time. It was only once it had been forcibly removed that she'd had to stand tall and face the world.

Her phone started ringing in the hallway and she rushed to answer it. She no longer instinctively looked for Pete's name and, glancing at the screen, she saw that it was Lottie. She smiled as she answered: Lottie had become a good friend, someone she could really be herself around and who she didn't constantly compare herself against, and it felt wonderful to have one of those again after so long.

'Ava is so excited about tonight,' Lottie said. 'She wants to know what Maggie is wearing. I can't believe it's started already, I thought we wouldn't have this until they were teenagers. They're growing up too fast!'

'I know,' Kate said, grinning. 'Maggie and Lily made me take them shopping so they could buy new dresses. I must say though, I really enjoyed it too.'

'Would you and the girls like to come over for Sunday lunch this weekend? Andy's ordered in a beef joint.'

'That would be lovely, thank you.'

'Fab, around oneish?'

'Perfect, looking forward to it. See you later for the disco.'

Putting the phone back down she made a coffee and sat at the kitchen table to do some work. What with the disco and the dinner planned for later that day she had the Friday feeling and was struggling to concentrate. She put the radio on and tried to get stuck into the press release she was writing but her mind kept drifting. What should she wear later? It was only a school party and dinner with some friends but she felt like making a bit of an effort. Should she sack off work and wash and blow dry her hair? She could make it up tomorrow evening. *Oh sod it*, she thought, closing her laptop. She was feeling reckless.

Upstairs she put some music on and jumped into the shower, taking her time and savouring the empty house. As much as she loved having the girls around, she enjoyed the time when she had the place to herself. She no longer felt lonely, even at night. The nightmares still came sometimes but they were less frequent now. She'd bought new bedsheets and covers, trying to make the bed her own and she often had little visitors, who crept into her bed and snuggled up beside her at night. Pete used to say that children should sleep in their own beds and had never allowed the girls to sleep with them but now she found that she didn't mind it at all. In the morning she would wake up surrounded by children and teddies and would smile. No, she couldn't possibly be lonely, the house was full of life.

Padding out of the bathroom she did her hair and make-up before putting on some smart jeans and a top. Looking at her phone she saw that it was 2pm – another hour before she had to collect the girls and bring them home to change before the disco started at 4.30pm. Really, she should try to squeeze an hour of work in but she fancied bunking off so she decided to walk up to the Broadway and have a mooch around the shops. She was just picking up her keys when she heard a knock on the door. It was probably Erin, she thought. She was working from home today and had said she might pop round for a cuppa. Never mind, the mooching could wait.

She opened the door with a grin, looking forward to catching up with her sister but her smile evaporated when she looked at the two uniformed police officers standing on her doorstep. Her heart started to pound.

'Mrs Garland?' one of them, the woman, asked.

'Yes, that's me, what is it?' she replied.

The officers introduced themselves. 'May we come in?' the man asked.

'Oh, yes, of course.' Kate led the officers to the living room, feeling her palms becoming clammy and her breath quickening. Was this about Pete? She felt instinctively that it was. They all sat down and she looked at them nervously.

'Mrs Garland, can I ask when you last saw your husband, Pete Garland?'

'Five months ago,' Kate replied. The date she had last seen

him was etched into her memory forever. 'Can I ask what this is about?'

The two officers looked at each other.

'Mrs Garland,' the female officer began. 'Your husband has been reported as a missing person.'

# 20

## CLAIRE

He had been an easy target, really. Unhappily married, desperate for a sliver of affection, it hadn't taken much to turn his head. Not that she'd planned it, she had no interest whatsoever in ruining a marriage and messing up other people's lives. She'd never had an affair with a married man before and doing so hadn't exactly made the list of her future goals. But then she met Pete and everything had changed.

She'd been in between jobs when the email came through from the recruitment company offering her a role as receptionist on the front desk of a big media company in the City. It was easy work and good money, so the next day she polished her heels, slipped into her pencil skirt and strode through the doors of the imposing building, clattering over the shiny floors and taking her place behind the glossy black marble desk. She liked the receptionist jobs because it was the perfect opportunity for people watching. And this place was just like all the others – each morning City workers piled in, clutching their takeaway coffees and playing with their phones, barely noticing her as they walked past her desk towards the neat rows of lifts behind her.

Occasionally someone would look up and see her; some of the men might give her a double take, liking what they saw, but most of the time she was invisible and she didn't mind a bit. It meant that she could watch them all, these rat-runners so absorbed in their own lives that they didn't even notice what was going on around them. She enjoyed studying them, imagining what kind of lives they led, and giving all the men an attractiveness score out of ten when she was feeling particularly bored. When Pete walked in – a nine, she decided immediately – she expected him to walk on by like all the others, so it came as a surprise when he caught her eye and paused at the desk.

'First day?' he asked her. She smiled politely and nodded, introducing herself. He gave off an aura of authority and she sensed immediately that he was quite important in the company but she had never been intimidated by senior management. They were just people who burped, farted and cried like everyone else.

'Welcome on board.' He smiled and then he was gone, piling into the lift with all the others and whizzing up to what she imagined was a top floor office. She forgot about him straight away and turned her focus to the next passer-by until the phone rang and she had to get down to work.

Over the next few days he continued to greet her politely each morning and soon she began looking forward to seeing him. He was easy on the eye and projected a confidence that she found attractive. Most men her age were either arrogant or insecure and she was bored of them. But she sensed that Pete was different and began wondering if she'd been too quick to dismiss older men in the past. He always arrived at the same time every day and she found herself checking her watch in anticipation of his arrival. A few minutes beforehand she'd duck down behind the desk and reapply her lip gloss.

But that was all it was at first, just a little something to look forward to in an otherwise pretty dull day at work, something that enticed her out of her bed a bit earlier to straighten her hair and pick a flattering outfit. It had happened at previous jobs, these harmless little crushes on people which made the day pass quicker, and nothing ever came of it, so she had no intention of this being any different. She generally kept herself to herself at work, made enough polite conversation for people not to think she was weird, and that was all. She wasn't interested in office politics and gossip around the water cooler and she'd never dipped her pen in the office ink so to speak. The thought of other people gossiping about her was unappealing. Perhaps it was because her mum had been a television actress but she'd learned from a young age to keep her private life as private as possible.

But then one day Pete came in early. She had only just arrived at work and was eating breakfast at her desk – against the rules but she rarely saw anyone else at that hour. There was another hour to go before the floodgates opened and everyone started pouring into work so his arrival surprised her and she found herself quickly brushing the crumbs of her croissant from her face and her blue silk shirt and hoping that he wasn't the type to report her for flouting the rules. But he smiled his usual greeting and walked on by, her transgression unnoticed or ignored.

'You're in early,' she said, conversationally.

He paused and turned back to look at her. 'Big meeting, lots to prepare,' he said, hesitating and then walking back over to the front desk. 'How's it all going then? Finding the ropes okay?'

'Oh yes,' she replied, 'everyone's really friendly.'

When his stomach rumbled loudly it broke the tension immediately and they both laughed. She gave him some of her croissant and they chatted for a while. Then, glancing at his watch, he said goodbye and he was gone. After that he always stopped by for a chat. She liked it, and she liked him. So when she got a round-robin email reminding everyone that it was Free Drinks Friday in the bar on the ground floor that evening – a monthly event held every payday – she was interested. Claire didn't usually mix business with pleasure and very rarely went to work events, especially ones where everyone tended to get blotto on free booze and do things (or people) they would sincerely regret the next day, but she started wondering if Pete would be there. When she finished work, instead of grabbing her bag and making her usual quick exit she found herself in the ladies' toilets touching up her make-up and straightening her skirt, before heading out into the lobby and strolling into the bar area on the other side.

The room was already full of people, buzzing from the prospect of free drinks and payday, and she scanned it quickly, looking for his face among the crowds. She felt disappointment kicking in when she realised that he wasn't there. Still, the night was young, so she got herself a gin and tonic and went to mingle with some of the PAs, who had always been friendly enough to her. As she half-listened to their tales of photocopier woes, she continued to watch the room but he never came and after an hour and a half, she'd had enough. She made her excuses and left, feeling annoyed with herself for even caring.

Over the weeks that followed, Pete started to come into work early more often. Meetings, client calls to prepare for, lots to catch up on, he always had an excuse. She had given up on the lip gloss. His visits to the front desk started to last longer. One day he brought in pastries, proffering the bag of warm, tasty indulgences at her before helping himself and leaning against the desk with one elbow to eat it. She told him that almond croissants were her favourite and the next day he brought one in for her. These small gestures lingered on her mind for the rest of the day.

In her defence, she hadn't known he was married at first. She had figured he was about ten years older than her but he didn't wear a ring and many men of his age were unmarried or divorced. It was only when he mentioned a skiing holiday he'd been on with his wife and kids that the penny dropped and she felt a crushing sense of disappointment that she couldn't explain, given that this was meant to be a harmless crush. For the rest of that day she felt grumpy and she went home that evening and opened a bottle of wine, her mind whizzing through the possibilities. Was he trapped in an unhappy marriage? Was he a serial adulterer? Or was he simply making polite conversation with her and she was being an idiot for thinking that it was something more? She didn't know the answer yet, but she realised that she wanted to find out. *It's still just a game*, she told herself, *a bit of attention, something to pass the time at work, nothing more*. But by the time the next Free Drinks Friday came about she couldn't resist asking him if he was planning to go.

'Oh, those things? I never go,' he said, rolling his eyes. Then he seemed to think about it again and added quickly, 'Maybe I'll pop in tonight. It's good to do some networking.'

She knew she shouldn't do but she felt ridiculously excited all day, a sense of anticipation growing inside her, butterflies fluttering around her stomach. The evening could not come soon enough. As soon as the clock hit 5pm she was out of her chair and in the loos faster than Usain Bolt, brushing her teeth, reapplying her make-up and spraying perfume. She got herself a drink and found some people to chat to while she awaited his arrival. She smiled and laughed at the right points in the conversation but she was distracted, looking around constantly for him. An hour passed and then a second hour. As the night progressed, she felt herself getting more drunk and more disappointed. Neither were what she'd had planned for the evening. Finally, she'd had enough and made her excuses before walking back through the reception area towards the revolving doors which would take her out of this stupid bubble of a life she had created in this building and back to reality again.

'Leaving so soon?'

Her stomach lurched at the sound of his voice and she turned around to see him looking at her and grinning, ruefully – she thought, although she couldn't tell with him yet. And looking so bloody hot. That was the moment, she realised on the way home, the moment when she knew that she was going to sleep with him. But it wasn't going to be that night because she was too annoyed. So she simply replied: 'Yes, got other plans, enjoy!' swung on her heel and walked away, leaving him standing there and, she sensed, watching her go.

On Monday he was at the office at 8am with an almond croissant and she felt almost immediately that something unspoken had shifted between them. Over the following weeks their conversations became more intimate, the tiny flirtations that had been so subtle at first suddenly seemed more obvious. When the next Free Drinks Friday was announced, he forwarded the email to her, simply saying: 'Going?' She knew she was grinning like an idiot as she hit reply and typed: 'Yep'. It was the first and only email he ever sent her. That evening when she entered the bar, everything felt different. She saw him almost immediately, chatting easily to some colleagues. She caught his eye as she walked past him towards the bar to order a drink and within seconds he was by her side, as she had known he would be. He ordered a gin and tonic for her and a beer for himself before turning to look at her.

'You're looking very pretty,' he said and the line took her back to that film, *Love Actually*, when Alan Rickman has a thing with his PA, and without even thinking she leaned in and whispered the line from the film in his ear: 'It's all for you.'

Pulling back she looked at his unreadable face and panicked for a second, worried that she had gone too far and scared him off.

Then, without any visible reaction, he simply whispered, 'Outside in twenty minutes' before walking away and back over to the group of colleagues he'd been talking to previously. She quickly drank her gin and scuttled outside, avoiding eye contact so that she wouldn't be drawn into any conversations, while butterflies fluttered around her stomach and she felt more excited than she'd done in ages. Half an hour later, she was still waiting outside, shivering in the cold and cursing the bastard when he dashed out and rushed over to her, full of apologies for keeping her waiting.

'I didn't want it to look too obvious,' he told her. 'I've never done anything like this before.' His frank confession immediately thawed her coldness towards him.

'Me neither,' she replied.

They looked at each other, suddenly nervous and unsure what to do. 'Drink?' they both said at the same time and laughed. He gestured for her to follow him and they walked together but slightly apart, zigzagging down the small side streets of London, for about ten minutes until they came to a pub so hidden that she hadn't even known it existed. Inside, it looked like it hadn't been redecorated since the eighties and there wasn't a single City worker to be found. She knew at once why he had brought her here – no one would see them, so they were safe from prying eyes.

Still, she found a little booth right at the back that was hidden from the rest of the pub while he went to the bar to get their drinks. When he came back he slid in next to her and the sudden closeness of him sent sparks of electricity through her. In all their previous interactions they had been divided by the chastity belt of the front desk. Their legs touched and she looked at him, sensing that he was feeling the same.

They never finished their drinks. She took him back to her flat in a taxi and they went straight to her bedroom, all the nerves from earlier banished. The sex was not as good as the fantasy she had played over and over again in her head, because it could never live up to that, but it was good enough. Afterwards, they lay there next to each other, unsure what to do. She looked at him and he smiled but she could tell he was grappling with something internally. The moment between them had passed, and she had lost him again to his other life.

'Are you okay?' she asked him.

'Yeah, I'm good, I'm just... it's just that I've never done anything like this before,' he said. 'I'm not sorry it happened,' he added quickly as he looked over at her, 'it was amazing, you're amazing. It's just a lot for me to process.'

She touched his arm. 'It was amazing,' she said. 'And you don't owe me anything at all. If you need to go now, then go. Don't worry about me, okay? I get it and I'm fine.'

He looked at her gratefully, clearly relieved she had given him an out. Ten minutes later he was gone and she was alone in her flat again. It was never going to be romantic, sex with a married man, she knew. And that was all it was to her, she told herself, she had wanted to have sex with this man and now she had. Tick. Time to move on.

And yet she felt strangely bereft, a feeling that she couldn't shake off all weekend. The following night she went out with some friends and as she sat in the crowded, trendy restaurant in King's Cross, laughing and joking, her thoughts kept wandering back to him and the previous evening.

When Monday came about, she found herself feeling nervous, unsure about what, if anything, was next for them.

She opened her emails and saw she had a message from the recruitment company asking how she was getting on and if she wanted to stay on for another three months. *Best to go*, she thought, *nip this in the bud now and get on with my life. No good can come of this.* And she was just about to reply to say no thanks, she didn't want to stay, when Pete walked in. The minute she saw him, she knew that they had unfinished business.

'Are you free on Wednesday?' he had asked her. Her heart had literally soared at the sound of those words, like music to her ears.

Later that morning she got a WhatsApp message from an unknown number. *Looking forward to Wednesday*, it said. She quickly saved the number to her phone under the name PG and returned to her email to the recruitment agency.

```
Hi Jess,
   Lovely to hear from you! Everything's
going great here thanks, I'm very happy
to stay on for another three months.
Please feel free to send over the new
contract.
   Best,
   Claire.
```

## 21

## PETE

On Wednesday, just three days before he was due to fly to Greece with Kate and the girls, he broached the subject with Claire nervously, waiting for her wrath. She looked at him in incomprehension. 'You're leaving your wife in a couple of weeks and you're still going to go on a cosy family holiday to Greece with her?'

'What can I do, Claire? It'll destroy the kids if I don't go and it'll probably be the last holiday that we all have together. I owe it to them. It's just a week and then I'll be home and I'll be all yours, I promise.'

She looked furious but managed to swallow down whatever angry words were threatening to spill out, saying simply, 'I don't think it's on, I really don't.'

'I understand,' he said as soothingly as he could, 'but think of it as one final trip, to mark the end of our marriage before you and I start our new adventure.'

'And what about the sleeping arrangements then? Will it be sex on the beach after the kids have gone to bed?'

He laughed. 'Hardly, Claire, we're all sharing a room, the

four of us. I can guarantee you there'll be none of that. Anyway, there's been none of that for a long time, as you well know. The only woman I'm sleeping with is you.'

She seemed a bit placated by that and he added, 'Look, Claire, it's for the girls, all right?'

She nodded reluctantly but still looked annoyed. Although she didn't mention it again until the end of the evening, it was obvious that it was on her mind but he'd played the 'children' card and she knew that she couldn't challenge him on that. When he was leaving, she wrapped her arms around him and whispered into his ear, 'You'd better not come back and tell me that you're in love with your wife after all.'

He squeezed her tight. 'It won't happen, I promise.'

On the way home he contemplated the ridiculous situation he had managed to get himself into. How had he ended up here? The rollercoaster ride that had thrilled him so much to begin with was now scaring him – it was too fast, too unstoppable. Not that he didn't love Claire, he did, but everything else was terrifying. He was leaving the woman he'd been with for over fifteen years, leaving his children, his job, his friends and his life. And did he even want to move to France or was he just doing it to please her? He'd thought he was on board, he really had, but now he wasn't sure again. It was like a constant conveyor belt of emotions, one after another, and it was starting to overwhelm him. He thought he'd felt suffocated before in his marriage but now he found there were times when the anxiety over what he was planning to do overwhelmed him so much that he struggled to catch his breath. When he was with Claire it was okay because her excitement was infectious but the minute he left her the doubts started coming back, thick and fast. Was he getting this all wrong? Had he fucked up completely? What had seemed like something so far away in his future to worry about was now just weeks away and he couldn't push it to the back of his mind anymore.

On Friday, his last day at work before the holiday, Dan cornered him on his way out of the office to get a sandwich. 'Have you told her yet?' he asked.

'No,' he admitted. 'We're going away tomorrow and it'll be our last family holiday together. I want the kids to enjoy it and to have fond memories of it. Then as soon as we're back, I'm going to tell her.' It wasn't true, but Dan didn't need to know that.

'Well, have a good holiday,' Dan said as he slapped him on the back. 'Rather you than me, mate.'

He got home to chaos. The girls were so excited about the forthcoming trip that they were running around like tiny little maniacs, squealing, shrieking and jumping up and down on the sofa while Kate dashed around trying to pack for them all. She looked at Pete and smiled. 'It'll be worth it when we get there.'

He was dreading the trip. When they'd booked it a few months back he'd been enthused by the prospect, keen on the idea of a make-or-break holiday to help sort his head out. But since then so much had changed. Now he was going away with a woman who he no longer loved but still didn't take any joy in hurting, pretending everything was fine, while the woman he did love was at home, pissed off with him. Going to the fridge and helping himself to a drink, he resolved to simply keep his head down and get through the week without any drama.

It was easier than he'd thought it would be in the end. After all, he'd been lying to his family for months, what was another week? The girls had a blast, playing in the pool most of the day, napping during the early afternoon heat, and making new friends. He and Kate both focused on the children's enjoyment, being friendly to each other and looking to outsiders like a perfectly happy, harmonious couple while on the inside the void still remained, which was just like it had been for as long as he could remember. A couple of times, when they were sitting outside the hotel bar with a cool drink and the children were off running around the gardens with their new pals, he wondered if she'd ever bring up the state of their relationship. Did she even want to fix it? Or was she simply happy in this permanent state of denial? Had she resigned herself to a life of survival rather than enjoyment? She never said a word and he certainly wasn't going to mention it now.

They went to bed not long after the children did most nights. Pete told Kate that he was exhausted from all the sun and swimming and she didn't question it, she was tired too. The days of hiding in the hotel bathroom sharing a bottle of wine while the children slept in the bedroom were long gone.

It was a pleasant enough family holiday – not the life-changing one he'd had in mind when they'd booked it, but not a complete disaster either. He came back feeling just as confused as ever. It confirmed his feeling that their marriage was over, they had simply fallen out of love and run out of things to say to each other. He didn't think they could get that back. But he still battled with the enormity of what he was planning to do in just a couple of weeks and the effect that it would have on his family.

There was another option on the table, he thought, a more honest and civil break-up where he stuck around to deal with the fallout and handled it all properly, which might help him sleep better at night. But Claire, amazing, beautiful Claire, would never forgive him if he abandoned their plans now and he couldn't risk losing her too. No, he'd gone too far to put the brakes on now. He had to plough on, whether he liked it or not. The thought had started keeping him up most nights and, when he did finally fall asleep, he'd wake up sweaty and panicking. There were times when he thought that he might be losing the plot. Other times he just wanted to run away from it all and hide somewhere no one would find him.

But now he felt even more sure that not telling Kate everything was the best course of action. No need to confess the whole story right now, he could simply tell her that he needed some time away. It was kind of true. Claire never had to know about it, yet it would give him a bit more time to work through the doubts in his mind. The more he thought about it, the more appealing the idea seemed to him. There would be no tears and recriminations, not right now anyway, no ceremonious goodbyes.

No, on the day he was due to leave, he'd simply pack a few clothes and toiletries, leave Kate a note and go. He'd withdrawn some money from their ISA already, which Kate never checked, and would just deposit it back in if he came home again. Deep down he knew he was putting off the inevitable, but he didn't care right now. All he had to do was to act as normal as possible for two more weeks. It wasn't too difficult – they'd survived Greece and the one good thing about having a wife who you never confided in anymore was that it was easy to hide even the biggest secret.

Claire seemed to have got over her annoyance too. When he saw her for the first time after Greece she'd barely even asked him about it, wanting only to focus on their own upcoming travel plans. She'd won after all, he thought, she'd got what she wanted. She wasn't interested in knowing about the intricacies of their family holiday, only that he had come home to her and that he still wanted to move to France.

They continued making plans and slowly he started to feel excited again, as he always did when he was in her company, like young lovers planning to run away to Gretna Green together. They decided to get the Eurostar so that they could spend a few days together in Paris first. 'Where else to start our amazing new adventure than in the most romantic city in the world?' Claire had said.

Behind her, on the wall, he saw she had been crossing off the days until they left on her French art calendar. Fifteen, fourteen, thirteen, twelve, the countdown was on. And still he was trapped between the two women in his life, not being completely honest with either of them and not entirely sure if he was being honest with himself either.

## 22

## CLAIRE

They'd been together for a few months when she broached the idea of moving to France with Pete. She'd always dreamed of leaving the rat-race of London behind and going to live somewhere remote and beautiful, setting up her own B&B business to make some money. She'd adored her dad's place in France and often dreamed of what it would be like to live there, but when he died she was heartbroken and couldn't bring herself to visit it again, even though it had been left to her. She hated the idea of it falling into disrepair, yet every time she steeled herself to go and started looking at flights, an image of her dad sitting in his favourite chair, smoking a pipe and doing a crossword came into her mind and she just couldn't go through with it. The thought of walking into that empty, abandoned house and knowing that he wouldn't be there was too much for her to handle.

But since she'd been with Pete, she'd started dreaming of them going there together. Somehow it felt more bearable with him by her side. She was in love with him, she knew that now. She'd tried to fight it, to tell herself that he was married and that it was just about sex, but it was a battle she was never going to win. She'd never really been in love before, she'd had plenty of boyfriends but they'd all come to nothing, usually because she got bored and decided to move on. But Pete was different. She didn't know if it was because he was more mature, because she was older and ready to settle down or if they were just a good match, but she was desperate to be with this man and being his bit on the side was no longer enough for her.

She wasn't stupid: she knew that the majority of married men who had affairs never actually left their wives and she wasn't naïve or arrogant enough to think that her situation was any different. *But it can't hurt to ask*, she told herself. And if it all went tits up, she could just move to France on her own and get on with her life.

Sometimes she thought of Pete's wife and children, continuing to live their lives completely unaware of this other life that Pete was living with another woman, and she would feel a pang of guilt and remorse. But then she reminded herself that the marriage was already unhappy, already broken, before she came along. And, she told herself, it was better for the children to have two happy, divorced parents than to have two miserable, together parents. She wasn't particularly maternal and had no interest in having children of her own but she'd make an effort with the kids, build a relationship with them and encourage Pete to spend time with them as much as possible. This would help to alleviate her guilt at what she was asking him to do.

When she first mentioned it to Pete she wasn't at all surprised when he dismissed the idea immediately. After all, it was pretty out there. But she had played her hand slowly and carefully and to be honest it didn't take that much persuasion in the end. They'd had that little bump, when she'd pushed him too far and he'd called it off with her but after a minor panic immediately afterwards she'd known he would come back. Their relationship was too important to throw away, she knew it and he knew it. Within a couple of months, he was not only on board with the idea, he'd got a job and handed in his notice at work. She literally had never felt happier in her life. She could see them together in that farmhouse, curled up together by the log burner in the winter and sitting out on the veranda in the summer, drinking wine, enjoying each other's company, far removed from the relentless hamster wheel of London and far away from his wife too.

They would grow old together there – the ones that got away, their friends would say, the ones that were brave enough to choose a better life. As it got closer to their agreed departure date the excitement practically overcame her. She gave her notice to the temp agency and to her landlord and started sorting through her stuff, giving as much as possible to charity so that she was only taking the bare minimum of things to France. She wanted to shed her old life like unwanted clothes and start again afresh on the continent. She didn't even care if they never got married: all she had ever wanted was him. And now she had him!

The night before they were due to leave, she sat alone in her flat, looked at all the empty space around her and thought, *This is it, I'm never going to be alone again.* She couldn't resist sending him a quick message:

Looking forward to seeing you tomorrow xx.

His response came almost immediately:

Literally counting down the minutes. Can't come soon enough xxx.

The next day she was up and dressed bright and early. As she closed the door to her flat for the last time and put the key through the letterbox, she sent Pete a quick message to let him know she was on the way and then paused, looking at the battered old blue door and revelling in the moment. *This is actually happening*, she thought, *dreams really do come true*. This time tomorrow, she and Pete would be in France, far removed from London, real life, the commute, the complication of Pete's family. *What will we be doing?* she wondered. *Sipping coffee while eating a freshly baked croissant in a Parisian café? Or still in bed, wrapped around each other, the whole day ahead of us, full of possibilities?* She couldn't stop grinning as she walked down the steps and out on to the street, wheeling her suitcase behind her as she headed towards the station.

She made her way to St Pancras Station and found a seat in the café where they had agreed to meet at 9am. As she sipped her skinny latte and looked around at the thousands of people rushing around on their way to work, she felt somehow removed from them all already. *This isn't my life anymore*, she thought, *I'm destined for better*. She imagined Pete emerging from the crowds, walking towards her with that heart-breaking grin he had, and she felt like she was going to explode with joy.

She checked the time on her phone – he was five minutes late. *Typical Pete*, she thought, *he's always keeping me waiting*. Five minutes turned to ten and then to twenty. The first stirrings of doubt began to form in her mind. She checked her phone to see if he'd messaged her but there was nothing. She looked around, scanning the crowds in front of her, desperately looking for his face but it didn't appear.

Forty minutes later, he still hadn't showed up and he hadn't responded to her message asking where he was either. Her mild concern was rapidly developing into full on panic. What the fuck was going on? They were going to miss the Eurostar at this rate. Had he got last-minute cold feet? She had been so convinced that he was beyond that but now she began to wonder again. Could something have happened between yesterday and today to change his mind? Or perhaps something had happened to one of the kids which had delayed him, but he'd be coming later? But why hadn't he messaged her? Should she get on the train? Should she wait? Jesus, it was forty-five minutes now and her head was spinning. The caffeine from the second coffee she'd had while waiting for him had added to her nerves and she was feeling jittery and edgy.

There was no going back now. She had no flat, no furniture and no job. She literally had the bags she carried with her and that was it. She was going to France, with or without him. Only she hadn't allowed the possibility of it being without him to enter her mind before. Now it was all she could think about.

Suddenly she heard the familiar beep of her phone. She felt an immediate flood of relief when she saw his name come up. *He's just running late*, she thought, *no need to overreact*, *it's all going to be fine*. Then she read the message.

Sorry, I can't do it. I can't leave my wife and children, they mean too much to me. You have to understand. Please don't contact me again. I'm changing my number. I'm so sorry. Goodbye x.

It felt like someone had punched her in the stomach. For a few seconds she couldn't breathe as she stared at the message on her screen. She felt the shock permeate every inch of her body and she wanted to run to the toilet and be sick. She typed back:

What the hell, Pete? Is this a joke? It's not funny.

She pressed send and waited for the two ticks to appear, indicating that her message had been received. But seconds turned into minutes and there was no sign of them. He must have turned WhatsApp off. She immediately threw all caution to the wind and called him, something she had never done before. She was relieved when it rang, a chance to talk to him, but the feeling quickly drained away from her as the phone continued to ring, unanswered, before going to voicemail. She immediately hit redial but the same thing happened.

'Shit,' she said aloud. 'Shit, shit, shit.' She looked at the time. If she didn't head to the Eurostar terminal now she was going to miss her train. She had to make her mind up and it had to be now. She threw some coins on the table for the waitress, stood up and walked towards the terminal.

She made it on to the train by the skin of her teeth. She stowed her bags, took off her coat and sat on one of the two seats that she had reserved. Looking at the empty one next to her she felt both enraged and defeated. How could he have done this to her? How could she have been so stupid as to let him do this to her? She'd thought he was this amazing man, that she'd finally met someone special but he was a coward just like the rest of them. Full of bullshit. And now here she was, completely alone, on the fast train to a new life that she didn't know if she wanted to live on her own.

She thought of her dad's house and all the work that was needed to make it liveable in. Could she do it by herself? Could she really live there all alone and start a business? Money wasn't a problem, she had enough in savings from her parents, but would she go mad on her own out there in rural France?

How dare Pete betray her like this! How dare he! He'd had ample opportunity to change his mind before it was too late, why wait until now? God, she was angry. She picked up her phone and tried to call him again. It went unanswered. She tried three more times, not even caring if Kate answered anymore, but it continued to ring out.

She went on to Facebook and looked for his profile. They weren't friends but she knew he had one from when she'd done the usual online stalking of him when they first started hooking up. But it wasn't there anymore, he must have deleted it. She tried Twitter and LinkedIn but there was nothing there either. She didn't have his personal email address and his work emails were probably being forwarded now. She had no other way of contacting him. *Bastard! Bastard, bastard, bastard!*

Would he change his mind, she wondered? Would he call her in the next few days and tell her he'd made a massive mistake and that he was on the way? She allowed herself to hope for a minute, visibly sitting up in her seat at the thought before sinking back down into it. When a married man says they're not coming, they're not coming. It was over.

Her dream had burst as easily as a flimsy balloon at a child's birthday party. She thought about her friends in London. They had known she had a boyfriend and that she was moving to France with him but they didn't know he was married. She wasn't one of those girls who had a tight-knit group of gal pals who gossiped and told each other everything. She preferred to keep her personal life to herself. She'd had a leaving dinner with them a few days ago, they had hugged her, given her presents and told her to keep in touch. The gap she'd left behind would soon be filled by something else as they got on with their lives. They would forget about her and London would forget about her. She felt instinctively that she couldn't go back. She could only go forward.

So France then, or somewhere else? The world was her oyster and the thought filled her with hope all of a sudden. She had no ties, no family, money in the bank, she could literally go wherever she wanted, do whatever she wanted. She would go to Paris, regroup, consider her options and then make a decision.

Screw Pete and his unhappy marriage that he had just

committed himself to for the rest of his life. He would regret this in the years to come, he would remember this as the moment that could have changed his life forever, and he was too chickenshit to go for it. *He's the loser, not me.* And clinging on to that thought, she looked out of the window as London and the UK sped away from her.

# 23

# PETE

Today was the day he was leaving his wife. His passport was burning a hole in his jacket pocket and his holdall, which he'd hastily packed while Kate was in the bath the previous evening, was waiting in the wardrobe. He woke up with a sense of both dread and excitement. He'd tossed and turned for much of the night before eventually falling into a fitful sleep, plagued by a strange dream in which he was walking through Covent Garden naked while everyone stared at him and Kate and Claire looked on, eating croissants together and laughing at him.

When he woke up, he almost wanted to tell Kate about it: she loved a good dream analysis and would probably be able to tell him what it meant but of course he couldn't breathe a word. This realisation almost made him feel wistful, like he had already lost her even though he was lying only a few inches away from her.

A few minutes later the girls bounded into the bedroom, wriggling between them and snuggling under the covers. Kate stirred and sat up, looking briefly across at him before slipping out of bed. 'Rachel's coming early today to take the girls to a breakfast fundraiser at the school. I'll go and help them get ready'.

He nodded and reached for his phone, checking his messages to see if there was one from Claire but there wasn't. He wondered what she was doing right now. She was an early riser so she'd probably be up and about already, getting dressed and finishing her packing. Maybe she'd have some music on and she'd be singing as she packed, in good spirits and excited about the day ahead. He was so envious of her then, her lack of baggage and total freedom to do this without any guilt or fallout.

While Kate was in the bathroom he crept to the wardrobe and checked his holdall. He'd packed light, just some casual clothes and toiletries. He had the money that he'd taken from their ISA, which he'd put into his personal bank account a few weeks ago, so he'd have plenty of cash to tide him over until he started his new job in a few weeks. He didn't want to withdraw any money from their joint account or use their credit card because he knew Kate would be checking it like a hawk and he didn't like the idea of her knowing where he was and what he was spending money on.

The previous Friday had been his leaving party at work. Kate had no idea, of course, she thought he was on a boys' night out with some of his workmates. There had been a fairly impressive turnout, he'd been at the company for years and everyone wanted to wish him well. Claire had asked him whether she should come but he'd told her not to. No one at work knew about them apart from Dan and Carl and so he'd pretty much have to ignore her all night so that they didn't arouse any suspicion which would be increasingly difficult the more he had to drink. He supposed it didn't matter who knew about them anymore but he still felt like he had to keep up appearances, right until the very end and he didn't want people gossiping. He wanted to be remembered as Pete Garland, the upstanding family man who was leaving because he'd got a better job, not for any other reason.

As the night wore on, people started to leave in dribs and drabs, giving him a hug, shaking his hand, slapping him on the back and wishing him well, until it was only him and Dan left, nursing their pints in a corner of the pub.

'Are you absolutely sure about this?' Dan had asked, as he'd known he would.

'No,' he admitted. 'But it's happening now.'

'It's not too late to back out, you know. You could still change your mind.'

'We're leaving on Monday. The tickets are booked. It's done, Dan.'

'But it doesn't have to be, if you're having second thoughts, that's all I'm saying.'

Poor Dan. He'd been a good friend and he'd tried not to judge him too much but it had been clear all along that he simply couldn't get on board with what Pete was doing. A few years ago, Pete would probably have felt the same himself. The thought of abandoning his family and running off with another woman would have been appalling to him. But so much had changed since then.

'I'm having second, third and fourth thoughts,' he confessed. 'But deep down I still feel like I'm doing the right thing. You know, we only get one shot at life and I want to spend it happy, not stuck in an unhappy marriage with a woman who doesn't love me anymore. Given some time, I genuinely think Kate will agree.'

Dan snorted into his pint. 'All right, Pete, you tell yourself that.'

'Look, you don't approve, I get that and I appreciate it. But I want you to know that I'm going to be the best father to my girls that I can be. I love them, Dan, I do.' He realised that he was more drunk than he'd thought and the booze was making him feel emotional. He had to swallow a few times to stop the tears from coming.

'I know you do, Pete, I know. What a situation you've got yourself into, mate.'

They clinked glasses in a morose cheers and looked down at their drinks. Soon after, they hugged it out and went home. There was nothing left to say.

He'd spent the next two days being the usual weekend dad. He'd come so far, there was no point in changing the plan now. The letter he'd written to Kate was hidden among a pile of work papers, ready to be put into position on Monday morning. On Sunday, Kate took the girls to a party and he had a couple of hours to himself. Switching on his laptop to browse the sporting news he had a sudden urge to delete all of his social media accounts. When news got out that he'd left Kate, he imagined that everyone would be clamouring on to Facebook or Twitter to try and gain some clues as to where he was or what he was doing. *Best to delete them all and not give them any ammunition whatsoever*, he thought. He quite liked the idea of becoming anonymous, with no digital footprint. One by one he went onto each social media platform and deactivated his accounts. It was strangely cathartic.

On Friday he'd gone out in his lunchbreak and bought a new phone and a pay-as-you-go SIM card. Currently no one had his new number, not even Claire. When the time was right, he would call Kate so that she had a way of contacting him if there were any emergencies and so that he could speak with the girls. He'd decided to leave his old mobile phone behind – he didn't want to be fielding calls and messages from Kate and all his friends when they found out that he'd done a runner. It would still be there, waiting for him, if he decided to come back.

He looked at the clock. He'd better have a shower: it would

soon be time for him to leave. He glanced over at Kate, who had returned from supervising the girls and was getting dressed in silence, feeling such a mixture of emotions that he could barely contain them. He was fizzing over with excitement at what lay ahead, at the thought of Claire making her way to St Pancras Station, waiting for him in the café they had agreed to meet at. He was as excited as a child on Christmas Day and Claire was definitely the best present he could have asked for. But he also felt jittery and nervous and part of him just wanted to hide under the covers and never come out. It felt like he had an angel on one shoulder who was continuously warning him against doing this while the devil on the other side was jumping with glee and telling him to ignore the warnings. He just had to stop procrastinating and go now; he felt like the walls were closing in on him and if he didn't leave soon, he would never escape.

'I'll see you downstairs. I'll put the coffee machine on,' Kate said, before heading to the girls' bedrooms to make sure they were ready. As soon as he was sure that she was in the kitchen, he grabbed the letter he'd written her and put it on her pillowcase. He figured she wouldn't see it until later that day, when he was long gone. *Just breakfast left*, he thought, *then I'm out*. By the time he got downstairs the children had already left with Rachel. He panicked for a moment, realising that he hadn't even had a chance to say goodbye to them. *Jesus Christ, what the hell am I doing?*

*Calm down*, he told himself, *you'll speak to them really soon. You're not leaving your children, just your wife*. Still, he felt awful about it.

He helped Kate make breakfast and they worked together in a synchrony that only couples who have been together for years can do. He felt like they were preparing the last supper but he had no interest in savouring the moment. Right now, all he wanted to do was get the hell out of there before he changed his mind. The house now felt like a prison that could trap him at any moment. He ate his toast as quickly as possible while Kate made small talk. *She has no idea what's about to happen*, he thought. *She thinks it's just a normal day.*

As soon as he'd finished, he wiped his mouth, stood up, kissed her and prepared to leave. Just a few more steps and out of the front door and he'd be gone. For better or for worse, the decision would be made. He started walking down the hall, his shoes clattering on the tiled floor. The front door was in sight – just five steps, then four and it would be over. He could see the familiar shape of his holdall that he'd put by the front door on his way downstairs, covering it with his coat so it looked less conspicuous. Everything would be better once he was out of the family home, once he saw Claire and she reassured him with her words and kisses. Just a couple of steps to go now.

'Were you ever going to tell me about her? Or were you just going to sneak off like a coward and leave us all behind like discarded toys you no longer want to play with?'

He stopped dead in his tracks. What did she say? Had he heard her correctly? No, he couldn't have done, she didn't know anything. Did she? *Fuck, fuck, fuck!* His body was frozen but the adrenaline started to course through his body, like a deer that realises it's been caught. The last thing in the world he wanted to do was to turn around and face her but he knew, with a sinking feeling, that he had no choice. Slowly he forced himself to look at her. She was standing in the hallway, looking straight at him with pure hatred on her face. And in that moment he knew for sure that, despite how careful he'd been, somehow she had found out about Claire.

'How did you know?' It was a terrible opening line but it was the only thing that he could think of to say to her. He had already determined, in the microsecond he had to react, that there was no point in denying it. She clearly knew and pretending otherwise would just be digging himself deeper into a hole. But right now he had no idea what, or how much, she knew. Half of him felt trapped, in that hallway, with no way of escaping the truth that was finally staring him in the face. But he also felt something else – was it relief? He had been living a lie for so long that it had weighed him down like stones in his pocket, forcing him deeper into the depths of deceit and lies and perhaps now he could finally be free of it.

'Oh, I'm sorry, Pete, did you think you were so clever that I'd never work it out? Or was it that I was just too stupid?' She was practically spitting the words out.

'Neither, Kate,' he spluttered. 'I didn't mean that, I'm sorry.' He felt like a dog, hanging its head in shame, tail between its legs. He could only submit.

'What I don't understand is exactly what your intentions are. Are you planning to run off into the sunset with your younger model, never to be seen again or were you, at some point, planning to own up to your responsibility and be a father? Tell me, Pete, because I'd really like to know.'

Had she read his letter already? No, that was impossible, he'd only just left it on the bed and she'd been downstairs the whole time. Had she discovered it over the weekend, read it and put it back? *Yes*, he thought, *maybe that was it*. In that case she didn't know everything. He breathed a sigh of relief. Yes, she only knew what he wanted her to know and although he wished to God she hadn't seen the letter until after he'd left, it was damage limitation at least.

'Kate,' he began, choosing his words carefully. 'I'm so sorry that you've found out like this. The truth is, I just need some time away, to sort my head out. Of course, I wasn't planning on abandoning you or the girls. I just thought a couple of weeks away from each other might help to clear our heads, you know? Our marriage, well, I don't need to tell you that it's not what it should be. I've not been happy for a long time and I don't think you have either. We need to address this and maybe we need a clean break or maybe we'll come back stronger, but we need time to think.'

She laughed in his face, not with amusement, but with contempt. 'Stop the bullshit, Pete, you're going away with HER for goodness' sake.'

Bloody hell, she knew everything! But how? He was scanning the various options. Had Dan told her? No, he didn't approve but he'd never do that. Had *Claire* spoken to her? No, that was ridiculous. He kept coming back to the same thing – she must have read the WhatsApp messages between him and Claire on his phone. But how? He'd changed his password and he was so careful not to leave it lying around. But that was the only possible explanation.

He felt his legs buckle beneath him and he sat down, on the cold hallway floor, leaning up against the front door – which just minutes ago had been so tantalisingly close. It was over now, he realised. There was no point in pretending otherwise. The image of Claire waiting for him at the Eurostar was slowly slipping away, already becoming a distant dream that he couldn't quite reach.

'I've been miserable, Kate,' he said, looking down at the red and white tiles, fixating on the mosaic patterns so he didn't have to look at his wife. 'I've been miserable for a long time. And then I met her and I just felt alive for the first time in so long. And it made me realise just how depressed I've been and how I need to do something about it. And the longer it went on, the harder it was for me to tell you. And I feel awful, I really do. I never wanted this to happen and I didn't go looking for it. But it did happen and I'm sorry.'

She didn't say anything and slowly he raised his eyes to look at her. She had sat down too, leaning up against the stairs, her head in her hands.

'Do you remember that night we first met?' she asked. The question startled him because of all the things he had expected her to say, it wasn't that.

'Of course,' he replied.

'I saw you, walking back from the bar with a cocky swagger and you told me to sit on your lap and I thought, *What an arrogant prick he is.* And then I fell in love with you and I thought, *No, he's not an arrogant prick at all, he's amazing, he's my Pete.* But you should always trust your first instincts, shouldn't you?'

*How petty of her*, he thought, but fair enough, she was angry and she had every right to be. He tried another tack. 'Are you honestly telling me that you think we're happily married and that everything is okay between us?'

'Of course I fucking don't!' she exploded. 'We can barely stand to be in the same room as each other and you haven't so much as touched me in years.'

'I haven't touched you? You haven't wanted to go anywhere near me, Kate. It feels as though you actually hate me sometimes. Even saying good morning to me is an effort to you. I put up with it, for years, because I knew you were going through a hard time and I wanted to be there for you, but it affected me too.'

'Oh, I'm sorry, Pete, I'm sorry that while I was struggling with motherhood, hating myself and barely being able to make it through the day that it was *so* hard for you. You who got to swan off to work every day and go to swanky dinners with friends and clients as if your life hadn't changed at all. It must have been so very hard.'

Despite himself, he was starting to feel frustrated with her.

This was just so typical of the new Kate and her 'oh woe is me' attitude. Why couldn't she just buck up like everyone else did? 'Kate, our children are five and seven years old. Everyone gets the baby blues but I'm not sure that you can still use it as an excuse.'

He knew it was harsh but it felt so good. They'd spent so many years avoiding confrontation and now all the unspoken words were flooding out and he could finally say the things that he'd been thinking for so long. He watched her face as she slowly composed herself and planned her next move.

'Anyway, Pete, we've digressed. What I'd like to know, as I asked you before, is what your intention is?'

'I just want some space,' he said. 'I want to take some time out and work out what it is that I want. I don't want to spend the rest of my life being unhappy and I don't think you do either.'

'So, are you telling me that you're not leaving me to be with this woman then? That you're just taking a breather?'

'I don't know,' he answered honestly. 'My plan is to go away and work it out.'

'With her?'

'With her.'

'And who exactly is "her"?'

'Does it matter?'

'It does to me.'

He sighed deeply. 'It's no one you know. Just someone I met.'

'Do you love her?'

'Yes.'

She nodded, as if resigned. 'Do you know, Pete, if you'd handled this like a gentleman, if you'd come to me and told me how you were feeling, I would have understood. We could have confronted it and dealt with it. We've been in each other's lives for so long that we owe each other that. But instead, you decided to deceive me for months on end, humiliate me and then scuttle off with your lover without so much as a goodbye to your children. That's unforgivable.'

Now it was his turn to laugh. 'You would have understood? Are you kidding me? You'd have made my life hell, punishing me for the humiliation that I've caused, blaming me for your own embarrassment. All you care about is what other people think. You want everyone to think we're the perfect couple, living in the perfect house, with the perfect children. You really don't care what's actually happening behind closed doors.' He risked a glance at his watch. Could he still make the train? Suddenly, he wanted to leave even more than ever. They weren't going to resolve this right now, sitting on the floor of their hallway, hating each other.

As if on cue, the wind deflated from her sails and she clutched her knees and started sobbing. 'What happened to us, Pete? When did it all go so wrong?'

He knew this was his fault, that he'd been a shitty husband to her but he was in self-preservation mode now and instinctively wanted to put the blame on her.

'It went wrong when you started resenting me even though I'd done nothing to warrant it,' he said. 'I've always tried to be a good husband, and a good father, but it was like I could do nothing right. For the last few years it's like you're just tolerating me being in your life for the sake of the children. You don't really want me around.'

'So rather than ask me what's wrong you just find someone else, is that it?'

'I tried to ask you,' he insisted. 'I tried so many times, but you just shut me out. It's like you gave up on our marriage long ago but couldn't even be bothered to discuss it. And to be honest, Kate, you kind of gave up on yourself too. I don't know what happened to you but you're not the woman I fell in love with, not anymore.'

'How do you think I've been feeling, Pete? Why do you think I've been like this?'

'I don't know.'

'Did it ever occur to you that I was struggling too? That I've been struggling for years watching you live your life like everything's okay while mine is crashing down around me?'

'I gave you everything you wanted, Kate, but it was never enough.'

'It's not about the fucking money, Pete! It's not about the fancy house or the holidays. It's about having a husband who's there for me.'

'I was there for you!'

'How? By sleeping with another woman?'

He sighed. They were going around in circles. This was why his idea to leave without a confrontation had been a good one. They could have saved this conversation for when they'd both calmed down and it would have been a lot more rational.

'Look, Kate, we're both angry, we're both hurt and upset. Maybe I should just go now, and we can talk again in a couple of weeks when we've both had time to calm down.'

'Okay,' she agreed, which surprised him. 'Only, if you really need time to calm down and think about it, you can't go away with her. Surely you know that?'

'So what do you want me to do?'

'Go anywhere, take the time you need, I'll take some time too. I'll tell the girls you've gone away on business. Come back in a couple of weeks and we'll talk again.'

He knew it was a perfectly reasonable request, in fact it was bloody decent of her given everything. For a second he saw the Kate he used to know – the fair, rational person who looked for the positive in every situation. *Should I do it?* He thought. *Should I give her this?* Then he thought of Claire. She'd be absolutely livid. Would she ever forgive him? She'd been amazing up until now but this was pushing it. He was in limbo between two women and he had no idea which direction to go in. But maybe he owed it to Kate to do this for her. All of a sudden the idea of an option C seemed appealing. Perhaps Kate was right. Perhaps some time on his own, away from both women, was what he needed to finally make a decision.

He looked his wife straight in the eye and nodded. 'All right,' he said.

# 24

## CLAIRE

The train emerged from the darkness and just like that, she was back. The English landscape whizzed past her, each field taking her closer and closer to Pete. There would be no ceremony, no welcome party when she arrived in London. No one even knew she was coming. Claire rested her head against the window and looked out at the countryside. It looked exactly the same as it had when she had last seen it – but for her, everything had changed.

It had been five months since she was last on the Eurostar, heading in the other direction towards her new life. Her mind drifted back to that day. She had been in bits when she realised Pete wasn't coming and, after her initial burst of defiance had quickly worn off, had spent the first half of the journey crying quietly and avoiding eye contact with other passengers. Everything she had imagined, anticipated and hoped for had been snatched away from her in an instant and she felt, for the first time in her life, utterly lost. She was used to being on her own and was usually content in her own company, but she had never really known what it was like to feel truly alone until then.

But she had always prided herself on being strong and

independent and after an hour of self-pity she had wiped her eyes, taken a deep breath and given herself a stern talking to. *Screw him*, she thought. She was young and beautiful, with money in the bank and no ties to anyone or anywhere. She could literally do anything or go anywhere she liked. She was truly free and how many people could say that? It wasn't a terrible situation to be in. By the time the train arrived in Paris, she was feeling almost positive. He was the loser in all this, not her.

But then checking into the hotel, she felt another wave of grief for the future that had been taken away from her and she lay on the bed and glanced across to the other side where Pete should have been, smiling back at her and beckoning her to him, and she allowed the tears to come again. She hadn't cried in years and now they were all coming at once, a river spilling down her face, down her body, on to the bedspread. She cried, she raged, she thumped the pillows and then she collapsed, exhausted. After a few minutes she went to the bathroom to clean herself up, then picked up her coat and purse and went downstairs, exiting the hotel on to the busy Parisian street.

She wandered around for a while and then found a bar, feeling the rush of warmth as she walked in and ordered a glass of red wine. She looked around at the rest of the customers, all in groups and pairs, chatting animatedly among themselves, not even noticing the British girl sitting there, alone, the world having crashed down around her. It was amazing how she could go from feeling hopeful to hopeless so quickly, she thought. Was this going to be her lot for the next few days, weeks and months? She couldn't bear it. This was why she hadn't fallen in love before, why she had always called off relationships before they got too serious. It was agony.

One minute she was thinking about jumping on a plane and heading off to Australia – it was spring there, what a wonderful time to go back to the country she had loved when travelling – and the next she was thinking of Pete, his face, his smile, his arms wrapped around her, enveloping her in the lemony smell of him, and realising that she may never see him again and everything else just seemed futile. Perhaps she should go to her dad's house and wait for him there? Maybe he would come.

She sipped her wine and let herself imagine for a minute that Pete was there with her, sitting opposite her, clinking glasses and saying cheers as they realised that they had actually done it. She indulged in the thought that she had won, that she had got him all to herself, that they had their whole future ahead of them and that the only thing they needed to think about was where they were going to go for dinner that evening. But the image quickly evaporated. It was no good to think like that, she was on her own now and she might as well get used to it. She thought about her dad's house. Maybe it was just what she needed right now, a bit of time alone, a project to get stuck into. She could refurbish the house while healing her wounds and then make some major life decisions after that. If she felt happy there she could start the B&B business she had been dreaming of. If it was too lonely being there on her own, she could walk away at any time and make a new plan. As the wine warmed her insides, she felt more resolute. Yes, she had a plan. She ordered another glass of wine and a steak and frites, Pete's favourite dish, and afterwards she went outside and took a walk along the River Seine, absorbing the city, its lights, people, colour and vibrancy. She breathed it in one last time.

She travelled south the next day, not wanting to stay in Paris any longer without Pete there with her. She checked into the B&B they had stayed in together just a few weeks before and walked down through the village to her father's house. The front door was stiff and she had to use her shoulder to push it open.

Inside, she looked around at the dark, dusty rooms,

running her fingers along her father's belongings, his writing desk and his dark leather Chesterfield armchair, breathing in the scent of him which was surprisingly only slightly masked by the musty smell of a house uninhabited for a long time. He was the only man she had ever loved, her father, until Pete. Her two great loves, gone from her life, one by tragedy and one by choice. She located the back-door key, hidden among a pile of papers on the kitchen table, and stepped out onto the veranda. Even though it was a cold, grey autumn day and the neglected garden had become overgrown and wild, the view was still breath-taking. Unspoilt, untouched countryside, save for some farmhouses and gîtes, surrounded her. All she could hear was the trees blowing in the breeze and, in the distance, a dog barking. Her dad was gone, Pete too. She was alone again and she would have to get used to it. Looking around she nodded to herself, this was as good a place as any to do that. She took one last look around and then, shivering, went back inside.

She started work on her dad's house the next day. Armed with cleaning products she scrubbed and polished every floor, every surface, until her hands were red raw and her knees were bruised from crawling on the unforgiving stone floor. She returned to the B&B each evening exhausted, collapsing into bed and feeling grateful for the sleep which came easily after the day's exertion, fighting off the intrusive thoughts that were swirling around her head and threatening to keep her awake.

She went into autopilot mode, making calls to builders, electricians, painters and decorators. Her French, which had become rusty, improved with each day and the friendly B&B owners, who had quickly realised that all was not well but were too discreet to ask, practised with her over breakfast each day, encouraging her, correcting her and praising her.

On dry days she tackled the garden, pulling out weeds,

attacking hedges with vigour and slowly transforming it back to its former glory.

Within three weeks the house was habitable enough to move into. She spent her days clearing out her dad's old stuff and decorating to make it homely. One day she walked into the village for some fresh bread and cheese and saw a little white car parked on the street, with a handwritten 'for sale' sign stuck on to the inside of a window. On a whim she called the owner and two days later she was behind the wheel, driving to the nearest city to go shopping for things for the house.

The days went by quickly, but the nights were long. Winter was coming and the darkness that enveloped the house felt almost claustrophobic. She would light a fire and sit in her dad's battered old armchair, clutching a glass of red wine and trying to immerse herself in a book but her mind always wandered. She was usually pretty content in her own company but her relationship with Pete had opened the door to another way of life and she now missed it acutely. Occasionally she would have a wobble and try to call him but the phone was always switched off. She assumed he had changed his number, a startlingly obvious indication that he had banished all trace of her from his life. After a few glasses of wine she would google him, desperate to find a photo, information, anything that could connect her to him but there was nothing. His social media profiles were still gone and he didn't have a profile on the website of the company he had accepted the job offer from. She even called them once, asking to speak to him, but the receptionist told him that there was no Pete Garland working there and never had been.

She assumed that it would get better over time, this near-constant feeling of grief for the idea of a life that she had lost. She told herself that she would heal eventually and find happiness in her solitude again. But she had too much time during those long, lonely evenings to overthink and overanalyse, and she found herself wondering if she truly had been happy before or whether it was just a foolish sense of pride that she clung on to.

'Look at Claire, she doesn't need anyone in her life to make her happy,' her friends would say after yet another heartbreak, and their envy and praise would make Claire glow with pleasure. But now it all just seemed pathetic. Who was she to think that she was any better or different to everyone else? We all needed someone in our lives. Time passed, quickly and slowly, quickly and slowly again, and the healing didn't come. The days turned to weeks and then to months.

At Christmas the people she had come to know in the village couldn't have been kinder or more generous to her, they had all loved her father and remembered her from her regular visits many years ago, and she received plenty of offers to dine with them in their homes. But she politely declined them all and spent the day alone.

By February the house renovation was nearly complete and she'd started working on the outbuildings, hoping to get them ready for the summer season so that she could rent them out. Most days she walked to the village, stopping to say hi and chat to the locals that she had come to know. Occasionally she would sit and have a coffee with them, feeling proud at how good her French had become. She really wanted to be happy and she tried, she really did. But her heart wasn't in it.

And so here she was, five months after she had boarded the Eurostar alone, on her way back to London again. She just had to see him, to talk to him again, before she could truly let him go. It was an itch that she had to scratch no matter how high the stakes were for her and for him. And given that he had changed his number and she couldn't reach him by email or social media he had left her no choice at all. She was going to have to go to his home and confront him.

She'd looked up his address in his work file when they had first got serious and made a note of it because knowing where he lived had made her feel closer to him somehow. She had checked it on Google Street View so she could see what his house looked like and picture it in her mind when he wasn't with her. But she had kept well away, the north–south divide unspoken but clear in both their minds – north London was Pete's family's domain and south London was hers. Now she was going to cross that bridge and invade his other life and she felt a mixture of excitement, anticipation and terror at what she was about to do.

The train pulled into St Pancras and she grabbed her holdall, stepped on to the platform and made her way towards the Tube station, heading down the escalator to the Northern Line which would take her to north London. Once on the Tube she looked glumly around her, feeling no joy at being back in the capital again. She hadn't missed this place with its busy people, dirty trains and constant crowds. She had come for one reason and one reason only, and that was to talk to Pete. But despite her distaste for London after months of rural living she had accepted that if she had to move back for him, to be with him, she was prepared to do it.

When she had first gone to France she had been incandescent with rage at Pete and the way he had betrayed her so brutally. But her anger towards him had dissipated in the time that they'd been apart. She'd started looking at the situation from his point of view and realised that she'd been asking too much from him by wanting him to move away from his children for her. She'd pushed him too far and paid the price. But maybe if she offered him an alternative solution – they could stay in London, live apart even, and he could be close to his children and be a bigger part of their lives, he might reconsider. She had wondered many times if he missed her. She desperately hoped that he did but there was only one way to find out. It was like taking a protective bandage off, being back here again and she felt exposed and vulnerable. But she had to know one way or another – she couldn't go on with the rest of her life until she knew for sure whether he had said no to the move to France or to her entirely.

The train pulled into Highgate, Pete's stop, and she jumped off. Up on the street, she opened Google Maps on her phone and started following the directions towards Muswell Hill, where Pete's family home was. All around her were mums heading towards the open space of Highgate Woods, pushing babies in prams or helping toddlers with scooters. She felt like a foreigner, completely excluded from this life, this other world that Pete was a part of. A wave of uncertainty washed over her. Had she made a huge mistake in coming here? Should she have left him alone? *Too late to back out now*, she told herself resolutely, and she continued following the directions on her phone, each step bringing her closer to Pete.

She reached their street, a typical suburban, tree-lined road with pretty red-brick townhouses and searched for Pete's house. And then there it was, right in front of her, number 8. It was a lovely house, she thought grudgingly, Kate had clearly put a lot of effort into it. It looked immaculate, with grey-potted olive trees on either side of the stained-glass front door and a beautiful pendant light hanging down from the porch, where two neat little sets of wellies sat side by side. A family home, that's what it was, she realised with a sinking heart, Pete's family. She swallowed the bile that was creeping up into her throat.

*What now?* She looked around. She couldn't just knock on the door without knowing who was in, she needed a safe space to watch and wait, somewhere she wouldn't be seen.

Glancing across the road, she spotted a little alleyway which led down the side of a house. She put her head down and headed towards it, leaning against the brick wall. Yes, she could see the house from here but she looked a bit stalker-ish. She hadn't really thought this through very well, naïvely assuming that there would be a coffee shop opposite the house that she could camp out in, but this was a residential street and there was nowhere to hide.

*I need a car*, she thought, and pulled out her phone to search online for the nearest rental company.

Two hours later she arrived back in the street, parking her hired grey Ford Fiesta a little way down the road from Pete's house, where she had a good view of the front door but wasn't too conspicuous. She leaned back in the seat, took a deep breath and waited. She felt like a police officer on a stakeout and wished she'd bought more snacks, but she didn't have to wait too long before the first sign of activity. Just after 3pm a woman left the house and hurried off down the street. It must be Kate. She studied her carefully, this woman who she had never really thought of as competition, or thought of much at all, to be honest, until the day Pete had chosen her over Claire. Since then, she hadn't been able to think of much else. There was no denying that she was attractive and she certainly knew how to dress. She was wearing skinny jeans and a long grey coat, accessorised with an oversized silk scarf. She looked glamorous but understated, perfect for what was probably the school run given the number of other mums walking down the street in the same direction, pushing younger children in prams and chatting together.

Once again Claire felt a pang of jealousy at not being a part of this other life, where it seemed to become a member you had to have a big house, a wealthy husband, at least one child and to shop at Boden.

She looked at the clock and guessed that she had about half an hour before Kate returned with the children. Now was her chance. She sprang from the car and strode towards the house, feeling the nerves building up inside her with each step closer. When she reached the path that led to their front door she panicked and almost kept on walking but then she steeled herself. She might not get another opportunity like this. Taking a deep breath, she knocked on the door, realising that she had no plan whatsoever for what to do if anyone other than Pete answered. But she needn't have worried because no one came to the door. After a minute, she knocked again but there was no answer. Nobody was home.

She quickly hurried back to the car, feeling conspicuous in this quiet neighbourhood and wondered if there were any curtain-twitching neighbours watching her. She didn't feel safe again until she was back in the car. She waited and watched and soon enough, the mums and prams started to return, this time accompanied by children, talking, skipping and laughing together. A few minutes later she saw Kate, holding two young girls by the hand.

*My God, they look like Pete.* The shock hit her hard. Both girls were chatting animatedly with their mum and laughing at something that she had said to them. They looked so happy, she thought, so innocent and sweet. She had an image of them greeting Pete with cuddles when he came home from work each night, embracing him with their innocent, unconditional love. His own flesh and blood. Of course he couldn't have left them and moved to France. She had been stupid for thinking otherwise. Now she just needed to speak to him, to tell him that she understood, that she wasn't angry with him but with herself.

Kate and the girls walked up the path and into the house, closing the door to the outside world – and to Claire. If he wasn't at home, he must be at work. Which meant that he probably wouldn't be home until at least six o'clock, if not much later knowing him. She considered her options and decided to leave and return again in a few hours. The less time she spent parked outside his house the less suspicious it would be. She turned the car engine on and pulled away from the kerb, following the directions on her phone towards the hotel she had booked. After she'd checked in and dumped her bag in her room, she drove back to Muswell Hill, parked up in the Broadway, and had a mooch around the shops, stopping at a café to get something to eat and looking around at all the yummy mummies and their children, having tea together. She wondered if Pete had been to this café with his kids and guessed that he probably had. The thought made her feel depressed and she quickly paid the bill and left. She decided to head towards Alexandra Palace – she had been to a concert there years before and remembered that it had a big park and views over London. A bracing walk was just what she needed to clear her head. When she reached the top, she stood and looked out over the impressive London skyline. All those millions of people out there, going to work, living their lives and here she was on the edge of the city, neither in it nor out of it, with no idea of what the future held for her.

She looked at her watch and was relieved to see that it had gone five thirty. She'd had enough of killing time in this alien neighbourhood where she didn't belong. She walked back to the car, started the engine and headed back towards Pete's house. This time she had to park a little further down the road, but she still had a good view of the house. She put her earphones in, turned on a podcast about how to start a B&B business, and waited.

Four hours later, she was still waiting, and she was tired, fed up and desperate for a wee. She didn't think that she had missed him returning home, so she considered the alternatives. Perhaps he'd gone out for dinner? Could he be on a business trip? And then she thought, what if he'd left Kate after all? What if he didn't even live here anymore? Could she literally be sitting here for days on end only for him never to show up at all? She had been so desperate to see him that she hadn't even considered the possibility that he wouldn't be there. She felt like a bloody idiot. What was she doing, sitting outside this man's house waiting for him to come home? There must be a better way.

And suddenly she realised – Dan, his former colleague. They were thick as thieves and she was sure he'd known about their affair even though they'd agreed not to tell anyone. She could tell by the way he acted around her, he always seemed a bit nervy and reluctant to engage in conversation. And she could easily contact him using his work email: the generic format was ingrained in her mind after months of temping at the company. It was a risk contacting him but he'd always seemed like a nice enough bloke and she was only asking him to pass a message on to Pete, not to do anything else. The worst thing that could happen was that he'd tell her to sod off and so what, she'd been through worse than that over the last few months. Why hadn't she thought of this before? She immediately pulled out her phone and composed a message:

Dan, hi it's Claire, I used to work on reception? I'm so sorry to contact you out of the blue, and on your work email too, but I need your help. I'm back in London for a few days and I really need to get hold of Pete but I don't have up-to-date contact details for him. I know you may not want to pass on his details to me and I completely understand that but is there any way you can just tell him that I'm in town and that I really need to see him? My phone number and the details of where I'm staying are below.

Thanks so much for your help, Dan.
Claire x

She hit send before she could change her mind. It was nearly 10pm by this point and there was no way she'd get a response until morning, so she decided to drive back to the hotel and wait. She started up the car and despite the anti-climax of not seeing Pete today, she felt a glimmer of hope at the idea of hearing from Dan in the morning. Tomorrow could not come soon enough.

Claire was having coffee in a café near to her hotel when the email from Dan arrived. It was 10am and she'd been hitting refresh pretty much continuously since 8am so her nerves were frayed. Still, he hadn't kept her waiting too long, which she took to be a good sign. She could barely contain her excitement at the fact that he had replied to her. She opened the email and devoured the contents.

Claire, I'm really surprised to hear from
you like this. I thought Pete was with
you? What happened? Did you guys have an
argument? He didn't tell me he was back
in the UK, when did he leave France?
   I'm afraid I can't help you, none of
us have spoken to Pete since he left the
company a few months ago. We all just
thought he'd done a runner to be honest
and was somewhere with you in the depths
of the continent. I've been in touch with
his wife Kate a few times and I'm not

going to lie, I've been pretty pissed off with him that he's made no effort to contact her or see the children at all. It's pretty shitty behaviour. So if you do see him again, please tell him to strap on a pair and get in touch with his wife and kids. The girls were devastated when he left.

Sorry, Claire, I don't mean to take it out on you but I think you've got more of a chance of hearing from him than me and he needs to hear this.

Dan.

She read and re-read the email, perplexed, trying to figure it out in her head. Dan thought Pete had gone to France; she thought he'd stayed with Kate. Neither of these things had happened, so where the hell was he? This didn't make any sense whatsoever. She looked at Dan's email signature, found his number and immediately dialled it. He picked up after three rings.

'Hello?'

'Dan, it's Claire.'

'Oh, hi, Claire.' He seemed surprised to hear from her.

'Look, I don't know what's going on but Pete never came to France. He left me waiting at the station and never showed up. He sent me a message telling me he'd changed his mind and that he was staying with Kate. I haven't heard from him since.'

The silence went on for so long that she thought he'd been cut off.

'Dan, are you there?' she asked.

'I'm here, Claire, I'm just really confused. He definitely didn't stay with Kate: she hasn't seen him since September. I've spoken to her a few times and I'm absolutely sure about that. So if he's not with you, where is he?'

'That's exactly what I want to know.'

'This is pretty messed up, Claire.'

'I know.'

'And he left his phone at home and deleted all his social media accounts too.'

'I know. I've tried all of them.'

'Do you think he's just done a runner? Did he stick two fingers up to everything and just head to a beach in Thailand to be on his own?'

'Possibly, but it doesn't sound like Pete. I can't understand why he'd do that and not make contact with anyone. For a few weeks maybe but it's been months and no one has heard from him. I'm freaking out a bit now, Dan.'

'He told me he'd got a new job, some tech firm, do you know which one it was?'

'Yes, but I checked and he definitely doesn't work there. That's why I came to London, I couldn't think of any other way to reach him. It wasn't until I got here that I thought to email you. I should have thought of it ages ago, I'm kicking myself now.'

'So what do we do now?'

She thought for a moment. 'I don't think we've got any other choice. We're going to have to call the police.'

## 25

## KATE

She looked at the police in surprise. 'What do you mean, "a missing person"? He's not missing, he's in France with his girlfriend.'

The male officer shuffled in his seat, looking embarrassed while the woman spoke. 'I appreciate that this is a very delicate situation, Mrs Garland, but we were contacted by a woman who claims that he disappeared some months ago and no one has heard from him since. Can you tell me exactly when you last saw your husband?'

'Monday September 7th,' she replied without hesitation. 'He'd been having an affair for months and he left me. I found a note in our bedroom telling me that he had met someone else. I haven't heard from him since.'

It wasn't the full story but everything she had said was true and the police didn't need to know about the confrontation that they'd had that morning or the agreement they'd subsequently made. No one did but her and Pete.

'Do you still have the note?' the officer asked. She nodded and went to retrieve it from its hiding place between the pages of a book in her bedside table. She'd thought about throwing it away a number of times but had never actually done it. The officers both read it before turning back to her. 'Have you tried to contact him?'

'I tried everything,' she replied. 'He left his phone at home and deactivated all his social media accounts. I messaged all his friends and family and I sent him a number of emails. I contacted one of his friends from work, Dan, and he told me that he'd left his job the week before. Eventually Dan agreed to meet me in person and he told me the whole story about Pete's relationship with this woman – Claire. I assume it's her who has reported him missing. Are you saying that he didn't go with her after all?'

The officer simply replied, 'From what we understand, Mrs Garland, no one has seen or heard from your husband since the morning of September 7.'

She stared at the police officers, not knowing what to say to them. The secrets that she had been keeping from everyone for so long about what really happened that morning were threatening to burst out of her and she had to use every ounce of strength she had to hold them back. 'I have no idea where he is,' she said. 'He walked away from our marriage and our life. He made it very clear that he didn't want to be contacted. He lied to me repeatedly. I assumed he'd run away with this woman and now you're telling me he hasn't. I don't know what to think.'

'You say he left his phone behind? Can we take a look at it, please?'

'Of course,' she said and went to retrieve it. 'It'll need a charge.'

'What about his bank accounts? Has he withdrawn any money at all?'

She explained about the money taken from their ISA a few weeks before he left. 'Since then, he hasn't withdrawn any money. I assumed that he'd opened a new bank account. He hasn't given me any money either, I've been relying on our savings until I can earn enough money to pay for the mortgage and bills.'

'What about his passport, driving licence, those sorts of things?'

'All gone, I searched the house from top to bottom after he left and he'd taken them with him.'

'And you say he hasn't been in touch at all?'

'No, I haven't heard a thing. As you can imagine I was hurt and furious. We have two young children who asked for him almost constantly at the beginning. I didn't know what to say to them, it was horrendous. I was desperate to get in contact with him and find out what was going on. I even tried his mother, who he's estranged from, but she hadn't heard from him either. For the first few months I sent regular emails to him begging him to reply but he never did. I don't even know if he read them.'

The female officer looked at her sympathetically. 'Does he have a laptop or computer at home, Kate?'

'Yes, he has a laptop. Would you like it?'

'Yes please, we'll need to take his phone and laptop away. We'll also need to search the house and take a sample of his DNA from something like a toothbrush or hairbrush, anything he left behind that we can use.'

'That's fine,' Kate said. She looked at the police officers. 'So, what do you think has happened to him?'

'That's what we're going to try and find out. We'll need a list of all of his friends and relatives, work colleagues and so on – anyone that he may have been in contact with. Can I ask, did you notice any changes in his mood or behaviour before he left?'

'Well obviously you know that our marriage wasn't in great shape, given that he was leaving me for another woman,' Kate said. 'But honestly? No. He seemed absolutely fine, happy really.

Now I know why of course. So no, he wasn't depressed, if that's what you're asking.'

'Were you arguing a lot, Kate?'

'Not at all. We actually got on fine. We weren't passionately in love but we rubbed along okay together. I was so distracted with the children that I didn't realise it wasn't enough to keep us together until it was too late.'

'Did he have any history of mental health problems?'

'Pete? No. He's about the most level-headed person you could possibly meet.'

'Is there anyone Pete might have fallen out with?'

'Not that I know of – well apart from me and all of my family and friends but that was after he left,' she said, laughing dryly.

'Can you think of anywhere at all that he might have gone?'

'Nowhere that I haven't tried already. I've spoken to everyone I can think of and none of them have heard from him. I'll give you all of their contact details.'

The officer nodded. 'That would be helpful, thank you. What about places that he loved – maybe somewhere you went on holiday regularly? A holiday house?'

'No, we never went to the same place twice and we don't have a holiday house. I'm sorry I can't be more helpful, I'm extremely thrown by all this.'

The woman looked at her kindly. 'I understand, Mrs Garland. I think that's all we need for now, thank you for your time.'

As they stood up to leave, Kate asked, 'So what happens next?'

'We'll search the house and take a look at his phone and laptop. We'll speak to his friends and family and we'll also run some checks to see if we can trace his movements over the last few months. We'll keep you updated and you can contact us at any time if you have any concerns or questions, okay?'

'Okay, I understand, thank you.'

'We'll speak again very soon, Mrs Garland.'

After they left, she sat on the sofa, shaking. She'd relaxed, she thought, she'd finally relaxed after months of being on edge and this was her punishment. Just as she thought that things had settled down, this had happened. What on earth did she do now? She looked at the time – it was nearly 3pm. She had to get to school to pick up the girls. They'd be so excited about the disco but she knew that there was no way she could keep up the pretence of normality this afternoon. She needed time to think and to process what had just happened. With shaking hands, she picked up the phone and called Lottie.

'Lottie, I'm so sorry, I've just been sick. No, I'm fine, I think it was something I ate for dinner last night. Look, I'm so sorry to ask but is there any chance you can pick the girls up and take them to the dance for me?'

Lottie was full of concern. 'Of course I can, Kate. I'll swing by and pick up their change of clothes on the way to school. If you're feeling peaky just leave them outside the front door for me. Look after yourself and I'll drop them home after pizza. I really hope you feel better soon.'

'Thank you,' Kate said weakly, hanging up the phone and curling up into a ball on the sofa. It was finally time to confront the truth. Everything she had felt over the last few months – the shock, anger, fear, loss, guilt and the sense of betrayal was real but she hadn't been honest with Erin or the police about what had really happened that morning. The only two people who knew were her and Pete. But it had been there, etched into her memory, all along. The deal they'd made and the promises he'd given her. It was time to face what had really happened to Pete after she last saw him on Monday 7 September.

## 26

## PETE

'All right,' he heard himself saying to Kate. 'I'll take some time out, on my own, to figure things out. How much time?'

'As much as you need,' she replied. 'As long as it takes for you to decide what you really want. Do you want to fight for this marriage, to fight for all that we built together and our children, or do you want to end it?'

'And what about you? What do you want to do?'

'I need some time to work that out, too.'

He nodded. 'Okay.'

'Where will you go?' she asked.

'I'm not sure,' he replied. 'I'll rent a holiday cottage, it's out of season now, it won't be difficult. Somewhere in the middle of nowhere where I can be alone, just me and my thoughts.' As he was saying the words he was thinking of Claire, who would have arrived at the station by now and would be waiting for him to join her. He had to tell her that he wasn't coming. 'I just need a minute,' he said.

She looked at him and nodded, the cogs turning in her head as she realised what he needed to do. He went upstairs to their bedroom and sat on the bed. Looking at his phone he saw a message that Claire had sent earlier.

Just closed the door to the flat for the last time. Heading to the station. Can't wait! Will get you a cappuccino 😊 xx

He hadn't cried for years but as he looked at the message he felt the tears pricking his eyes and before he knew it, he was sobbing. How had he got into this whole sorry mess? He was being pulled in so many different directions and his mind was whirring through the options, unable to settle on the right one for more than a minute or two before it was moving to the next. Downstairs, just moments ago, he was decided but now, looking at her message he was torn again. What was the point, really, of going off on his own when he could be with the woman he loved? Was he really that unsure about whether he was doing the right thing or was he just scared? What if he decided after a week or two that Claire was definitely the one for him, but she didn't want him anymore? What if Kate didn't want him either and he ended up completely on his own? Shit, shit, shit, what should he do?

When he looked up Kate was standing in the doorway looking at him in stunned silence as he clutched his phone and sobbed.

'Jesus, Pete, you really do love her, don't you?'

In spite of himself, he nodded.

'So, what's so amazing about this woman that you can't bear to leave her waiting for you but you can bear to leave me and your children, your flesh and blood?' Her earlier anger that seemed to have dissipated was back with a vengeance. 'Is it because she's young and beautiful? Does she not nag you like I do, Pete, is that it? Because let me tell you, we all end up nagging in the end. You might think you're free of the old ball and chain but you're just putting on a new one, you'll see.'

'Kate, come on, you know it's about way more than nagging. It's about the state of our marriage.'

'Let me guess, she gets you. She, like, *gets* you in a way that I don't anymore. Or perhaps I never have. Is that about right?'

It was so close to right and, feeling completely out of control for the first time in his life, he shouted back: 'Yes, that is about right, Kate. She does get me. She loves me. She's interested in me, my life, my feelings.'

'And I'm not?'

'No, you're bloody not!' He was really getting into it now. 'All you care about is keeping up appearances. As long as everything looks shiny on the outside that's good enough for you. It's like you're a hollow shell, all beautiful on the outside and empty inside. You don't care about what's really going on behind closed doors. Because what is going on behind closed doors, Kate? Nothing – absolutely nothing. We never talk, really talk, to each other. I don't know where you are but it's not with me.'

He was feeling completely hysterical now, torn between panic that Claire was waiting for him, wondering where he was, and relief that all the feelings he'd kept to himself for so long were coming out.

'And whose fault is that, Pete?'

'Yours!' he said incredulously. 'It's your fault, Kate. It's been like living with a cold fish rather than a wife for the last few years. Are you surprised, really, that I had to look elsewhere for love?'

'A cold fish? Did you really just say that?'

'Yes, I did. When was the last time we had sex? When was the last time we even kissed or cuddled?'

'The last time we attempted to have sex, you couldn't get it up. I know why now.'

'Of course I couldn't get it up, I was afraid of rejection. From my own wife. Because you look at me with such contempt I feel like a failure, all the bloody time.'

'You feel like a failure? What about me, Pete? I already know I'm a terrible mother and now I'm being told I'm a terrible wife too – no, even worse, I'm a cold fish.'

*Here we go again with the I'm a terrible mum card.* She'd pulled this one out so many times over the years that he'd grown tired of it. She was pathetic. 'Why do you think that is, Kate? Maybe it's because you have a nanny looking after our children every day while you sit around staring into space or shopping for lampshades. Perhaps if you spent more time with them you'd be a better mother.'

He would never forget the look on her face, as long as he lived. Immediately he knew he'd gone too far. 'Look, Kate, I'm sorry, I shouldn't have said that. You're a brilliant mother, the children absolutely adore you. You just need to let this whole issue go and move on. It's all in your head, that's all. No one else thinks it.'

'Apart from you, clearly.'

They were getting nowhere and he was starting to calm down again now. This argument had cleared his head and he knew more than ever that he had to get away from this house, from Kate, once and for all. He had already calculated that he was going to miss the Eurostar but he could easily catch one later that morning and meet Claire in Paris. Had he decided, then? Was that what he was going to do? He thought again about being alone in a holiday cottage by the beach, just him and his thoughts. He had a couple of weeks before he started his new job and, in any case, he could work remotely, wherever he was. Maybe he could go fishing, he used to love that and he hadn't done it for years. Perhaps it was finally time to put himself first, before either woman. He'd had a mad, crazy few months, he was on the verge of losing it and he needed some time to just calm the fuck down. But then he thought again about Claire, about the life they had planned, and his heart ached.

'Look, we clearly have a lot to say to each other, a lot of things that we probably should have said a long time ago. Maybe if we had, we wouldn't be where we are now. I think I should go now, give us both time to cool down, and we'll talk again.'

'Go where, Pete? Where are you going to go?'

They looked at each other but she knew the answer before he'd even spoken. Perhaps she even knew a few seconds before he did. Defeated, she turned away from him and walked back down the stairs. He took a minute to compose himself before following behind her, eyeing his holdall which was still on the floor by the front door. All he had to do now was pick it up, open the door and leave.

Just as he reached the bottom of the stairs he heard her speak. 'Is she a good fuck, Pete, is that it?'

*Oh, for God's sake, can't she just let it go now? This is getting ridiculous.* All he wanted to do was to end this conversation and get out. But before he could stop himself, he swung around to face her. 'Yes, she's a great fuck. She's the best sex I ever had. Literally ever. Which is quite refreshing after being married to a cold-hearted, uncaring, frigid bitch like you for so long.'

Kate looked at him with such hurt and shock that he almost reached out to comfort her, to tell her that he was sorry and that he didn't mean it. But before he could, her expression was quickly replaced by contempt. 'I'm sorry that I've been such a disappointment to you for all these years, Pete. Well, I'm delighted for you. Clearly you've successfully traded me in for a new model with no previous history. Although does she know that you come with some baggage? She might not be so keen to look after two children. That's assuming that you still want to be a part of their lives now you're living the dream?'

'You know what? She can't wait to meet the girls – she's really looking forward to getting to know them and spending time with them. She wants to be a big part of their lives. I think she'll make a brilliant mum, the girls are going to absolutely adore her. She has so much love to give and she's already planning for them to come out and spend the holidays with us. So you'll get what you want in the end, Kate. You'll get to be all alone and miserable, wallowing in your perfect, pristine house without any of us around to spoil it for you.'

And with that he leaned down to pick up his holdall and hoist it onto his shoulder. He knew he'd been a bastard but he no longer cared. France was calling and he could almost taste the wine and cheese he'd be eating in Paris in a few hours. He'd call Claire on the way to the bus stop and tell her that he'd missed the train but that he'd catch the next available one. Perhaps she'd even wait for him at St Pancras so that they could travel together. He pictured her beautiful, smiling face, greeting him at the exit to the underground station, clutching a coffee for him and opening up her arms to him. He felt a rush of pleasure at the image, which would be a reality in less than an hour's time.

*Yes*, he thought, *yes, I've finally made my decision once and for all.* And then everything went black.

## 27

# KATE

S he hadn't meant to kill him. That was literally the last thing she ever wanted to do. To deprive their children of a father was unforgivable, no matter what he had said or done to her. But she had been so incandescent with rage at the horrible vitriol that was coming out of his mouth, the way he had described her, the way he had suggested that this whore would be a better mother than her and in that moment she just wanted to hurt him. That was all – to hurt him like he had hurt her with his words. It was like she'd finally exploded after years of bubbling under, and she was temporarily out of control, a maniac with one sole purpose – to punish the person who had caused all her pain. It was only for a few seconds but it was enough. Horribly, horribly enough.

She'd found out about the affair a few weeks before. To be fair to him, he'd played it out well because she hadn't suspected a thing before that. It was probably testament to what a sham their marriage had become that she didn't even notice her husband had been cheating on her for months.

But then one Sunday morning when he'd taken the girls

swimming, she heard a phone beeping and out of curiosity she followed the sound to the coat rack. Rifling through his coat, she found his phone nestled in a pocket. He must have put it in there before he left and forgotten about it when he decided not to bother with a coat. Looking at the screen she saw a message from someone called C. It was a link to a website and, underneath, the words:

Three weeks tomorrow x.

The message itself was fairly innocuous but her interest was piqued. Before she could stop herself she'd entered the password to his phone, which she'd known for years. When it came up as incorrect, she frowned. When had he changed his password? She felt a growing sense of unease as she stared at the phone and was suddenly determined to get into it somehow. Taking it back into the kitchen she looked at the clock. She still had another forty-five minutes before Pete would be back.

Staring at the phone she ran through some ideas for passwords. How about the girls' dates of birth? She tried a combination of them both but again she got the incorrect password message. She tried his favourite football club. Wrong. She tried again with the number one at the end. Wrong. She tried her own name. Wrong. She would run out of attempts and lock the phone if she wasn't careful. She scanned through the list of possible options in her mind.

Then she remembered an old password he used to use, years and years ago, way before marriage and children. A combination of the name he'd given to his first ever car, Diana, and his year of birth. She'd laughed so hard when he'd told her. 'Who calls their car Diana?' She tentatively typed the password in and, to her relief, the home screen appeared. She was in.

She immediately opened WhatsApp, reading the message from C and clicking on the link that she had sent. It was for a hotel in Paris. *Was C his PA?* she wondered, was this a business trip? But she already knew deep down that it wasn't. She scrolled right up to the beginning of the message thread, past months and months of messages until she got to the top. Then she started reading.

Twenty minutes later, she reached the end. She hadn't even realised that she had been clutching her chest with one hand the whole time. Her heart was pounding, her hands were clammy, and she struggled to catch her breath as she tried process what she had just read. *The bastard, the absolute bastard.* The messages had started off brief – just random days and times but as time went on they had become longer and more explicit.

She didn't have all the pieces of the jigsaw puzzle but she had enough to see the general picture. He was having an affair with this 'C'. And they were planning to go to Paris together in three weeks. Was it a dirty weekend away or something more? When she saw how long ago the first message was she felt sick. They'd been at it for months. She couldn't believe this was happening, yet the evidence was right there in front of her.

*What do I do now?* She looked at the clock and realised that she had to decide because Pete would be back soon. Closing her eyes, she took a few deep breaths to calm herself down and made a snap decision – she wasn't ready to deal with this right now, she needed time to get her head around it. If she confronted him now, she'd have to do it with the girls around and she knew she'd absolutely lose it. No, she needed to calm down first and to work out how she was going to approach this. She'd put the phone back, she decided, and pretend like nothing had happened for now. Standing up quickly she had to clutch the back of the chair to steady herself. But then Pete would know that she'd read the message, she thought. *Shit shit shit.* Could she mark it as unread? She pressed a few buttons and breathed a sigh of relief when it worked. Then she put the phone back in his pocket.

There were hours left to go before the girls went to bed. After that, she could have it out with him but until then she'd have to act normal. How the hell was she going to do that when she knew what she did? She wanted to scream and yell, to throw every insult under the sun at him the minute he walked through the door. *The bastard, the utter bastard!* How could he have done this to her? And to their children? All this time, she had been trying so hard to make the perfect family home for them and it had all been for nothing – he'd been enjoying a whole other life with another woman. *Maybe I could find a way to forgive a one-off fuck*, she thought, *we're hardly love's young dream at the moment and I'm not naïve, these things happen.* But this was totally different. He wasn't coming to her admitting his mistake, begging for forgiveness and asking for another chance. No, quite the opposite, he was in deep with this other woman. A couple of messages had unsettled her. Was he thinking of leaving them? Was this Paris thing more than just a few days away? It was hard to tell because the messages were usually vague but she had a sinking feeling that there was more to it. She felt in the pit of her stomach that he had checked out on their marriage. What was she going to tell the girls? What was she going to tell her friends and family? She'd be left to face the music, alone and humiliated, while he swanned off into the sunset.

*And what have I ever done to him but try to be a good wife and mother?* she thought angrily. *I've always been loyal to him. I gave up my career to raise our children, I stayed at home so he could continue to live his old life like nothing had changed. And this is how he repays me?* But even as she told herself that she was blameless, she knew her words were only half truths. She felt the last shred of self-confidence that she had only just been hanging on to start to rip apart. Who was she kidding? She was hardly the dream housewife. Yes, she had done these things, but she had failed at it and she had resented it. She had blamed him – he knew it and she knew it. And this was her comeuppance.

But she didn't deserve this. No one deserved this. The lies, the deceit – they'd been together for over fifteen years, he owed her more than this. He had never actually told her that he was unhappy and he should have spoken to her first, he should have confronted the situation head-on and given them a chance to fix it before he went looking elsewhere. Would it have even made a difference, she wondered? Even if they'd still been as in love as ever, would his head have been turned by this woman anyway? Had there been other women? Did it simply come down to the fact that he was a cheater? How had it all come to this?

The sound of children dumping swimming bags on the floor by the front door and running into the kitchen jolted her out of her thoughts.

'Mummy, Mummy!' Maggie shouted, immediately climbing on to her lap. Kate wrapped her arms around her daughter and held on to her tightly, breathing in the familiar smell of chlorine and trying not to cry. 'What's for lunch, Mummy?' Lily, always ravenous after swimming, asked as she stuck her nose in the fridge.

Before she had a chance to answer, Pete walked in. He looked at Kate and frowned. 'You okay, Kate? You look pale.'

'I think I might be coming down with something, actually,' she replied. 'I'm feeling a little peaky.'

'Poor Mummy,' Maggie said, putting her little hand on her mum's forehead. 'Do you need some Calpol?'

She smiled weakly. 'Thanks, darling, I think perhaps I just need to rest up for a little bit and then I'll be just fine. So how about you and Daddy go out for burgers?'

The girls squealed with excitement and Pete didn't look disappointed either. He loved McDonald's and it was a rare treat in their household. 'Are you sure you'll be okay on your own?' he asked.

She nodded. 'I'm fine, you go.'

'Should we bring you anything back?'

'No, it's okay, I'm just going to go back to bed for a bit. I'm sure I'll be fine later.'

After he'd ushered the children back out of the house, Kate considered making a coffee before pouring a glass of wine instead, and sat down to decide on her plan of action. She would have to confront him tonight and tell him that she knew about the affair. He'd probably deny it at first but once he realised there was no getting out of this situation he'd have to admit it. Then what? She doubted that he was going to get down on his knees and beg for her forgiveness. Was it worth trying to persuade him to fight for their marriage? Did she even have it in her for a fight anymore? Should she just pack a bag for him and present him with it that night, telling him to go? Should she leave with the girls and go to Erin's house? *No*, she decided immediately, *this is our home and he is the one who has to go.*

So that was it. They'd have it out and then she'd kick him out.

*And shit!* They were meant to be going to Greece next week. *Well screw him*, she thought. *Me and the girls will go without him and we'll have an amazing time. And he can stay in miserable old London, shagging his mistress and doing whatever he wants. I don't care. He won't be my problem anymore, I'll have kicked him out.*

Except that she never did. She could never really understand or explain why. Was it because she preferred to stay in denial about her life and her marriage, because she was waiting for him to say something, or because she was simply too tired or too afraid for a confrontation? Either way, they had all trooped back from McDonald's, high on fast food and she'd simply put the kettle on and got on with her day. So many times she was on the verge of saying something, of confronting him and asking for the truth, but each time the words couldn't quite escape from her mouth. She hated herself, with every minute of every day that she pretended that everything was fine, she hated herself and what she had become. Yet still, she did nothing.

They even went on holiday together and the bastard pretended everything was fine the whole time. Oh, he was the doting father, tossing the girls around the pool and making them shriek with joy, chatting to the other parents around the pool, all the other wives cooing over him like they always did. Normally it made her feel proud, that he was hers, but now she just felt defeated. In the evenings he'd go to the bar and order her favourite drink, presenting it to her with a flourish. She waited for him to say something, or for her to say something, but neither of them did. It was like they were both actors in their ridiculous travesty of a life. One night there was a live singer at the hotel bar, crooning out some horribly cheesy tunes and some of the other couples got up to dance.

'Go on Mummy and Daddy, have a dance,' Lily pleaded. She looked at Pete and he looked at her, and then he scooped Lily up and carried her to the dance floor. 'I want to dance with my little princess,' he said, and she wrapped her little legs around him. So Kate had grabbed Maggie and taken her on to the dance floor. To any onlookers, they would have seemed like a perfectly happy family. Inside she was in bits. On the plane home, while the girls slept, she had sobbed quietly.

'What's wrong?' Pete had asked, looking at her in concern.

'Oh, it's nothing,' she replied. 'I always get sad after a holiday.'

He nodded, then grinned. 'Remember when we went to Thailand before the kids came along and you cried all the way home? I kept trying to console you but you weren't having any of it. You just kept saying, "It was just so lovely, Pete". Then we got home, you put the washing on, unpacked, poured a glass of wine and said, "It's *so lovely* to be home".'

The memory of the couple they used to be, the person she used to be, had made her sob even harder. He had put his arm around her, the first time he had held her all holiday, and said: 'It'll be fine, Kate. You'll be fine when we get home.' In that moment she had loved him and hated him in equal measures.

They got home and life carried on as usual. Hours turned to days and before she knew it the day that had been marked in her mind from the minute she saw that message from 'C' – *three weeks tomorrow* – arrived and she still hadn't said anything. She had lain awake in bed for most of the night, watching him sleep and contemplating waking him up to confront him. She almost did it several times, reaching out a hand to prod him awake, before withdrawing it again. The previous night he'd packed a bag and toiletries – he thought he'd been subtle but once she was alert for the signs of deception they were so obvious that she couldn't believe she'd missed them before. She hadn't breathed a word of what she'd found out to anyone, not even Erin. She was too embarrassed and too frightened to admit that it was really true. What the hell was she going to do on her own? The thought terrified her more than the thought of actually losing Pete.

But still she didn't say a word. Not even when he woke up, looked across at her to check if she was awake (she was but she was pretending not to be). Not when the girls bounded in a few minutes later and climbed into bed. And not when he enveloped both girls into a big bear hug. Not long after that, Rachel arrived to pick up the girls. It had been a strange coincidence that they had a breakfast fundraiser at the school the day that she knew he was due to go to Paris. Surely it was a sign that she should finally confront him? Lily and Maggie had asked her to go to the school event too but she knew that it was the very last chance she would have to talk to Pete. Somehow, she had always known that it would come down to the final moment.

When he walked into the kitchen she breathed in the familiar lemon scent of him for what, she realised, might be the last time in a long time. She wanted to throw herself at him, to beg him not to go, to stay and fight for their marriage but she didn't. Instead, she made breakfast. While they ate, she made small talk with him, watching him closely for any signs that he was going to break and tell her everything. But he seemed so normal, as if nothing was wrong. She couldn't understand it at all. She waited, and waited, willing herself to say something and finally, as he got up to leave, the strength that she had been lacking for so long finally surged up inside her.

'Were you ever going to tell me about her?'

She saw his whole body go rigid. She could practically see the cogs in his mind whirring as he tried to work out what to say and what to do. She had a fleeting moment of satisfaction about the fact that she had outwitted him, this man who thought he was so clever, before remembering that it was really her who had lost.

After that, it was all a bit of a blur. The furious exchange, the angry words spoken to each other. In that moment she had been desperate for him not to go with this other woman even though she knew that their marriage had fallen apart long ago. She couldn't bear the thought of him being with someone else. She felt all the rage and the resentment that had been sleeping inside her for so many years come to the surface. What a pretence their marriage had been! All this time they had been lying to each other – her pretending that everything was fine and him thinking she was a cold fish.

But it was when he mentioned the girls that she finally snapped. It was her raw spot and he'd hit it bang on. The idea of this other woman being a better mother than her – of the girls adoring her, of them loving this 'C' more than her. And he seemed so smug about it, the bastard. And something inside her snapped. As he turned to leave, to walk away from her and the life she had worked so hard to build she was seeing red, she was so furious, so she grabbed the first thing she could find – a stone ornament of a naked woman that she had bought from an art gallery and Pete had rolled his eyes at when he heard how much it cost – and she had whacked him over the head with all her might. And then again, and then again.

But she hadn't wanted to kill him. She had just wanted to hurt him, the way that he had hurt her with his horrible words. And when he fell to the ground with a sickening thud and lay motionless in the hallway, all the anger deflated from her like a burst balloon and she sat down on the floor next to him and stared at the unresponsive body of the man she had loved for half her life. She knew she should call an ambulance but she couldn't move. Her body was cemented to the floor. And surely she hadn't done much damage, she'd only hit him a few times and she wasn't particularly strong, he'd wake up any moment with a headache and be on his way. Time ticked on but still she sat and stared, unable to process the seriousness of what had just happened, completely incapable of accepting that she had just killed her husband.

Eventually the sound of the post being shoved through the letterbox and landing on the tiled floor, just centimetres from Pete's head, brought her back to reality with a sickening jolt. This time she looked at Pete, really looked at him, and finally understood that he was dead. Suddenly her body came back to life and she started scrabbling around in a panic and trying to slide her body backwards along the floor, to get as far away from him as possible. She put one hand to her mouth and stared at him in horror. What had she done?

She stood up and paced around the house, frantic, trying to

work out what to do next. *Perhaps it is all just a nightmare*, she thought, but every time she went back into the hallway, there he was on the floor. What had she done? What did she do now? Should she call someone? Erin? The police? Of course she had to call the police. But then they would arrest her and what would happen to the girls? They'd just lost their father and now they would lose their mother, too. They would be known forever as the girls with the murderer mother. Had she actually done this? Had she actually killed her husband? No, surely that wasn't possible. She walked slowly back up to him, peering at his face, still clinging on to the hope that he was just unconscious. Gingerly she put two fingers to his neck. No pulse. He was definitely dead. She backed away again, staring at him in fresh horror.

She ran up the stairs, desperate to get away from him. Thundering into their bedroom she sat on the bed, her heart pounding. Something on the pillow caught her eye and she turned to look at it. It was an envelope with her name written on it. She grabbed it and opened it, reading the words quickly. It was a note, telling her he was planning to leave her. He must have put it up there knowing that she wouldn't see it until later that day, after he was long gone. He was a bastard, a coward of a man. But still, he didn't deserve to die.

*Think*, she told herself, *think!* But she couldn't, her mind was a complete mess, suspended somewhere between reality and disbelief, unable to comprehend that less than a couple of hours ago she was having breakfast with her husband and now he was dead on their hallway floor. She went to the kitchen and poured a glass of whisky to try to calm herself down. As the liquid coursed through her body her breathing began to slow down and she started to focus again. She had to think.

What were her options now? If she called Erin right now to

tell her what had happened what would she tell her to do? She'd say to call for an ambulance. But it was too late for that now, he was dead. The only option was the police but how could she explain what had happened? Even if she could convince them it wasn't premeditated, she was still a killer, there was no doubt about that. She would go to prison. Their private lives would be splashed all over the newspapers, there would be a court case. Her life would be over, her children's lives would be ruined. Where would they live? Would Erin have them? Her new boyfriend Scott seemed lovely but would he agree to take in two damaged children who weren't even Erin's, let alone his? And she wouldn't cope in prison, she knew she wouldn't, she couldn't hack it. And why should she go to prison anyway, for an accident? She hadn't meant to kill him, it had been a terrible, tragic accident.

Should she kill herself? She deserved to die, after all she had taken someone else's life. Death seemed a better option than prison right now. But then what would happen to the girls? Robbed of both their parents in one day, having to grow up with the knowledge of what had happened. No amount of counselling would ever be enough. She would ruin their lives, too, with her cowardice.

*And whose fault is this really?* she thought, suddenly, angrily. *This is Pete's fault. He drove me to this with his lying and his cheating and his cruel words. If it wasn't for him, this would never have happened! I'm not going to let him ruin my life, why should I?* And although she knew that what she had done was inexcusable, it made her feel better. She felt the blame shifting to him and it comforted her immediately.

And then she thought again of her girls, her beautiful, sweet girls. She had to protect them, she had to do whatever it took to protect them. She had done a terrible thing and she would have to live with that for the rest of her life, that would be her punishment, but now she had to make this go away. For everyone's sake.

The sound of Pete's phone beeping made her jump. She reached into his coat pocket and pulled it out. It was a message from C.

Where are you?

This was it, this was the moment that would define her future and her girls' future. And in that moment, she made her decision. She was thinking sharply, concisely, for the first time in years. She quickly typed back:

Sorry, I can't do it. I can't leave my wife and children, they mean too much to me. You have to understand. Please don't contact me again. I'm changing my number. I'm so sorry. Goodbye x.

The phone rang almost immediately. And then again. She stared at it, willing it to stop ringing and eventually it did. She took another big gulp of whisky and felt better. That was the first problem solved. What did she do now?

The solution was almost too easy, she thought, after all he was leaving her anyway, the evidence was plain to see in the note that he had left her that morning, written in his own hand. Perhaps other people even knew about it. So why not act like it had happened just as he had planned it? How would anyone know any different? The only person who knew was this C person. But if there was no way of contacting him, she'd have to give up eventually. After all, it couldn't be the first time a man had chickened out of leaving his wife at the last minute. Would she come to their house? She doubted that Pete would have told her where they lived. It was risky, but it was her best option. And she might even get away with it. She felt a surge of relief that she had a plan.

So now she just had to work out how to get rid of the evidence. This would take some more doing. As she necked more whisky, she almost laughed at the ridiculousness of the situation. A useless housewife trying to work out how to dispose of her cheating husband's body. Her life was more unbelievable than the soaps she loved to watch because of their ridiculous storylines. There was no way that she could get him out of the house without being seen. They didn't have a garage and she wasn't strong enough to carry him out to the car and shove him into the boot without making a scene. Even if she wrapped him up in bags, it would look suspicious. The children would be home in just a few hours and she had to get rid of him by then. How was she going to do it?

She went into the kitchen and reached for the secret stash of cigarettes she kept in a high up cupboard for emergencies. Stepping out into the garden and lighting one she inhaled deeply with shaking fingers and looked around. Could she bury him in the garden? Was she even strong enough to dig a hole herself? She didn't think so. And one of the neighbours might see her from their window, too. What if she hid him in the house and did it late at night? But then where would she hide him? As she smoked, she looked at the tarpaulin that covered the old ponds. They had drained them years ago and had been meaning to fill them with soil as part of the garden renovation project but still hadn't got around to it. Suddenly she realised the answer was staring at her in the face. Stubbing out her cigarette she walked over to the tarpaulin, lifted it and peered down into the two holes beneath. They were big enough and deep enough, she thought. All she would need to do was to put him in one of them and cover it up with soil. Then she could build something over it and no one would ever know. It almost seemed too simple.

Before she could change her mind, she grabbed her keys and went next door to knock on her neighbour's door. She would pretend that she needed to borrow some milk, she thought. But no one answered. Then she went to the other side but again, no answer. They were all out at work or school. Now was her chance.

She grabbed Pete's legs and pulled him through the house, out of the sliding doors and on to the patio. It was exhausting and she was panting and sweating but adrenaline kept her going and she pulled and pushed until he was next to the hole. One last push and he was in. Then she ran back into the house, grabbed a bin bag and shoved his holdall into it, leaving only his coat, phone and the letter. She ran to the shed where they had bags of soil and started ripping them open and throwing the soil down the hole as quickly as she could so that she no longer had to look at his lifeless body. But it wasn't enough so she ran around the garden looking for old tiles and stones, anything that she could throw down there too.

When she was done, she looked down and all she could see was soil and rubble. It wasn't enough but it would do for now. She quickly covered it back up with tarpaulin and lit another cigarette. When she was done, she went back inside, washed her hands and picked up his phone. There were four missed calls, all from C. She deleted them and put the phone into his coat pocket along with his letter. She'd deal with them later. Then she scrubbed the floor and walls, removing all traces of blood like she was on autopilot, as though it was crayon marks or food stains from a toddler's grubby little fingers. She took the ornament to the kitchen sink and cleaned it thoroughly before putting it back on the sideboard, exactly where it had been before. Finally, she showered, dressed, and sat at the kitchen table waiting for the children to come home from school.

She just about made it through the rest of the day but as

soon as the girls were in bed, she had quickly worked her way through a bottle of red wine until she passed out on the sofa.

When she woke up in the early hours of the morning and the terrible reality of what had happened came back to her, she had realised that she needed to keep up the pretence of being the abandoned wife if she wanted to get away with it. There could be no loose ends. So, she had done what she thought she would have done under different circumstances – and she had played the role perfectly.

Even though no one was looking, she had checked their bedroom, called his phone and eventually discovered the note that she had already read, re-reading it over and over again. In the days that followed she had called his friends and family. She had emailed him even though she knew he would never read her messages. She felt that if there was ever an investigation into his disappearance then she had done everything right – but she lived in fear that she had missed something.

She had almost given up the pretence so many times. There were many moments when she didn't know if she would be able to keep it up. When Erin came around the next day she almost confessed to the whole sorry thing. Several times she picked up her phone to call the police and then changed her mind. And then Lily breaking her leg had thrown the whole thing into further disarray. Lily needed her more than ever now, there was no way Kate could hand herself in. In a way, it was a welcome excuse. By the time Lily was better, she had convinced herself it was all for the best after all. Everyone believed that Pete had left her; this C person hadn't materialised so she was in the clear and could finally get on with her life.

In the early days she was a mess. She couldn't eat, she couldn't sleep but she had to hold it together for the girls. She grieved for him, every day, but for the Pete she used to know, not the Pete who had lied to her, cheated on her and said all those mean things to her. They had become like two strangers, they didn't love each other anymore, not like they should have done. And, slowly, as time went on, somehow she found a way to cope. With each day that came and went she felt stronger and more capable. The resolve in her grew stronger and stronger. She was doing the right thing, she was protecting her family.

Every day she waited for the police to turn up on her doorstep but they never came. And as time went on, she began to relax a little more. She began to rebuild her life, telling herself that she had to make it count because she didn't know how much longer she had left. She had to be the best mum possible to the girls, she was all they had now.

She started seeing a therapist, navigating the tricky path of working through all her issues without ever discussing the biggest, most horrific issue that she would ever face.

She let Rachel go, she relaunched her career, all the things that Pete had wanted her to do but until now she hadn't had the strength to do. And despite everything, she actually started to feel better. She really felt like she was getting her life back on track and she could actually see a future for her and the girls.

Keeping up the pretence and lying to everyone, especially Erin and the girls, broke her heart but she kept telling herself it was the right thing to do. When Karen came into their lives she knew it was stupid to encourage it but she couldn't help herself. Despite everything she still wanted the girls to have a piece of Pete in their lives. She didn't want them to forget their dad. They would grow up thinking that he had abandoned them. When they were older and understood life a little more the realisation of that would hurt even more, perhaps they would even go looking for him. But they would never find him. No one would ever find him.

Still, her life sometimes felt like a ticking time bomb and she owed it to herself and her children to make the best of what she had, while she had it. The fear stayed with her, every day and worse at nights, but it got easier with each day that went by. She'd done what she had to do, to save her family and that was all there was to it. And, as time went on, she had almost made peace with it, had almost found happiness again despite everything, when that knock on the door finally came.

And now she had no idea what she was going to do.

# 28

## CLAIRE AND KATE

SIX MONTHS LATER

Claire shook the estate agent's hand. He smiled warmly at her and pocketed the keys that she had just given him.

'*Bonne chance, mademoiselle,*' he said, and she smiled back and turned away.

She had got a decent price for her dad's house in France. A British couple had fallen in love with it at first sight and had made an offer that same day. They wanted to relocate from London and start a B&B. They were going to live the life that Claire had dreamed of for herself and Pete. But that dream hadn't come true and she had finally come to accept that it never would. It was time to let go.

At first she had waited for news from the police, convinced that Pete was out there somewhere and would come back to her. She had stayed in that crappy little hotel in north London for three weeks, waiting for answers, but there was nothing. She kept calling for updates, only to be told the same thing each time. They would be in touch if there were any developments. In a moment of madness, she even considered getting in touch with Kate but she knew that it would be pointless – she doubted that she would agree to talk to her. Eventually, she decided to go back to France and wait there instead. Every day she had willed the police to call and say that they had found Pete, that there was an explanation for his disappearance. They had been very kind to her but they had no leads, no clues as to where he might be. He had disappeared off the face of the planet. Eventually they had contacted her to tell her they had not found any suspicious circumstances surrounding his disappearance. He was a grown man who had chosen to disappear. It happened. The case would remain open, they said, and they would be in touch if there were any developments.

Up until then she had still clung on to the hope that he would simply turn up one day and knock on her door, with some crazy explanation for what had happened. Perhaps it had all got too much for him and he needed some time out to think it all through. In her dreams, he always came back to her, not to Kate.

Something still niggled at her, something not quite right about the whole story. She couldn't put her finger on what it was. Was it the wife? Did she know more than she was letting on? The police didn't seem to think so. Dan definitely didn't think so. They had spoken on the phone a few times and she had called him to tell him that the investigation had reached a dead-end for now.

'Thanks for letting me know, Claire,' he'd said. 'What will you do now?'

'I don't know,' she'd replied. 'It still doesn't feel right, there has to be an explanation. A man can't just disappear off the face of the planet like this.'

Dan had sighed heavily. 'I understand how you feel, Claire, but I think Pete was a troubled guy, way more troubled than any of us really knew, and he had been living with the guilt of this double life for so long. Perhaps he just ran away from it all.'

'Have you spoken to Kate?'

'We've been in touch a couple of times. She's doing as well as can be expected. This whole thing was such a blow to her – she'd only just come to terms with the fact that Pete was leaving her for you and then she had to process this new information.'

'Do you think she knows more than she's letting on?'

'About Pete? No, definitely not. I spoke to her after he first went missing and she was absolutely distraught. There's no way she could have been pretending, she has no idea where he's gone – that I know for sure. If that's what you think, Claire, you're barking up the wrong tree, I'm telling you now.'

'Where do you think he went?'

'I really don't know. I've tried and tried to think but I just can't.'

'Do you think he'll ever come back?'

'I like to think so, I mean, he's got two children for goodness' sake. Surely he'll see sense eventually and turn up. I really wouldn't be surprised.'

And that was when she had realised the truth of it all. She was alone – it was Kate who would get everyone's sympathy and support, not her. And if Pete ever did turn up again it wouldn't be for her, it would be for his children. All this time she had been waiting for him but she would always be second best. And she didn't want to be second best. It was time to close the book on the whole sorry story and start afresh. Screw Pete Garland and his midlife crisis. Screw his wife. Screw them all.

So she had put the house on the market and started planning her new life, starting with a one-way ticket to Australia. She was going to go travelling for a while and see where the world took her. She had a very healthy bank balance now thanks to the sale of the house and she had no ties to anywhere. She was done with trying to settle down, it always ended in heartbreak. She had been right all these years to rely only on herself. Pete had been a temporary blip in her life but she was on her own again now, as she had always been. Perhaps she'd bump into him somewhere – maybe on a beach in Thailand or surfing in Byron Bay. Maybe he was living the dream somewhere after all. Maybe she'd always be looking for him, deep down, in every country she visited, in every new place she went to. Perhaps she'd scan the tables of every bar she went into, looking for the man she had loved with all her heart sipping a cold lager and reading a torn paperback, hoping that she would find him. Or maybe he didn't want to be found. She didn't know and she didn't think she'd ever really find out.

She left the estate agent with nothing but her passport, wallet and backpack, got into a taxi and headed for the airport. It was time to say goodbye to the past – to France, to Pete and to the life that had remained a fantasy. It was time to let go of her doubts and theories about what had happened to him. It was time to look to the future. And for the first time in months, she felt excited again.

Kate was in the park with the girls when she got the call from the police to tell her that the investigation into Pete's disappearance had been downgraded to low priority. It was the summer holidays and London was in the grip of a heatwave that had lasted for weeks without a drop of rain. There was talk of a hosepipe ban for the first time in years. The house pulsated with heat and they had fans in every room to keep themselves cool. The girls had been in heaven, splashing about in the paddling pool in the garden all summer and sitting on deckchairs eating ice lollies on the new decking that she'd had installed over the old ponds. She'd finally got the garden renovated and it looked amazing. She'd made it into a real entertaining space, perfect for playdates with friends and drinks with her school mum friends in the evening, with fairy lights twinkling in the trees and a big firepit for cooler nights. They had people round the house all the time now – the girls loved inviting their friends home to play and she had a gang of pals who came over for barbecues and drinks at the weekend.

Rachel stopped by from time to time for a catch-up and Karen visited once a month. Erin was pregnant after a whirlwind romance with her boyfriend Scott and the girls were so excited about meeting their new niece or nephew. Kate, who knew how overwhelming it was to become a mother for the first time, was already on standby, ready to help her sister out and make sure that she never felt alone like she had.

When the police had first told her that Pete had been reported missing, her life had been turned upside down all over again. She had been a nervous wreck and spent countless hours racking her brain, looking for the possible things she could have missed all those months ago, anything that could incriminate her. Had she finally reached her day of reckoning? The police had searched the house from top to bottom and contacted everyone Pete knew.

Karen had called her full of concern the minute officers had left her house. 'I can't believe this, Kate, what's going on?'

'I've got no idea,' she replied. 'All these months I thought he was with another woman in France and now I have absolutely no idea what happened to him.'

'It's exactly what his own dad did,' Karen said sadly. 'He just ran away from it all – from his life, from his responsibilities. It's like history repeating itself. I'm so sorry that this has happened to you and the girls, Kate, you deserve so much more.'

Of course she'd felt even worse then, but she'd come too far to give up now. She'd worked so hard to rebuild her life and she had to keep playing the part, now more so than ever while the police's gaze was on her. *Did I miss anything?* she kept asking herself. Having had a taste of a better, happier life she was more desperate than ever to get through this. She was terrified of losing everything she had.

But days turned to weeks and then to months and nothing happened. She waited for the police cars to pull up outside her house, for them to handcuff her and walk her out but they never came. Erin and Lottie, who had flocked around her protectively when she first told them the news, started mentioning it less and less. Everyone was simply getting on with their lives and as time went on, she started to breathe again. But still, she fretted. She tried to throw herself into work, and the children, and life. She tried to forget about the investigation. But she couldn't. Each day she plastered on a smile and carried on playing her part as the abandoned wife trying to put her life back together. Inside she was falling apart, living in a state of constant fear. It wasn't until that moment in the playground, when the police told her that the investigation hadn't unearthed anything suspicious, that she finally felt herself relax. She hadn't missed anything. She'd got away with it, for now at least. She could look to the future again.

So much had changed in a year. This time last summer they had been in Greece on that joke of a holiday where both she and Pete had pretended that everything was totally fine when their marriage, and lives, were falling apart. Looking back, she could barely recognise the person she had become. Next week they were going to Spain with Erin and Scott for a holiday and Lily and Maggie had been counting down the days. She was looking forward to some time off work – it had been hard trying to juggle work with the girls at home so much and in the end she'd decided to take the whole of August off so that she could focus on spending time with them. She would get back to work in September when school started again and she was looking forward to it. She had upped her rates and she was earning enough money to stand on her own two feet. She still dipped into their savings for big things like holidays or unexpected bills but she was becoming more and more independent. Now, when people asked her what she did for a living, she didn't shy away from the answer. 'I work in PR,' she would tell them. 'But I work part-time, around my girls.'

They were like the three musketeers now, a tight-knit trio of ladies who were joined at the hip. They even followed her to the toilet, incapable of being away from her for a second. She didn't mind. They still mentioned Pete, but it was much less frequent now. They had accepted that he was no longer in their lives, in a way that only young children can. Kate knew that there would be more questions, as they got older and became more aware of their dad's absence and the mystery surrounding his disappearance. She was ready to answer them, to assure them that their dad had loved them very much indeed. She hoped she would be enough for them.

Recently, Lottie had been trying to set her up with men. 'Oh did you know that Ely's dad is divorced? And he's *such* a nice guy. I was thinking of inviting them over one Saturday. Maybe you could come too?'

She had laughed at her friend's not so subtle attempt at matchmaking. 'Thanks, Lottie, but I think I'll pass.' She wasn't ready to even consider starting something with someone else. She wasn't sure she would ever be. She would never get over what she had done to Pete; it would always be there, in her conscience, haunting her at night when she tried to sleep, and she wasn't sure that she deserved to be with someone else. But as long as she and the girls were okay, that was what mattered.

She had thought about selling the house and moving away, to start a new life, but she couldn't risk anyone moving into the house and discovering Pete's body. She would need to stay here, trapped in this house forever, until either she met her maker or the truth caught up with her. But she had made the best of it, she thought. It could be worse.

After all, she had created the perfect home, filled with love and laughter which reverberated around the walls when the girls ran around, playing with their friends. When she stayed up late into the night, sitting on the deck with her new friends, drinking wine, gossiping and laughing. When Erin and Scott came round and she put her hand on her sister's bump and felt the baby kick, feeling a surge of joy at the new life that was being created. When Karen came to stay for the weekend and sat on a deckchair with a cup of tea, playing games with the girls and beaming with pride at her beautiful grandchildren. When she took her laptop outside and worked under the umbrella, writing stories and making calls to journalists, squealing with excitement when she successfully placed a story. When, after a long day, she lit the firepit and sat close to it with the girls, toasting marshmallows and listening to Disney songs. The house was teeming with life.

It was just what she had always wanted.

## THE END

# ACKNOWLEDGEMENTS

They say it takes a village to raise a child. Well, this book is my literary first-born and I couldn't have done it without a collective effort behind me.

To Alison Chandler and my writing course-mates at the Collage Writing Room, who gave me invaluable support, encouragement and feedback – and the proverbial kick up the backside I needed to turn my dream into a reality and actually put pen to paper.

To Jo Pinner and her friends who very kindly and helpfully answered my questions about missing persons investigations. And Emma and James Newall who cheerfully brainstormed the best place to dump a dead body with me over a few beers and helped me come up with the ideal spot. I literally couldn't have disposed of Pete without you. #accessory.

A huge thank you to my sister Zoe, who read my early manuscript and gave me the encouragement and confidence to believe that people might actually want to read it. Thank you for being in my corner.

Thanks to Bloodhound Books, who took a chance on a debut novel from an unknown writer and transformed 2020 from what was otherwise a pretty shocking year into the one when I achieved my life's ambition. And to all of the Bloodhound Books team for your support, positivity and professionalism through the publishing process. Thanks in particular to Clare Law, my editor, who spent many hours polishing up my manuscript and making it shine.

To my NCT gang who are absolutely nothing like the bunch in this book and who supported me so much in those early months of motherhood, making sure that – unlike Kate – there was always someone to talk, cry and laugh with. And not a glossy ponytail or activewear in sight.

And finally, to my husband Jon. For being my biggest cheerleader and sounding board. For reading my manuscript and teaching me some important grammar lessons (otherwise Kate's emails would have been disappearing into the digital ethos and they'd all have been towing the line). For holding the fort while I disappeared off to write every weekend. For taking the kids to gymnastics so I could snatch another couple of hours of work. For believing in me.

# A NOTE FROM THE PUBLISHER

**Thank you for reading this book.** If you enjoyed it please do consider leaving a review on Amazon to help others find it too.

**We hate typos.** All of our books have been rigorously edited and proofread, but sometimes mistakes do slip through. If you have spotted a typo, please do let us know and we can get it amended within hours.

info@bloodhoundbooks.com

Printed in Great Britain
by Amazon